CHAIN OF VIOLENCE

As Lesley Egan:

CHAIN OF VIOLENCE
CRIME FOR CHRISTMAS
LITTLE BOY LOST
RANDOM DEATH
THE MISER
A CHOICE OF CRIMES
MOTIVE IN SHADOW
THE HUNTERS AND THE HUNTED
LOOK BACK ON DEATH
A DREAM APART
THE BLIND SEARCH
SCENES OF CRIME
PAPER CHASE
MALICIOUS MISCHIEF
IN THE DEATH OF A MAN
THE WINE OF VIOLENCE
A SERIOUS INVESTIGATION
THE NAMELESS ONES
SOME AVENGER, ARISE
DETECTIVE'S DUE
MY NAME IS DEATH
RUN TO EVIL
AGAINST THE EVIDENCE
THE BORROWED ALIBI
A CASE FOR APPEAL

As Elizabeth Linington:

FELONY REPORT
SKELETONS IN THE CLOSET
CONSEQUENCE OF CRIME
NO VILLAIN NEED BE
PERCHANCE OF DEATH
CRIME BY CHANCE
PRACTICE TO DECEIVE
POLICEMAN'S LOT
SOMETHING WRONG
DATE WITH DEATH
NO EVIL ANGEL
GREENMASK!
THE PROUD MAN
THE LONG WATCH
MONSIEUR JANVIER
THE KINGBREAKER
ELIZABETH I (Ency. Brit.)

As Egan O'Neill:

THE ANGLOPHILE

As Dell Shannon:

CASE PENDING
THE ACE OF SPADES
EXTRA KILL
KNAVE OF HEARTS
DEATH OF A BUSYBODY
DOUBLE BLUFF
ROOT OF ALL EVIL
MARK OF MURDER
THE DEATH-BRINGERS
DEATH BY INCHES
COFFIN CORNER
WITH A VENGEANCE
CHANCE TO KILL
RAIN WITH VIOLENCE
KILL WITH KINDNESS
SCHOOLED TO KILL
CRIME ON THEIR HANDS
UNEXPECTED DEATH
WHIM TO KILL
THE RINGER
MURDER WITH LOVE
WITH INTENT TO KILL
NO HOLIDAY FOR CRIME
SPRING OF VIOLENCE
CRIME FILE
DEUCES WILD
STREETS OF DEATH
APPEARANCES OF DEATH
COLD TRAIL
FELONY AT RANDOM
FELONY FILE
MURDER MOST STRANGE
THE MOTIVE ON RECORD
EXPLOIT OF DEATH
DESTINY OF DEATH
CHAOS OF CRIME

CHAIN
OF
VIOLENCE

LESLEY EGAN

PUBLISHED FOR THE CRIME CLUB
BY
DOUBLEDAY & COMPANY, INC.
GARDEN CITY, NEW YORK
1985

All the characters in this book are fictitious,
and any resemblance to actual persons,
living or dead,
is purely coincidental.

Library of Congress Cataloging in Publication Data

Egan, Lesley, 1921–
Chain of violence.

I. Title.
PS3562.I515C46 1985   813'.54
ISBN 0-385-19807-8

Library of Congress Catalog Card Number 84-21158

First Edition

For Gertrude, with much affection

Make a chain:
For the land is full of bloody crimes,
and the city is full of violence.
Ezekiel 7:23

CHAIN OF VIOLENCE

CHAPTER ONE

Varallo got back to Glendale headquarters at four-thirty on Saturday afternoon. He dropped off some evidence at the lab, without much hope that they'd be able to make much of it, and went up to the communal detective office. He found O'Connor fuming to the other detectives in, shaking a copy of a local sheet, the *News-Press,* at them. "Libel!" O'Connor was saying. "Well, for God's sake, not exactly libel but of all the ridiculous— Of all the outrageous—" He thrust the paper at Varallo. "You haven't seen this damn thing—" The *News-Press* was on the street at around four in the afternoon. "My good God, this is the silliest— I swear to God, if I'd thought that damfool female would turn out a story like this—"

"Oh, now, Charles," said Jeff Forbes peaceably. "It's very nice of the little lady to say such sweet things about us." O'Connor uttered an explosive snort. "Sure, a little bit unrealistic, but what do civilians know?"

"Unrealistic!" said O'Connor.

Varallo contemplated the headline. One of the editors at the *News-Press* had conceived the idea of running feature articles on various aspects of community services, and for the past week all the men at headquarters had been plagued by questions from a diminutive brown-eyed blonde interfering with routine and taking up time. This was the result, in Saturday's paper. GLENDALE'S FINEST, ALL DEDICATED MEN OF HONOR, said the headline. He scanned the column, grinning. "Don't fuss, Charles. Unrealistic all right, but what are the odds?"

"My God," said O'Connor, "making us look like a bunch of knights in shining armor— It's ridiculous!" As usual at this time of day, he needed a shave, his bulldog jaw blue, and his tie was crooked and his shirt rumpled.

It was Joe Katz's day off, and everybody else was out on something except for Leo Boswell and their female detective, Delia Riordan. Forbes slid farther down in his desk chair, stretching out his lank long legs, and said, "The bit I like is at the end—the quote from Charles."

"Oh, yes, very nice," said Varallo, and laughed. The byline was Mary Beth Hannaford, and she had certainly gone all out to give the local police force a superlative public relations job. "Lieutenant Charles O'Connor says, 'This is a noble choice of career for any citizen dedicated to public service, a rewarding and interesting professional job.' "

"I never said such a thing!" said O'Connor violently. "Would any peace officer in his right mind say such a thing? Making us out to be a bunch of saints—" He uttered a loud snort, running a hand through his curly black hair. "Noble career!"

"Ha," said Jeff Forbes sleepily. "I can think of other words."

"I liked the part," said Delia Riordan, "at the end. About how grateful the citizens should be—"

Varallo had just gotten there. "Oh, yes, very nice," he said, grinning. "All our citizens should be grateful to have such a dedicated body of honorable police officers to combat the terrible evil of crime in our modern society." He sat back and lit a cigarette. "The civilians. Well, regardless, it's nice to have the pretty things said about us. Don't carp, Charles."

"Evil!" said O'Connor. He had one hip perched on Katz's desk. "Evil! My God. Yeah, for God's sake, the civilians— They don't know the realities. It isn't once in a blue moon we get a whiff of the pure brimstone. What the hell are we coping with day by day? Human nature!" By his tone he might have uttered a fearful obscenity. "The foolishness, the stupidity, and the mindless violence, the lack of any common sense— This piece of sentimental twaddle— My God!" He stabbed out his cigarette violently.

Varallo laughed. "Don't fuss, Charles. If it reassures the citizens that our hearts are in the right place, all well and good."

"It just annoys me," said O'Connor, "making out that everything's black or white. Human nature— It doesn't always add up that way." He lit a new cigarette. "And what was the new one you've been out on?"

Varallo passed a hand over his tawny blond crest of hair. "The minister again," he said. "And of course no suggestive lead. This time he knocked the woman down, she's got a broken arm. We'll have to get a statement from her tomorrow, I'd just got the bare facts when the ambulance came. He got about seventy bucks and some jewelry. He left the usual religious tracts, I dropped them off at the lab. A Mrs. Abbott, up on Olmstead. But we seem to be getting an M.O.: she'd just got home from the market."

"Oh," said Delia. "Same as the first two. Funny in a way, Vic." The first two robberies had occurred in the last ten days, and the victims had told the same stories: the polite solicitor at the door making a pitch for a missionary society, and when the screen door was opened, the brochures offered, he had marched in and pulled a knife, threatened the victim, and gotten away with cash and jewelry.

"Funny isn't the word," said Varallo. "She gives us the same description, by the little I heard, well dressed, a clerical collar, a little dark Vandyke beard. And he just waved the knife around, didn't really offer any violence, just threats. She tried to go for the phone, and he knocked her down against a table, rifled her handbag, and went. I got there just as the ambulance came, the Traffic man saw she was hurt. This time he left a brochure about the Salesian Missions."

"And of course," said Forbes, "no hope of prints off that sheet of paper."

"Well, probably no." The first victim had been given a pamphlet about a missionary society of the Faith Baptist Church, the second a pamphlet about a Methodist missionary society. Both of those had been dead ends; neither society sent out door-to-door solicitors, and both brochures had been posted in the lobbies of local churches for the taking. "Get a statement from her tomorrow," said Varallo, "not that there'll be anything in it." The thankless job of coping with the day-to-day crime could be discouraging.

John Poor came in and sat down at his desk; he looked disgruntled. "So, more paperwork," he said sourly, "and it'll never come to anything. Though I think it's another one in the series—all the earmarks, place in a fancy residential area, some heavy stuff taken —TV, stereo, couple of fur coats, small appliances, cameras . . . They probably have a pickup to move the big stuff, it was an outsized color TV, and that makes six already. If you could say an M.O., looks like the same ones—very slick, very pro. The householders were at an anniversary party, didn't get home till 2 A.M., didn't discover the burglary until this morning. Burt's been up there hunting for prints, and of course there's nothing. But I kind of think it could be the same ones who pulled these six or seven jobs the last couple of months. Not that that's any help." He yawned. "I think I'm getting spring fever. The hell with everything."

"And I," said Delia, "have just decided I'm going to take tomorrow off. I was going to wait until Tuesday, but I'm so sick and tired of being in this mess, I'll take tomorrow off and finish it."

"You might just as well," said Varallo. And Mr. Beal appeared in the doorway of the big detective office.

"I'm a little early," he said, "but it's Saturday and we're going out for dinner. Come on, Rosie."

Rosie, the little woolly black mongrel, was curled up beside Boswell's desk. She got up obediently and went to the door. Up until last year, Rosie had been owned by the chief of police of a little town way north in the state; when he died and his daughter brought her down to Glendale, Rosie had lost no time in finding the police station. She seemed to have the idea that she belonged in a police station, and after she'd run away several times a compromise had been reached; Mr. Beal, her owner's husband, dropped her off every morning and picked her up in the afternoon. Rosie was content to stay at home nights as long as she could spend her days at the police station. She trotted out amiably with Mr. Beal.

It was getting on toward the end of shift, and it had been a slow day with nothing much accomplished. There were the usual ongoing things to work, the perennial heisters, the dope dealers, one unidentified body found in the street on Thursday night, and possibly they'd never find out anything about that one: an elderly man with nothing on him but a little small change and a half-full bottle of sherry, probably just another wino dead of natural causes. There was a little spate, a good deal more than usual, of angel dust floating around school playgrounds and elsewhere; possibly somebody was manufacturing it locally, but if so there weren't any suggestive leads. Among the various heists, it seemed to be the same pair who had pulled off several in the past couple of weeks, but so far there weren't any useful leads to those either.

At least tomorrow they'd have Katz back, and Gil Gonzales. And on Saturday night, it was on the cards that some new business would show up for the detectives.

Delia stood up. "I think I'll take off early. See you on Monday."

She went down to the ladies' room and renewed her lipstick, powdered her nose; she reflected impersonally that the latest beauty operator had done a good job on that casual cut and permanent; she didn't quite look the thirty-three she had turned just a couple of weeks before. Not that she could lay claim to any beauty, she thought, neither plain nor beautiful, ordinary dark hair and

fair complexion, ordinary blue eyes, a very ordinary-looking girl—
Well, she thought ruefully, perhaps not quite a girl anymore. She
started down the stairs and thought to herself vaguely that there
were stopping and starting places in life, as she had thought before; right now she was at a new starting place, and on a new
course that would probably go on for most of the rest of her life.

All those long years of proving herself as an L.A.P.D. policewoman, the long hours of study, acquiring all the useful skills to
make her more efficient, the fluent Spanish, the courses in police
science, and most of the time working the swing shift, so unavoid-
ably she had lost contact with friends— You couldn't say it had all
been for nothing, but of course it had all been for Alex. It had had
to be the thankless police job, for Alex. Alex Riordan, losing his first
wife after twenty years of childless marriage, marrying a girl half
his age to lose her in childbirth a year later. Delia didn't know
much about her mother. They had managed, with a succession of
housekeepers, until the year he was sixty-five and Delia was thirteen, and he had gone out on his last call—Captain Alex Riordan,
Robbery-Homicide L.A.P.D.—and taken the bank robber's bullet
in the spine. That had been a bad time, until they had found Steve,
ex-Sergeant Steve McAllister, L.A.P.D., just short of twenty-five
years' service when he had lost a leg in an accident: a widower
with a married daughter. The three of them had been together for
fourteen years and more; the new leg hadn't hampered Steve
from manipulating Alex's wheelchair, and Alex had always liked to
cook. Of course, of course it had had to be this job for Alex, pretending to be the son Alex never had.

Neil had seen that from the first, and hadn't he tried to make her
see it—stubborn, blind, foolish Delia resisting him all the way. She
and Isabel Fordyce had been best friends all through school, and
Neil not really a superior elder brother to Isabel—a friend, until he
was something else. How desperately she had held out against
him, blindly committed to the all-important job for Alex—and
how he and Alex had hated each other, of course.

And it hadn't been until over four years ago that she had, in one
devastating moment, realized the truth: that the little victory she
had won was meaningless. Neil coming to say good-bye—and she
had known, starkly, that she had nothing at all in return for the
sacrifice of resisting him. In the years of hard work on the job, all
her friends had drifted away. She hadn't even talked on the phone
with Isabel for a year before that last time of seeing Neil; and a
month after that she'd had the last letter from Isabel, the note

telling her noncommittally that Neil had married a Spanish girl he'd met in Ecuador; he'd been directing an archaeological dig there for the University of Arizona.

So it had come to her that it had all been for nothing. The promise of a meaningful life, a woman's life, exchanged for nothing but the thankless, sterile job. So all that was left to her was that job: but it was something, a job she could do well. And Alex was proud of her; Alex and Steve loved her.

And then that had changed, all in a moment, like the patterns in a kaleidoscope. It had been three years that Alex had had the crippling stroke, and had to be in the convalescent home, helpless and paralyzed. Sometimes he had known her, increasingly he hadn't. When it became evident that he was never coming home again, Steve had gone back to Denver to live with his daughter. He wasn't much of a letter writer, and Delia seldom heard from him.

And then, last December, Alex had slipped away to some other place. One thing the long time of living alone had given Delia was time for reading for pleasure; she had read voraciously, and she could no longer believe that Alex had been dissolved into nothing. There was too much evidence about that, which had nothing to do with orthodox churches. He had just gone somewhere else, the Alex she had known—irascible, stubborn, opinionated, and tough —and he was all right. Somewhere.

It was, of course, ridiculous to go on living in the big old two-story house in Hollywood. It had long been clear of any mortgage and was in a good residential area. She had put it on the market two months before, in February, and it had sold within a month. The escrow had closed two weeks ago, and she had bought the condominium in Glendale— As she'd planned, a bright, new apartment, closer to the job, easier to housekeep in, more cheerful. She had been moving household goods in bits and pieces for the past four days, and had thought she'd make the final move on Tuesday, her day off, but she was increasingly sick of the dank, dark old house in Hollywood; better do it and get it over.

Downstairs, she went down the corridor to the lab, at the back of the station. Rex Burt was just straightening from a microscope at the workbench, Gene Thomsen contemplating some negatives just out of the dryer. "Well, what can we do for you?" asked Burt genially.

"A little favor," said Delia. "I'm moving."

"We'd heard about it," said Burt.

"And there isn't much to move—I sold all the furniture and got new. But I'd be very much obliged if you could bring the van over sometime tomorrow—there's just one thing—"

Burt cocked his sandy head at her. "Don't tell me, let me guess," he said. "You've still got that idiotic bird. And the cage is too big for a car."

"Well, yes," said Delia. "That is, no, it wouldn't fit. And it's the last thing to be moved."

"Listen," said Burt, "we're not supposed to use the van except on official business."

"I know, but just as a favor to a fellow officer—"

"Oh, hell," said Burt resignedly. "All right, all right. Unless something urgent turns up overnight— I suppose we could come over in the morning. Give me the address again."

"Waverly Place," said Delia meekly. "Thanks very much, Rex."

It was the end of April, and the weather was warm and pleasant; in a couple of months the summer heat would hit southern California. At least the wild and wet winter was over. And in this new spring, she had come to a new starting place in life.

She stopped at a restaurant in Atwater for early dinner, and got to the old house in Hollywood after dark. As she went in and switched on lights, she shivered; it was cold and dank. Well, it held memories; it had been home to her all her life; but now it was just a bare, empty old house.

"Hello, Henry," she said.

As usual he came back at her readily. "Hello, Delia dear, you're a very pretty girl, dear! Give us a little kiss!" But Henry sounded rather subdued, and no wonder, she thought, looking around the empty rooms. All that was left in the big old house was the four-poster bed that the new owners had bought with the house—and Henry. Henry was a large blue and yellow macaw, brilliantly colored and decorated. His former owner had been a homicide victim last December, and her heirs had repudiated Henry with loathing; Henry had, in fact, been left without any family at all. Just, Delia had thought, like herself. "I say," said Henry somewhat morosely, "let's all have a little drink."

"Never mind, boy," said Delia. "Tomorrow we're going to a nice new place, you'll like it."

"Awk," said Henry glumly. She filled his dish with sunflower seeds and peeled an orange for him. There wasn't any food in the house except Henry's seeds and fruit; she'd been having all her meals out for two days, all the kitchen contents ferried over to the condo. She scratched Henry's bright head, and he teetered on his perch and ruffled his bright blue wings at her.

All three of them were on night watch on Saturday night—Bob Rhys, Dick Hunter, and Jim Harvey. Saturday nights could bring cops a little spate of work, but most of it would be for Traffic: the accidents and bar brawls and drunks. They sat around until after nine, when they got a call to a heist at a pharmacy out on Glenoaks Boulevard. Rhys and Hunter went out on it.

The pharmacist had been alone in the place, just about to close up. He was a thin, middle-aged man named Abel, and he was shaken and scared but had kept his head. "I know the crime rate's up, but I've never been held up before— I'll have to check the stock to tell you what they got away with, they took a lot of amphetamines and some other stuff as well as what was in the register. There were two of them, just young punks, maybe seventeen, eighteen—"

"Could you describe them, Mr. Abel?" asked Rhys.

"Well, I can give you some idea— One was bigger than the other, he was maybe six feet, thin, dark hair— They weren't in here very long and I was shook up— He had a gun, I've got no idea what kind except it was pretty big— The other one had a knife. It was the bigger one did all the talking, and he kind of ordered the other one around, told him to go in the back and get all the pills— No, I can't say I'd recognize a photograph, there wasn't anything distinctive about either of them, just a couple of young punks. There might have been seventy or eighty bucks in the register."

"What about the other one?" asked Hunter.

"Well, as I said, just a couple of punks. He wasn't as big, he didn't say anything, just held this big knife. I guess they both had dark hair— Yeah, they were white— Just old clothes, jeans and sweatshirts. Oh, and one other thing, I don't know if it was them, but just after they went out, I heard a motorcycle take off out on the street."

"Did either of them touch anything here, the counter or the register?" asked Rhys.

"No, the big one got me to open the register and hand over the cash, and the other one just collected all the bottles and packages from the back. He had a big paper bag, he put everything in that."

So there wasn't, probably, much point in calling a lab man to dust for prints. If the punks were that young, they probably wouldn't show in Records. Rhys asked Abel to come in and make a formal statement, which was about all they could do. In the car, he said to Hunter, "That pair again. And no damn place to go on it."

This was the fourth time in six weeks detectives had heard about the pair of heisters, young punks in their teens, one with a gun, one with a knife. It was possible they had pulled more heists, but in the other four jobs the victims had reported a motorcycle taking off just afterward. They had hit two other pharmacies, a twenty-four-hour convenience store, and a fast-food place at closing time, and so far had gotten away with a sizable haul, quite aside from all the drugs, which would be eminently salable on the street. And there wasn't one thing for the detectives to do about it but write the reports. The computers downtown at L.A.P.D. headquarters didn't know anything about such a pair; it was on the cards they were too young to show in Records.

They went back to the station and Rhys typed the report. For a Saturday night, it was a quiet shift. In a couple of months, as the summer heat built up, shortening tempers, business would step up. Tonight, though Traffic was busy with the accidents and drunks, they had only one more call, to a mugging on South Central. The victim had been beaten rather drastically, and the paramedics had taken him away before Hunter and Harvey got there, but there was a witness and an identification. The victim was one Thomas Berger, and he owned the small bar at the corner of Magnolia and Central, acted as his own bartender. The witness was Bernie Curran, and he'd had a few beers but was perfectly rational.

"Listen," he said, "it was dark and I couldn't no ways describe 'em to you, but I seen the whole thing, and it must've been some guys knowed Tom, see, know he'd be taking all the money from the register for the night deposit at the bank—when he closed down the bar, see—and look, ordinarily I wouldn't have been there this late—this is a neighborhood sort of place, Tom gets the regulars in mostly, guys from around here drop in for a couple of friendly drinks, shoot the breeze some, maybe a few hands of gin —but my wife's off visiting her mother, and I stayed until Tom shut down. I come out to my car, I'm parked just up the street, and just as I'm unlockin' the door I hear Tom yell and I look back and see these guys beating on him—he'd just come out the front door, see. There were two of 'em, one of 'em had a club of some kind. And I yell at 'em and start to run back, but they'd already got Tom's bag —the bank bag, see, he had the money in. They took off and so I called the cops from the pay phone on the corner. The way they ran, they must've been young fellas, but no way could I tell you what they looked like. My God, I hope Tom isn't hurt bad, but the first cop said better get an ambulance—"

The Traffic man was Lopez; he said, "He didn't look too good. He was unconscious and bleeding pretty bad."

Hunter asked Curran to come in and make a statement tomorrow. They went back to the station and Harvey talked to Emergency at Memorial Hospital. Berger was still unconscious with severe head wounds, but Emergency thought he would make it and might be able to answer questions tomorrow. It was nearly the end of shift; let one of the day men write the report on it.

As usual on Sunday morning, O'Connor took the outsized blue Afghan hound, Maisie, up into the hills for her weekly run; she bounced around, long legs flying. She didn't get as much exercise as a big dog should and was reluctant to get into the car for the ride home. At the house on Virginia Avenue, he turned her into the backyard to play with four-and-a-half-year-old Vince and went in to put on a tie. Sunday was supposed to be his day off, but he generally went into the station to see what was going on.

Katharine was on the phone in the hall, and as he came past her she was saying, "Well, we owe the Poindexters, they had us to dinner last month—" O'Connor growled at her and she looked up. "Just a second, that was Charles—you know how he hates dinner parties and dressing up—"

"Now, Katy— I can't stand that Goddamned stuffed shirt, and just because one of your ex-teacher pals happens to be married to him— Who are you talking to?"

"Laura, naturally. It's nothing to do with you—I'll tell you about it sometime. Anyway, it was really about Simon Farren. Well, that's what I thought, but, Laura, it wouldn't look terribly queer, would it? I mean, if I had three or four other people—"

"What the hell are you talking about?" asked O'Connor querulously. "What do you mean, about Farren? What about Farren?"

"Never mind," said Katharine. "Go away, I'll spell it out for you sometime." When O'Connor came back from the bedroom, she was still talking; not for the first time, he decided he'd never fully understand females. The last thing he heard her say, as he headed for the back door, was "But it really wouldn't look like a plot, would it— I mean, people do introduce people to their friends— Well, I see what you mean, Laura, but after all—"

Females, thought O'Connor. But they would go their own way.

On the way downtown he was thinking harder about the angel dust showing up all over town, and nothing to say where it was coming from. The two major gangs in this area, the Guerreros and the Eldorados, had been known to do a little dealing in pot, uppers and downers, and he was wondering now whether one or the other of them had started a little manufacturing on the side. PCP was very simple to make, if potentially explosive, but none of those characters were known for their excessive caution. The word was out to any possible street informants, any information appreciated; but if either of the gangs was involved, nobody with useful knowledge was going to risk a knifing by blowing the whistle to the cops.

At the office, Rosie was curled up beside Leo Boswell's desk, and Forbes and Gonzales were just sitting talking while Varallo was typing a report. O'Connor sat down at Katz's desk—he was more often in the communal office than his own private cubicle—and asked, "So what's new?"

Forbes passed over the night report. "I checked with the hospital just now—this Berger's been in surgery, isn't conscious yet. We'll be able to question him eventually, not that I suppose he can tell us anything. The heist looks like that same pair with the motorcycle."

"And no Goddamned place to go on it," said O'Connor.

Varallo ripped the triplicate sheets out of his typewriter, sat back and lit a cigarette. "And not much of anywhere to go on the minister that I can see. But I've got to go and see this Mrs. Abbott. I just heard the gist of it yesterday, she'd been knocked down and had a broken arm. The Traffic man called an ambulance, and I didn't get much out of her. I'd better call and see if she's home."

"You said she'd been to the market," said Forbes. "So had the other two, hadn't they? Or does it say anything?"

"Your guess is as good as mine," said Varallo. "See if she's got any more to tell us, but of course it's the same joker, with his missionary tracts. And this Curran's supposed to come in sometime today to make a statement."

Joe Katz came in looking annoyed and said, "Get out of my chair, Charles. I've got another damned report to write. The burglaries go on forever. And not that there's ever much of an M.O. on the run-of-the-mill burglary, I've got a kind of hunch this is another one pulled by the same jokers. I make it eight or ten in the last couple of months, the same earmarks in a vague sort of way— all big, fancy places in high-class areas, well, that says nothing, but by the loot it's got to be at least two men with a pickup or something. And they've got in the same way mostly: jimmy on the sliding doors, the back windows. I left John getting a list of the take, and it seems to have been quite a haul: two big TVs, stereo, couple of expensive cameras, and of course they haven't any record of the serial numbers."

"The stupid citizens," said O'Connor. "I have a suspicion, Vic, that my wife is hatching up some kind of plot with yours."

"Entirely possible," said Varallo. "Time will tell." He looked up the number in his notebook and began to dial the phone.

Gil Gonzales came in and said, "No rest for the wicked. Talk about the rate being up— Most people like to sleep in on Sunday morning if they can. Would you believe a heist pulled at 10 A.M. at the Rosedale Nursery? Of all the damned silly places to hold up— they'd only been open a couple of hours, he only got about forty bucks. And where the hell is the lab team? The owner says he pawed all over the register, somebody's got to print it, but there's nobody in the lab."

"Somebody'll be in eventually," said O'Connor, "I suppose." Gonzales sat down at his desk, absently stroking his neat little mustache.

Varallo put the phone down. "The lady's home," he said to Forbes. "Like to come and hear what she has to say?"

Burt and Thomsen showed up in the mobile lab van about eleven o'clock, at the old house on Waverly Place. Delia had spent the morning clearing out the very few odds and ends still to be moved. She stripped the bed and folded sheets and blankets in the back seat of the car, with the packages of Henry's seeds; all that was left in the cleaned-out refrigerator was Henry's fresh fruit and lettuce, and she put that in a plastic bag. She'd been ferrying everything else to the condo every night this week; now there was just one garment bag with winter clothes to get into the car.

Henry was still rather morose. He greeted the lab men with a wolf whistle. "Give us a kiss, dear! Scratch Henry's head, please!"

"How you put up with that damned thing," said Burt. "Well, where are we taking it?"

Delia gave him the address, the corner of Mountain and North Central. "You can follow me over."

"You'll be glad to get out of this place," said Thomsen, looking around the bare, shabby old rooms.

So she hadn't any time to dredge up old memories, before leaving for the last time the place that had been home all her life. And you didn't want to lose memories, but there were times it didn't do to dwell on them. Burt and Thomsen carried the cage out to the van, and Delia followed them with its stand. She had bought Henry a handsome new cage, but all the books about parrots said they should have large quarters, and the cage was about four feet by three, gilded metal with a smart gilded rectangular stand. Henry screeched and fluttered.

The van followed her back to Glendale. The condominium was in a fairly new, starkly modern building at the top of Central Avenue. She pulled into her allotted carport, and Burt found a slot for the van on the street. They carried the cage into the elevator, Delia trailing them with the stand. The building was silent, not a soul around: Sunday, and people sleeping late. Henry was usually an incessant chatterer, but possibly the elevator alarmed him; he was absolutely silent all the way up and down the hall into the condominium apartment.

"Say, this is nice," said Burt, looking around the living room. "You'll be a lot better off here."

"Nice view," said Thomsen. "Where do you want this thing?"

"This side of the balcony door." Delia placed the stand and they heaved the cage onto it. "Awk!" said Henry. "I like a little sugar in my tea. Yo-ho and a bottle of rum." He sounded a little more cheerful, to be in a furnished room again. "And thanks very much, Rex," said Delia.

"No trouble. We'd better get back and see if any new business has gone down."

After they had left, Delia brought up the odds and ends from the car and put them away. Presently she'd go out to the market, lay in supplies for the freezer and refrigerator. Last night she had made up the bed, and there wasn't much more to do. She sat down on the new couch and lit a cigarette, looking around at her new place in life with satisfaction, at the bright new furniture. Fortunately she had liked the drapes that were already here, a cheerful green and gold print. The new furniture was all in soft greens and golds, to blend with the drapes and the cheerful apple-green carpet. She had hesitated between this place and another condo a few blocks away, but that had been on the ground floor; this was on the fourth, and the balcony was a little larger. She had the idea that it was going to be pleasant to sit out there on nice evenings, with the panorama of city lights spread out below. And it was a security-guarded building; until it came time for air conditioning, it would be nice for Henry to be near the open door to the balcony.

She peeled and quartered an orange for him before she went out to the market. "Thank you, dear," said Henry. "You're a very pretty girl, dear." The books about parrots said that they didn't know what they were saying, just mimicked what they heard, but Delia wondered about Henry; he did come out with some appropriate remarks.

When she came back from the market with two loaded grocery bags and set them down to unlock the door, a man was just coming out of the nearest door down the hall. He was a thin, middle-aged man with scanty gray hair and large black-framed glasses. He gave her an incurious look. Delia took the bags in and shut the door.

"Hello, Delia dear!" said Henry. "Give us a kiss. I say, let's all have a little drink!"

And then the phone rang, and it was Laura Varallo. "Vic said you were getting it over with today—a good idea—and I'm dying to see it—"

"Come over on Tuesday," said Delia. "Yes, I'm practically moved—nothing much more to do. Come to lunch on Tuesday." It would be nice to have a first guest in the new place. Laura had been a good friend.

"Well, there isn't any more I can tell you," said Mrs. Bertha Abbott blankly. She was in her sixties, fat and gray-haired and motherly-looking. This was a fairly large house in a very good residential area in north Glendale. She looked at Varallo and Forbes and touched the cast on her right arm. "I told you how it happened— I'd just got back from the market, I was putting things away in the freezer and refrigerator, when the doorbell rang—and the man was dressed like a minister, I mean he had on a straight white collar, you know, and he was very polite— Oh, a description, I don't know, he was a white man, he had a little beard, what used to be called a Vandyke, and I really couldn't say about any age—he wasn't very young or very old. He said something about a missionary society and I wasn't interested but you have to be polite. I opened the screen door to take the brochure and that was when he pushed right in, and he had a knife, he asked for money—and I expect it was foolish but I was mad, I told him to get out and I shoved at him—" She took a breath. "And that's when he knocked me down, he didn't hit me really hard, but I was off balance and I fell against the coffee table— And he said again he wanted money, and so I got my handbag and gave him all the cash I had, and he took my engagement ring and another diamond ring I was wearing."

"Did he touch your handbag?" asked Varallo.

"No, I just handed him the money— I think there'd have been about sixty dollars."

They pressed her for a further description, and all she could say was that he had been middling tall and possibly in his thirties. "I don't belong to any church," she said. "Missionary societies—well, I know some of them do good work—and you have to be polite—"

CHAPTER TWO

The larcenous minister, by the M.O., didn't show in any local records, by what the computers downtown could say. They got a description of the two diamond rings from Mrs. Abbott, and back at the station added that to the current hot list for pawnbrokers, but there was nothing unusual about the rings and it was a forlorn hope that they would be spotted. Meanwhile there were other things to do. The victim of Thursday night's heist at a liquor store had picked out a mug shot, and they hadn't found that one yet; he'd moved from his last known address in Records, and they had just gotten a new one from his parole officer yesterday. Varallo and Forbes started out to check that. He was an Adolfo Hernandez, with several counts of armed robbery with L.A. As they were going out, Curran came in to make a statement on that mugging. Gonzales talked to him; there wasn't, of course, anything in it to give them any leads.

O'Connor spent quite a while on the phone with a Narco officer downtown, and he didn't get any useful ideas. All Central Narco could say, with their feelers out to every police division in the county, was that there did indeed seem to be more angel dust floating around than usual. It could be that there was a manufactory somewhere around, and it could be anywhere in the county or out of it. The foolish powder was a perennial problem, but in segments as it were. The high-class stuff, the cocaine, was largely a problem for the L.A.P.D. divisions, and a big headache; the show-business people, the big business executives, were into that, having the money; and there were always the venal pharmacists, the complaisant physicians issuing prescriptions for the uppers and downers. Glendale, if not the nice clean town it used to be, didn't get so much of that; but there was always stuff being peddled in the street.

Boswell and Gonzales went out hunting heisters. Lacking any firm identification, the slow way to do it was to look for men in

Records with the right pedigrees, haul them in and lean on them; sometimes they caught up to them that way.

Varallo and Forbes found Hernandez in a cheap apartment in Eagle Rock. He was the expectable young tough, and they didn't get anything out of him on the questioning. He had a record, two counts of armed robbery with L.A.P.D. and Pasadena. But the liquor-store owner had made a positive identification from the mug shot; they could hold him twenty-four hours without charging him, and arrange a lineup tomorrow. Varallo started the machinery on a search warrant for the apartment—they had to go through the motions—and Forbes took him over to the jail.

The day dragged on to five o'clock, and O'Connor was just starting to leave when Communications relayed up an urgent All Points Bulletin. "This is a hot one," said Sergeant Dyer tersely. "We just got the word from Hollywood. There was an L.A.P.D. man shot an hour ago, making a pinch for armed robbery. A Sergeant Hollister, he was dead at the scene and his partner's in Emergency with a couple of slugs in the body. There's an A.P.B. out, it's Luis Barrios, quite a little pedigree, there's a make on the car," and he added the plate number.

"Goddamn," said O'Connor, "let's hope somebody drops on him quick." And the Traffic shift had changed at four o'clock, the squads wouldn't have been briefed on this, but the A.P.B. would go out on the radio. Every lawman in the county would be on the lookout for this one, a cop killer.

Forbes had just left; nobody else was in at ten to six, and Varallo finished arranging for the lineup tomorrow morning, when a new call went down, a homicide. "Damn it," he said to Sergeant Bill Dick on the desk, "it's the end of shift." But things came along at inconvenient times, and he called Laura to say he'd be late and went to have a preliminary look at it.

The address was Acacia Street south in town, and it turned out to be an ancient court consisting of eight ramshackle units. The uniformed man was Whalen, and he had a woman in the back of the squad. He said cynically, "Educated guess, they're both hookers. This one is Edna Quigley, she found the body and called in—may have messed up the scene some before I got here. The body's an Alicia Taylor."

The place was shabby and cluttered and dirty. Whatever else she was, the Taylor woman hadn't been much of a housekeeper. The body was in the front bedroom, lying on a disordered double bed in a tangle of dirty sheets, the body of a woman probably in her thirties; it was hard to say whether she'd been good-looking or not, her tongue protruding from a swollen mouth and the face bloated and dark. It looked as if she'd been strangled manually, the autopsy would say, and not recently. Varallo didn't waste much time looking around; this was a job for the lab. He went out to the squad and talked briefly to Edna Quigley. She looked about thirty-five, with bleached blond hair and a round, insipidly pretty face wearing too much makeup. She was still crying a little, hiccuping and sobbing. "We were going out to dinner together," she told Varallo, "I just talked to her on the phone yesterday afternoon. We usually got together about once a week, Allie and I knew each other for years, she was my best friend, I guess you could say. This is just awful, I can't believe Allie's dead, I got such a shock when I saw her—"

"Do you know anyone who might have had a reason to kill her?" asked Varallo.

"Well, of course I don't, that's just crazy— I came to pick her up, we were going out to the Tam-o'-Shanter for dinner, and the door was unlocked and I went in, and there she was—" She dissolved in tears again. "Everybody liked Allie, nobody'd want to hurt her! I just can't believe anybody'd kill her like that—"

"Did she have a job?" asked Varallo.

"Well, no, not right now."

"What about any boyfriends?"

"Well, she had a couple, I guess. I don't know any names." She looked at him sideways; she was recovered enough to be evasive.

"Did you use the phone in there to call the police?"

"Well, sure, what else?"

Varallo said, "Then we'll have to get your prints for comparison with any others there might be." He spelled that out.

"I haven't done nothing," she said shrilly, "you can't make me get fingerprinted, I'm not a criminal—"

"No, but we'd like your cooperation," he said patiently. "You'd like to see whoever killed your friend caught up to, wouldn't you?"

"Sure I would. Allie never did nobody any harm, it's just awful her getting killed—"

Varallo called the lab from the squad, and twenty minutes later Ray Taggart showed up in the mobile van. "It's all yours," said Varallo. "Get some photographs and then you can call the morgue wagon. But first you can print the witness." Edna Quigley submitted to the printing reluctantly, and Varallo got her address and let her go.

It was seven-thirty when he got home to Hillcroft Road, and Laura said, "I had to marry a cop. Well, you can warm up meatloaf indefinitely. The rest of us had dinner an hour ago." The children came chasing up, six-year-old Ginevra and four-year-old Johnny. "I got a new story to read you!" said Ginevra excitedly.

"Not now, darling, Daddy wants dinner. He can hear it later."

"And Charles seems to think you and Katharine are cooking up something."

Laura laughed. "Maybe. I'll tell you about it later."

The night watch came on and heard about the new homicide when Taggart looked in as he came back to the station. "I picked up a few prints," he said, "but it remains to be seen if they do us any good. I sent the body in." Any evidence on this would probably come from the lab work.

Rhys called the hospital on Berger; he was conscious and could be talked to the next day. They sat around until nearly ten o'clock before they got a call; it was nothing to make them any work, a mugging on the street, a cab driver just coming out of an all-night restaurant on his way back to his cab. He had a bang on the head and was doing some cussing, and all he could tell them was that the mugger was big and young. "But I only had about five bucks on me. These damned thugs all around nowadays, Glendale used to be a nice quiet town."

Rhys and Harvey had just gotten back to the station when another call came in; Rhys left Harvey to write that report and went out with Hunter on that. It was an address on Chester Street, an old but well-maintained apartment building of about eight units. The squad-car man was Steiner, and he was looking concerned. "I called an ambulance, she says it was rape and you'll want evidence on that— Naturally she's pretty shook."

In the living room of the apartment, Linda Miller was huddled on the couch miserably. She was wearing a nylon nightgown and a shabby chenille robe. She was a rather pretty blonde in her early twenties, and she'd been crying, was still dabbing at her eyes.

"Of course I was a fool to open the door," she said drearily, "but I was half asleep—and when he said telegram, well, I've been worried about Mother, she hasn't been well and she was going in for a lot of tests. They live up in Lancaster, Mother and Dad, I mean. I'd been in bed about half an hour when the bell rang, and I asked who it was and he said, telegram. So I opened the door—and he pushed right in—I tried to fight him, but he was big and strong, he didn't hit me or anything, he just—you know—raped me." The ambulance attendants were just arriving.

"Can you give us a description?" asked Rhys.

"No—I don't know—he wasn't here long—and I was so scared . . . But," and she gave a little sob, "it was funny—after he'd—after he'd done it, he said he was sorry he had to do that, and I was a nice girl—"

"That's a funny one," said Hunter when the attendants had taken her out. "Would it be any use to print the place? By what we can gather, he probably didn't touch anything, just fell on her right off."

"You never know," said Rhys. "Talk to her again when she's a little calmer, see if she remembers anything else."

And the report on that took up the rest of the shift.

On Monday morning, Varallo collected the witness to the heist, the owner of the liquor store, and took him over to the jail to the arranged lineup, and he picked out Hernandez, with no hesitation, as the heister. "I'd know that ugly mug anywhere, that's him. Like I said, he came in about closing time and hit me for everything in the register, over four hundred bucks."

Varallo booked Hernandez in formally and back at the station applied for the warrant. The search warrant for Hernandez's apartment had come through, and he and Gonzales went to look at it, but nothing useful turned up there except the gun, a beat-up old Colt .32.

It was Forbes's day off. Delia talked over the previous night's rape with Varallo when he got back, looking over Rhys's report. "I suppose I'd better talk to the girl and see if she can give us anything more helpful. I checked the hospital, she was released this morning."

"And somebody'll have to see Berger, but that'll be a handful of nothing," said Varallo. "Has that Barrios got dropped on yet?"

"The A.P.B.'s still out," said Lew Wallace, looking up from his typewriter. "Let's hope somebody spots him." Rosie was curled up asleep beside his desk. "Charles went to talk to somebody at Central Narco, no telling when he'll be back."

Delia went out to find Linda Miller, and before starting for the hospital, Varallo went down to the lab. "Did Taggart pick up anything useful at that homicide scene?"

Burt looked up from the workbench. "Some pretty good latents not belonging to the corpse," he said. "Can't tell you anything definite yet, except for one thing. Those other prints, from the girl who found the body—Edna Quigley. Ray left a note to check them and I did that first thing. She's in our records, four counts of hooking."

"I figured," said Varallo. "What about the corpse?"

"Well, she's not in our files," said Burt. "I sent those prints downtown, see if she shows there."

"And I would take a bet," said Varallo. "And one like that, any of the johns she picked up could've done it and faded into the woodwork. Unless he left us some prints—"

"Let you know later," said Burt.

Varallo drove down to Memorial Hospital and talked to Tom Berger, who couldn't tell him anything about the muggers. He was a paunchy man in his fifties, with his head bandaged. "They jumped me just as I came out the door," he said aggrievedly; "all I can say is there were two of them, and one of 'em had a baseball bat or a two-by-four, something like that, I must've got knocked out right away—next thing I know I wake up here."

"Do you have any idea how much they got?"

"Yeah, sure, I had all the day's take in the deposit bag for the bank, I don't get rich at my place, but it's steady—I got a lot of regulars—it was about a hundred and twenty bucks. Saturday's the best day in the week. No, I got no idea who they were, how could I? Just a couple of damned robbers."

Anybody with a modicum of sense, of course, might figure that Berger would have the day's take on him when he closed the bar. He couldn't give any kind of description. This was another one that would get stashed in Pending indefinitely. Varallo thought sardonically about that newspaper story. Noble career indeed! It could be a damned discouraging job.

"Well, the way I told the cops last night," said Linda Miller, "he wasn't here long, it was all pretty fast, and I was scared. I didn't really get a good look at him." She had looked relieved to welcome a female detective, and said now a little shyly, "I'm just as glad to talk to another girl about it, Miss Riordan, it was sort of embarrassing. And I was still pretty shook last night."

"Well, that's understandable," said Delia encouragingly. She had talked to an intern at Emergency that morning, and the girl had been raped all right, and furthermore had been a virgin.

"I just couldn't go to work this morning, I called Mrs. Greer and explained, and she was nice about it." Linda Miller worked at a local savings-and-loan company.

"You can't describe him at all?" Aside from the rape, she hadn't been hurt. "And you said he apologized to you?"

"Yes, it was weird, real weird. As soon as he'd—you know, done it—he said, I'm real sorry I had to do this, you're a nice girl. And he just went out. Well, he had a kind of round face, he was young, maybe in his twenties, and he had blond hair, kind of long. He was just sort of ordinary." She twisted her fingers together, looking down at the floor. "I tried to keep my head, I called the police, but I don't suppose there's any way you can find out who he is— Oh, I'm positive I'd never laid eyes on him before. And like I told the other cops last night, I'd been worried about Mother, so has Dad, that was why I opened the door when he said telegram— I should have thought, if anything was wrong Dad would have phoned, and they don't deliver telegrams any more— And I just can't tell them about this, they'd have a fit and want me to come right home, and I'd never get as good a job up there— Well, one thing I will say, I'll never open my door again to somebody I don't know!"

"Do you think you'd recognize a photograph?" asked Delia.

She said doubtfully, "Well, maybe. I don't know. Do you want me to look at photographs?"

"It's just a chance, if you would recognize him," said Delia. There was a collection of mug shots of the sex offenders in their records, and a much bigger collection at Central Headquarters downtown. "And the sooner you look, the better the chance that you might pick him out."

"Well, all right," said Linda. Delia took her back to the station and in their Records office settled her down over a book of mug shots, waited while she leafed through it slowly. But in the end Linda just shook her head.

"I don't think any of these is the one, but honestly I didn't get a very good look at him, Miss Riordan. I don't think he's any of these."

"Well, it was just a chance," said Delia. "Would you feel like looking at some more pictures downtown?"

"I don't think it'd be any use. Honestly, I can't say I would recognize him. It was all so fast, and I was half asleep when he got in."

Delia took her home. By then it was long after one o'clock and she'd missed lunch. She stopped at the coffee shop down the block from the station and found Mary Champion there, from their Juvenile office, and joined her. "I understand you got yourself moved," said Mary. She was a rather hard-bitten, dark woman in her forties, with twenty years of police work behind her. "How's the new place?"

"Oh, just fine," said Delia. "Just fine. It's been fun buying all new furniture."

"New lease on life," said Mary sympathetically. "I'll drop by and see it someday."

"Any time," said Delia. "I've got a lovely view from the balcony."

Mary finished her coffee and opened her bag to powder her nose. "Well, I'd better get back and finish that report. Another of the little darlings sent in by the school principal, high as a kite, and I just got rid of an irate parent."

"Wanting to know," said Delia, "why we can't stop all the dope floating around."

"That's just what. If they only knew. And that *Times* editorial yesterday fulminating about how senseless the drug laws are, like prohibition, just creating the problem by making it profitable for the dealers."

"My good Lord!" said Delia. "Don't go quoting that to Charles. He must have missed it, or we'd have heard an explosion."

"Augean stables," said Mary with a grimace, "but what are we supposed to do, let the animals run wild in the jungle? Well, see you."

Delia dawdled over a sandwich. When she got back to the station, she found the communal detective office empty except for Varallo and Gonzales, talking to a sullen Edna Quigley. She was sitting in the chair beside Varallo's desk, a thin blonde with too much makeup and a tight black skirt hitched over her knees. She was eyeing the men warily and resentfully.

"Come on," Varallo said hardly, "we know all about both of you, Edna. You've got four counts of soliciting with us, and Alicia Taylor turned up in Records downtown, five counts, and one of petty theft from a client. You claim she was your best friend, so you knew that."

"Well, you've got to live," she said. "All right, I knew that."

"Was anybody running her?" asked Gonzales, and she flared up at him.

"Jesus, no, she never got tied up to any pimp any more than I did! Nobody ever ran either of us."

"Strictly free enterprise," said Varallo. "So, do you know any of her johns?"

"Not to say know, how would I? She didn't have any real regulars, there were guys she knew just casual, but I don't know any names, just like Bill and Jack and Gary, like that. She used to hit bars all over town, pick up the johns, most nights. She'd just moved over here from Hollywood, mainly because I got her to, that's a real crummy town these days, Glendale's a lot nicer."

"Which bars?" asked Gonzales.

She shrugged. "Not the real classy places, with restaurants, the barkeeps at places like that chase you out if you're on the make. Places down South Brand, Central, San Fernando Road. Yeah, she had a car." They knew that; it had been towed into the police garage for lab examination. "No special places, I guess. We used to get together once a week or so, have dinner some nice place, take a night off. Listen, I don't know anything about her johns, listen, Allie was a good friend of mine, if I knew who might have done that to her, don't you think I'd spill it quick?"

"Did she ever say anything about one of them with the kinky ideas?" asked Gonzales.

She gave a dreary giggle. "Mister, grow up sometime. You run into that kind anywhere. But you mean, like some john wanted to tie her up, do the torture bit? No, she never said anything about one like that, and she wouldn't have stood for nothing like that, there's enough straight guys to pick up and she wasn't that far down. I can't tell you a thing, honest, I wish I could."

"You said you'd talked to her on the phone on Saturday afternoon. Did she say anything about where she was planning to go that night?"

"No, she never. Any of the places she usually hit, I guess. I wouldn't know."

They let her go after a while, and Gonzales slumped down in his desk chair, streching out his legs, and lit a cigarette. "Any john from anyplace," he said. "And unless he left some prints behind, and they're on record somewhere, we'll never know who."

Varallo looked at Delia. "Did you get anything else out of the Miller girl?"

"Not a thing. She couldn't pick any mug shots. But that's a little offbeat, the apologetic rapist. We might ask the computers if that M.O. has ever shown up before."

"Another nut," said Gonzales. "And nobody's dropped on that Barrios yet. Some more came in from Central a while ago, the gun was an S. and W. .38. And Hollywood picked up his car in a lot on Sunset, so nobody knows what he's driving now. He's got one hell of a pedigree."

"Armed and dangerous sums it up," said Varallo tiredly. "He's on P.A. from a fourth count of armed robbery, and he's done time for assault and manslaughter. They sent up some mug shots to post in the squads." He passed one over to Delia. "Isn't he a pretty boy?"

It wasn't an attractive face, square and tough-looking and scarred by an old case of acne. The terse description just added to the picture. Male Caucasian, five-eleven, a hundred and eighty, black and brown, wanted homicide, approach with caution.

They sat in silence for a while—apparently everybody else was out on something—and for the moment there wasn't anything else for them to do. There were a couple of court appearances coming up the next day, arraignments on cases cleared away a couple of weeks before.

O'Connor came in presently, looking glum, and said, "I've got half a mind to haul in a few of these gang members and lean on them. All the PCP— And God knows enough of the other kinds of foolish powder— If they're not manufacturing angel dust they're dealing in it."

"You don't suppose they'd tell us anything?" said Varallo. "Waste of time, amico. Now, if these were the bad old days when we could use the rubber hoses, we might get some useful information, but with the state of the courts now—"

"Waste of time," agreed O'Connor, and ripped his tie loose and leaned back; the chair creaked under his bulk, and the bulge of the .357 Magnum in the shoulder holster showed prominently. "Nothing new down, I hope?"

"Not that I know of," said Varallo. "Nice quiet day." The afternoon was drifting along toward the end of shift. He reached for the phone and called the lab and got Thomsen. "Have you sorted out any of those latents from that homicide scene?"

"Yeah, six pretty good ones, but they're not on record with us. I sent them downtown and to the Feds. We'll get a kickback sometime, wait for it."

Katz came in and said, "Get out of my chair, Charles. Now we've got another daylight burglary, all up in the air."

The burglary rate was climbing every day and there were seldom any leads, but over the past couple of months there had been an unusual number of daylight break-ins, all expectedly in the middle-class apartments where working people were away all day. It could be the same X on all of them, or half a dozen X's working independently. "Just more paperwork, damn it," said Katz. He got the report forms out but didn't immediately make a move at the typewriter.

"Just remember what a noble career it is," said Varallo, and O'Connor barked a savage laugh.

A messenger came up from Communications with a manila envelope. It contained the autopsy report on that unidentified body. Varallo scanned it hastily and said, "Damn all. Man about sixty, cause of death acute alcoholism. The city'll have to bury him. Damn it, I forgot to ask that Quigley woman if Alicia Taylor had any relatives to notify."

"No particular hurry about it," said Gonzales.

There were still a few heist men they were looking for desultorily, from three jobs a couple of weeks before; with only vague descriptions to go on, they were picking up men out of Records with suggestive pedigrees to question, but probably nothing would come of it.

"Damn it," said O'Connor, "it's either a feast or a famine. I think I'm going home early."

Nothing new went down the rest of the afternoon. Boswell came in about five o'clock with a suspect to question, and Varallo sat in on that, but they couldn't get anything out of him and he was just a possible; they let him go.

Delia stopped at the market on her way home, and got to the bright new apartment at a quarter to seven. As she came down the hall, there was a man unlocking the door of the other apartment next to hers, nearest the elevator. He was a tall dark man in a gray business suit; he gave her an incurious glance. There was something vaguely familiar about him, but she couldn't place him, didn't think she'd ever seen him before. As she opened her own door, she could hear Henry chattering away to himself in the living room. He seemed to have regained his normal spirits, and greeted her exuberantly. "Hello, Delia dear! You're a very pretty girl! Did you have a nice day? I say, let's all have a little drink!" Delia went to scratch his bright blue head. For all his fearsome great curved beak, Henry was affectionate and docile, even if he did talk too much. There was a strong cool breeze coming in the open balcony door. For the next couple of months, before the heat built up enough to call for air conditioning, she could leave the windows and the door to the balcony open, and Henry would enjoy the fresh air. She cast an appreciative glance at her nice view over the city, in April as yet uncontaminated by smog.

For no good reason, Varallo was tired; it had been a slow day. As he turned into the drive, the children were playing in the backyard; he waved to them. In the kitchen, Laura said, "You're a little early. I'll get the children in in a minute. You look as if you could use a drink before dinner."

"That's the best idea I've heard all day," said Varallo, bending to kiss her. He wandered into the living room and found the fat gray tabby, Gideon Algernon Cadwallader, asleep in his armchair. He lifted him out of it, and Gideon, affronted, stalked out. Varallo sat down and Laura brought him a tall brandy and soda. He surveyed her, his lovely brown-haired girl, and took a grateful sip. "And so what's the plot you're cooking up with Katharine?"

Laura laughed. "Well, it's not really a plot, Vic. It's about Delia. Now she's really all alone, and you know how it's been for her— All these years on the job, and mostly on swing shift until she got the job here— She hasn't any old friends at all, hasn't any friends except us and Katharine and Charles, and the people at the office. And she's really quite a pretty girl, in a quiet sort of way."

"Oh, I see," said Varallo, enlightened. "Find a boyfriend for Delia."

"Well, you needn't put it as crudely as that. But if she could meet somebody—somebody nice, who'd appreciate her—"

"Have you got anybody in mind?"

Laura sat down opposite him and regarded him thoughtfully. "Well, the nice eligible men are few and far between. We've just been talking about it. Katharine's idea is that Dr. Farren—you know, their pediatrician. They've had him to dinner and for some reason he and Charles hit it off—complete opposites, of course. He's only about thirty-five, and he's divorced . . . his wife was a drunk. No children."

Varallo grunted. "A nice boyfriend for Delia."

"Well, Katharine says he's a dear, so kind and a wonderful sense of humor."

"Did you ever stop to think that Delia might not be interested in a boyfriend?" Laura just looked at him pityingly.

"And what I thought of was that brother of Audrey Butler's." The Butlers lived next door on Hillcroft Road, and had been friendly; they were a little younger than the Varallos, with two

children. "We met him last month—Don Jenson. He works at the
Security-Pacific Bank, he just got transferred down here from
Santa Barbara."

"I don't seem to remember much about him."

"Well, Audrey wishes he'd get married, she says he's something
of a loner and a little shy."

"He doesn't sound as good a bet as the doctor. And exactly
what's your idea, produce him and say here's a nice prospective
husband?"

"Don't be silly," said Laura. "It's just to see she's introduced to a
couple of . . . of suitable nice men, and see if anything comes of
it. She's such a nice person, Vic, and when you think about it, what
chance has she to meet anybody on that job?"

"Except cops," said Varallo sleepily. "Boswell and Gonzales are
both bachelors, and Lew Wallace, but I suppose they've got their
own girlfriends. But come to think, there's Bob Rhys. Now, he's a
hell of a nice fella, and I know his mother'd like him to get married
and start a family, but maybe he's a born bachelor. And how would
they ever get together when Bob's on night watch?"

"Oh, for heaven's sake," said Laura, "she sees enough cops on
the job, she wouldn't be interested in dating one."

"Now, you look here," said Varallo seriously. "Delia's all right.
Maybe she's satisfied with her life just as it is."

"And maybe she just thinks so," said Laura. "Don't worry, it's
just to see she meets some new people, and a couple of eligible
men. Katharine's going to ask her to dinner, she thought it might
look queer because she never has, but now Delia's living in town,
closer—and I've talked to Audrey, she thought we could have a
cookout in their yard and if you brought Delia to take potluck and
it looked like a last-minute impulse—"

"Delia won't like it if you try to manage her."

"After all, people do introduce their friends to each other. We're
not going to make it obvious," said Laura with dignity. "I'll get the
children in. Finish your drink—dinner's all ready."

Monday was Dick Hunter's night off. The beginning of the week
was generally slow, but with the crime rate up in what used to be
the quietest police beat in the county, they couldn't count on that.
Surprisingly they got their first call half an hour after they'd come
on at six; it was one of the Traffic men, Bill Watkins. He said he was
calling from a pay phone. "Look, it's nothing for you," he said to
Rhys, "but the citizen's fit to be tied, she wants the full treatment,

yelling for detectives. It's a very funny damn thing, at that, but there's nothing anybody can do about it."

"What is it?"

Watkins laughed. "Technically I suppose it could be called assault, not that she's hurt. She had some of her hair cut off."

"What?" said Rhys.

"While she was waiting for a bus at Brand and Broadway," said Watkins.

They were both intrigued enough to go and look. Watkins had the citizen sitting in the squad parked in a red zone at that intersection. Her name was Bernice Dingman, and she was something of an eyeful, in her mid-twenties with a luscious figure, a face like a movie queen, and a luxurious head of beautiful chestnut brown hair, which fell to below her waist and was naturally curly. She was seething with rage, but Watkins had calmed her down sufficiently that she was making some sense.

"It was the beach, damn it," she told Rhys and Harvey. "Naturally I don't wear it hanging down usually, I do it up in a knot or a figure eight with braids. I don't go around like this on the job, naturally. I'm a nurse at Community Hospital, this is my day off. I've never had it cut since I was ten years old, I suppose you could say it's my one vanity, my hair. And we went to the beach today—Sylvia and I—Sylvia Singer, we went in her car, and she had to be home by six, she'd promised the baby sitter not to be later, and we got held up on the freeway, so I told her just to drop me off and I'd get the bus home, I live up on Spencer, and Sylvia lives in Eagle Rock. And coming out of the water, I'd just tied my hair back with a ribbon, it wouldn't matter just the little while I was on the bus. And I'd only been sitting there," she gestured at the bus-stop bench, "about five minutes when this—this creep came up behind me—I didn't know a thing until I felt a sort of tug—and look at it! Just look!" In the beautiful rippling chestnut brown cascade was an ugly gap where a thick wad of it had been chopped off roughly in the middle. "Naturally I jumped and looked around, and *there he was*—capering around like a lunatic with a silly grin and waving this great big piece of my own hair at me—he had a pair of scissors in his other hand—and then he ran off down Broadway."

There hadn't been anyone around, anyone else waiting for the bus or on the street. The stores along there would have been closed at six o'clock, and few people rode the buses. "Can you describe the man?" asked Rhys.

She was still mournfully feeling the gap in her tresses. "Only in a kind of general way. He was a big tall lanky fellow, young, and I can tell you one thing, he's a nut," she said forcefully. "Look, I'm a nurse, and I know about things like this—he's probably got a fetish for hair, the way some of the nuts do for shoes or underwear. He could be a sex fiend. But just look at what he's done to me— I don't know how I'm going to cover it up."

Of course she could be right about the fetishism, but equally of course there wasn't anything detectives could do about it, with not even a good description to go on. Watkins drove her home, and Rhys and Harvey went back to the station. Rhys was still writing a brief report on it when the radio, tuned to police frequency in the background, handed them some news.

That cop killer, Barrios, had just been identified as the heister who had held up a liquor store in Valley Division, out on Saticoy Street. He had taken a shot at the owner when he'd been slow in opening the register, and the owner had identified the mug shot definitely. And there was still no make on the car.

"Christ," said Harvey, "the Valley boys'll be out in force hunting. That's a wild one, Bob. He must know every lawman in the county is looking for him, and pulling a job like that—"

"Maybe he needs the money to go further on the run," said Rhys. "The hell of a thing! But there are a lot of people around out there, Jim—about eleven million in the whole county. He could go to ground somewhere and lie low for months if he doesn't head in any direction out of state. We can only do so much." And the word would be out on the teletypes, to N.C.I.C., in case Barrios did head out for elsewhere, but there were only so many peace officers to read the teletypes, notice the A.P.B.

"There was something on the news today," said Harvey. "That Sergeant Hollister's funeral is tomorrow."

"And God rest his soul," said Rhys seriously.

"He was thirty-six, he had a wife and three kids."

"Yes. Did you happen to notice that damfool article in the *News-Press* about Glendale's finest?"

"Oh, yes," said Harvey. "Silly. I can imagine what O'Connor said about it."

The radio went on muttering in the background; there was a little pileup on the Golden State Freeway, but that was Highway Patrol business. At nine-fifty they got a call to a homicide.

It was a bar on San Fernando Road, and the neon sign over the door said simply, BLACK AND WHITE BAR. The squad-car man was

Steiner. He said, "It was the bartender called in. His name's Mike Callaghan."

To match the name, Callaghan had a square, Irish-looking face and red hair; he was a middle-aged man with an incipient paunch and a rasping voice. Everybody else in the place—about fifteen customers—was Latin. "These Goddamned spicks," said Callaghan. "The last five, six years they're all we get in here, and excuse me, gents, I don't like to sound prejudiced but who's to say how many of 'em jump the border illegal to cash in on Uncle Sam's welfare? I got the guy's knife, here it is," and he produced a wicked-looking horn-handled knife with a blade about six inches long. The blade was stained. "They were sitting at that table there, talking Spick, and all of a sudden this guy stabs the other one, they'd been arguing about something I guess, talking loud—I will say, a couple of other customers helped me hold him down."

There was some I.D. on the corpse. He'd been Antonio Aguilar, twenty-four by the driver's license, an address on Harvard. There were all those witnesses to the killing; Rhys and Harvey spent a while getting all the names and addresses. This would make a hell of a lot more paperwork for the day boys. Finally, they got around to the knife wielder. He was a rather handsome fellow, tall and dark, and to Rhys's first question he said sullenly, "No sé. No English."

"Oh, hell," said Rhys. The courts were so damned fussy about the necessary warnings, protecting the criminal's rights. They ferried him down to the jail; one of the night jailers was a fellow named Dominguez who could talk to the prisoner. He read him his rights first, and relayed the answers to the night-watch men. His name was Eduardo Cantero. He and Aguilar had both worked at a small-parts assembly plant on San Fernando Road. They were both unmarried, living in cheap rented rooms. "He claims he's legal, he's got a green card," said Dominguez. "They were arguing about makes of cars. Cantero was going to buy a car, and he'd about decided on a used Chevy, and Aguilar said he was a damned fool, General Motors was no good, because they exploited their workers, and he'd better buy a Ford product—and Cantero says he just got mad, he didn't mean to kill him, he just lost his temper."

"My good God," said Rhys, "the things we do see." And that would make some paperwork for the day boys too.

CHAPTER THREE

Delia was off on Tuesday. The rest of them drifted in, and Mr. Beal dropped Rosie off at the front door of the station; she came trotting up the stairs after Gonzales. Varallo passed the night report around, and they all did a little cussing about this new homicide; it was nothing to work as far as investigation went, but there would be all the tedious routine to do on it, getting the statements from the witnesses, applying for the warrant; it could take the better part of a couple of days.

Varallo and Wallace had to be in court today, covering a couple of arraignments, and that could take an hour or the rest of the day; the judges didn't care how much police time they wasted. Technically the detectives were assigned to categories: Delia, Jeff Forbes, Varallo, and Gonzales to Robbery-Homicide; O'Connor, Wallace, and Boswell to Narco; Katz and John Poor to Burglary—but in practice, being shorthanded, they all handled whatever came along. O'Connor, Boswell, and Forbes started out to hunt up all those witnesses. Before leaving for the courthouse, Varallo thought a little about the larcenous minister. That one was barren of any leads, but he had pulled three jobs in ten days and showed some incipient violence; they'd like to catch up to him. The *News-Press* ran a short daily column listing the ongoing police calls, without details; Varallo thought it might do no harm to give the minister some publicity, to warn the citizens about his little operation. He called the paper, finally got connected to an editor, passed on the information, and asked cooperation. He was assured there would be a story in tonight's paper.

Chasing down all those witnesses and getting the statements from them took all the rest of the day, and they hadn't finished the paperwork by the end of Tuesday's shift. Varallo didn't get back to the station until after two o'clock; Wallace was luckier and got out of court by noon. By the grace of God, nothing new went down, but of course something would eventually.

Varallo had just finished taking a statement from one of the witnesses at the Black and White Bar at five-thirty, when Thomsen came in and laid a Xeroxed sheet on his desk. Forbes and Wallace were talking to other witnesses, Katz hunched over his typewriter, the big office humming quietly with business. "Say," said Thomsen, "we just got a kickback from some of those prints in the Taylor girl's place. The only make we've got, all the rest of the others N. G. This one showed up in L.A.'s records. Here's the package on him: he's a Carl Brock, one count of grand theft a couple of years back. He did a little time for it. I thought the last known address might be out of date, so I checked with Welfare and Rehab. He's just off parole about four months ago, there's a recent address."

"So, thanks so much," said Varallo. The address was on Brigden Street in Pasadena. He wasn't about to go out looking for Brock at this end of the day; leave it for the night watch. "You never raised anything off those missionary tracts, I suppose."

"What do you expect?" said Thomsen. "The sleazy paper, you wasted our time bringing them in."

The witnesses had all left by a quarter to six. Varallo passed the information on to O'Connor and Forbes. "That hooker," said O'Connor uninterestedly. "Nothing says this Brock is the john who killed her. Just more legwork."

Varallo left a note about it for Bob Rhys and they trailed out for home wearily at the end of shift, hoping that nothing new would break overnight.

Rhys read the note when the night watch came on and said to Hunter, "I suppose we might as well have a look at this guy before we get any new business." They took his car and went over to Pasadena, found the address on Brigden, which was a jerry-built newish apartment building. They found Carl Brock at home. He was about thirty, with a weakly handsome, girlish face and wavy blond hair, and he was alarmed at the flashed badge.

"Just a few questions," said Rhys. "You know an Alicia Taylor, you were in her apartment recently." The prints had been on the footboard of the bed.

"Taylor?" he said stupidly. "I don't know who you mean. Alicia— Oh, yeah. Yeah. That girl. What about her?"

"Were you with her last Saturday night?"

He looked from Rhys to Hunter warily. "No, I wasn't. Alicia— Yeah, that was her name, I just had to think a minute, but I don't know her. Not to say know her. I just picked her up in a bar in Glendale last week, you know, just the once."

"And went home with her for a one-night stand," said Rhys. "We know she was a hooker, and not a very high-class one. When was that?"

"Jesus, I don't know—but it wasn't Saturday, it was maybe a week ago tonight or Wednesday. How the hell do the cops know about it, and what's this about, anyway?"

"You left some fingerprints in her pad," said Hunter. "What were you doing on Saturday night?" They hadn't seen an autopsy report yet, but she had probably been killed that night.

"Saturday— Well, I was with some other fellas playing poker, at Bill's place. Bill Cooper." He gave them the address readily, Evanston Street. He said he and Cooper worked at the same place, a men's store on Colorado, and there had been three other fellows there; he gave them names but didn't know any addresses; probably Cooper would. "What the hell's all this all about?"

They didn't waste time telling him. Being in Pasadena, they looked up the address on Evanston and found Bill Cooper at home, at another small apartment. He was about the same age as Brock, a dark, stocky fellow, and he confirmed that Brock had been at Saturday night's poker party, gave the names and addresses of the other three men. "Sure, Carl was here, from around seven to 2 A.M., and did himself some good—he was hotter than a two-dollar pistol that night, he cleaned me out all right. Why the hell are cops asking?"

So it looked as if Brock had a substantial alibi and they'd been wasting time; but it had had to be checked out. They got back to the station at nine-fifty and met Harvey just pulling into the parking lot.

"You missed a new heist. A pharmacy out on Glenoaks, and by what the victim says it was that same pair again, the teenagers with the motorcycle. The pharmacist saw them take off in the street."

"Hell," said Hunter. "Not a smell of a lead on that. By their ages they won't be in Records."

"Just another report to write," said Harvey.

On Wednesday morning, with Wallace off, Varallo read the note Rhys had left for him and passed it over to Forbes. "Evidently that's the only set of prints the lab's tagged so far from the Taylor girl's place. Nowhere to go—except ask at all the bars where she might have picked up the john on Saturday night."

Forbes uttered a rude word. "Now, I ask you, Vic—any one of

forty places anywhere in town, and why would anybody have noticed a cheap hooker picking up an anonymous john? None of those places will be open until this afternoon, and it'd be a big damn waste of time asking questions. The damn thing'll end up in Pending eventually anyway."

Varallo agreed dispiritedly. O'Connor, as usual, wasn't in his office, but slouched at Wallace's desk with Rosie in his lap. There were still statements to get from a few more witnesses to that knifing, and Boswell and Gonzales had gone out on that. Delia was sitting at her desk smoking and studying a report, and Varallo eyed her absently; Laura was quite right, she was a good-looking girl in a quiet sort of way, the dark hair in a casual short cut, nice fair complexion, good figure in the unobtrusive plain clothes she wore for work, dark pantsuits or dresses. Thirty-three this month, and not looking her age.

The autopsy report came in on the Taylor girl, and there wasn't much in it. She'd been strangled manually, and the estimated time of death was between six and midnight last Saturday. They hadn't heard whether the lab had picked up anything else there; the lab always took its time. Varallo got on the phone and talked to Burt. "Listen," said Burt, "you've been reading too many detective stories, Vic. Sure, sometimes we can pull off the miracles. But in the ordinary place with the ordinary dust and dirt, what's to find for analysis? Nobody knows any of the rest of those prints, sorry."

"Just the anonymous john," said Varallo. "Well, thanks."

And the phone rang up in O'Connor's office; he put Rosie down and went to answer it. Thirty seconds later he bellowed Varallo's name. "All of you come in here and listen to this, I think it's going to give us some work." Varallo, Forbes, and Delia crowded into the little office.

O'Connor punched the amplifier on the phone. "Just say that again, I want my crew to hear it. It's a Captain Dawson in Lansing, Kansas," he added.

"—AWOL from Fort Leavenworth." The voice blaring out from the amplifier was loud and clear, a pleasant male baritone. "His lieutenant contacted us last night, after he talked to some of this guy's pals. And it doesn't look too good, Lieutenant. His name's Frank Orley, he's a buck private, on a first hitch, he's twenty-one, and he's got a clean enough record with the Army, nothing outstanding, the officer says he's not very damn bright but gets by. He's from California originally, a place called Culver City. And he got a Dear John letter from his girl about a month ago, and according to the pals he's been brooding on it ever since. He's been talking about killing her for throwing him over. She's just married another fellow. He went over the hill sometime on Monday, and he took along a gun belonging to one of the pals, a .38 Colt revolver and some ammo for it. Nobody can say whether he's maybe hitchhiking or hopped a car somewhere. If he's in a stolen car, he may be picked up but maybe not, too. And he could be some distance on the way."

"The definite threats?" said O'Connor.

"That's too right, he wants to kill the girl for marrying the other fellow, and the other fellow too. Reason we're calling you, it seems to be in your territory. None of the pals knew where she lives out there, but the lieutenant had a look at what he left behind, and there was the Dear John letter from a Frances Dane. No address, but he'd put her down as who to notify in case of death and it was an address in Santa Monica. The girl's not there, it's her mother's address, and the mother gave us an address in your burg just an hour ago. The girl's now Mrs. Frances Hendrix, and the address is Graynold Avenue."

"All right, I've got it," said O'Connor, scribbling. "He's heading west, hitchhiking or whatever—he could have covered a little distance but he won't be here yet unless he had money for a plane."

"Probably unlikely," said Dawson. "He wouldn't have had much over a hundred bucks on him, by what the pals say. But he sounds pretty damned desperate, and he may pull a robbery on the way. But there's a lot of territory between here and there, O'Connor, and all we can do is put out the want on him. God knows where he's got to. We just thought the girl ought to be warned—by the last thing he said to one of the pals, he's definitely out to get back to California and kill both of them."

"You're so right," said O'Connor. "We'll be on it, Dawson. You'll let us know if he's picked up."

"And let us know what goes on out there," said Dawson. "The Army'll have first claim on him, unless he does succeed in committing murder."

O'Connor put the phone down and said, "Goddamn it, the bastard could be here by late today or tomorrow. Quicker if he got a plane. The girl and her husband have got to be warned, and we'd better stake out that address. We can get a description of him from the girl. Goddamn it, I should have got the mother's phone. It's on the cards they both work and she'd know where. But try the address first."

Varallo and Forbes went over to the Graynold Avenue address. It was an old, dignified eight-unit place, well landscaped, in that good section of town. The Hendrix apartment, by the name slot on the door, was on the second floor, but nobody answered the bell. Downstairs, a door on the left of the lobby bore a sign, MANAGER-ESS, and a stout gray-haired woman opened the door to them. "Yes, I'm the manageress, I'm Mrs. Ramsey, what do the police want here?" She stared at the badge in bewilderment. Varallo explained economically, and she exclaimed, "Why, that's just terrible! A terrible thing—those two nice youngsters, why, they just moved in two weeks ago, they've just got married, they're such nice young people and you can see so much in love—this is a terrible thing—"

"Do they both work, Mrs. Ramsey? Do you know where?"

"Why, yes, she works at Robinson's in the Fashion Center, and he works at the Bank of America on Brand. This is terrible, I never heard of such a thing—"

In the car Varallo said, "Better talk to her first." They drove across town to that old and small shopping mall on Glendale Avenue. At Robinson's Department Store they talked to a Mrs. Conley in Personnel. Frances Hendrix was in the better dresses section, on the second floor. "We'd like to talk to her privately, is there an office we could use?"

"I suppose you could use the employees' lounge down the hall—I'll call her up here."

The lounge was a big room, rather bare of furniture, with a coffee machine, a soft-drink dispenser. She came to them in a few minutes; she was a very pretty girl in her early twenties, with a slim figure and blond hair, blue eyes and a tiptilted nose over a wide, friendly mouth. They got her to sit down and told her about Frank Orley, and she was alarmed and indignant.

"Frank!" she said. "But that's just crazy, I can't understand it, he hasn't any reason to feel that way. Saying he wants to kill me—and kill Ed! I was never engaged to Frank, we were just friends, I never even let him kiss me—he's just somebody I knew—"

"Had you dated him?" asked Varallo.

"Yes, a little bit, but it wasn't anything serious, not on my part anyway. We were in high school together—"

"That was in Culver City?"

"That's right, but Mother and I moved to Santa Monica in my

last year of high. Frank didn't graduate, he wasn't very smart in school, he dropped out and got a job at a gas station in West Hollywood. He was always asking me to go out with him, and I did sometimes before he went into the Army. I guess he was a lot more serious about it than I was, he said he wanted to marry me and I just told him not to be silly—I was sorry for him," she said honestly. "I always felt sorry for Frank. He's an orphan, he grew up in a lot of different foster homes and I don't think anybody really cared much for him, gave him much attention. That was the only reason I went out with him sometimes and said I'd write to him when he went into the Army. He didn't have anybody. I didn't really think a lot of him, I was just sorry for him. That was last year, and I didn't write very often, but he wrote to me—and I was a little worried about it, because he called me sweetheart and talked about getting married, and I never thought of Frank that way at all, it was just silly. And then I met Ed, that was about six months ago. I don't think I'd written Frank once since then, I was just being friendly writing him at all—you know." She was a nice girl, honest and open. "And of course when Ed asked me to marry him, and we decided to do it right away, I wrote Frank and told him about it. I said I wouldn't be writing again, because of getting married, and I just wished him luck—I tried to make it friendly. But he hasn't any reason to feel jealous, we were never anything but friends, I never cared a—a button for Frank that way. Do you think he really means it, that he'd try to kill both of us?"

"Well, his officer and the police back there seem to think so, Mrs. Hendrix," said Forbes. "Of course there's a want out on him and he may be picked up before he gets back to California, but it'll be just as well to take precautions. Does he know your address here?"

She was looking frightened now. She said, "Oh, my goodness, yes, he does. That last letter—I was just trying to sound friendly, I told him about Ed, and we'd just arranged to rent the apartment that day—I didn't mention the address but I did say it was the corner of Graynold and Glenoaks—and there's only the two apartment buildings there on the corner."

"That's unfortunate," said Varallo. "And we haven't got a picture of him, have you?"

"Heavens, no," she said. "But of course I can tell you what Frank looks like—he's about six feet and thin, with brown hair and a kind of long face—"

That was something if very general. "Does he know where you work?" asked Forbes.

"Yes, of course, I've been at Robinson's just over a year, I couldn't get a decent job in Santa Monica, and it meant I had to move up here, I've been in an apartment on Dryden, and Ed was living at home with his parents, of course, and we wanted something a little bigger—we couldn't afford a real honeymoon, we just got married two weeks ago—and moved into the new apartment—"

"It'd be just as well," said Varallo, "if you stayed home from work for a while, and your husband, too. Did you happen to tell Orley where he works?"

She said unhappily, "Well, I did," and she was looking more frightened. "Do you really think Frank's serious about this? I can't believe it, but if you say so—oh, dear, I'll have to explain to Mrs. Conley, and it'll mean losing pay—and what the bank will say about Ed taking off—"

"Well, it's just a precaution," said Forbes. "We'll hope he gets picked up soon, but until we know where he is—"

"Yes, I see," said Frances Hendrix. "Good heavens, I just thought —you said the police back in Kansas had called Mother—she must be frantic, if they told her this, probably trying to phone me, but we're not allowed to get calls at work—you want me to go home now?"

"I think so," said Varallo. They talked to Mrs. Conley, who was head of Personnel, and explained; Frances Hendrix didn't have a car, and they drove her back to the apartment and heard her lock herself in. There was a chain on the door. Then they went downtown to the Bank of America on North Brand and talked to Ed Hendrix.

He was one of the tellers there; he was a tall, dark, good-looking young man in his early twenties, with a solid jaw and shrewd eyes. As he listened to them he began to look frightened too, but for the girl. "This is just crazy," he said. "Francie'd told me about that fellow, she was sorry for him—kind of a dim-witted fellow, not much on the ball, I gather. She'd never gone steady with anybody but me, there wasn't anything between them that way. What she told me, I gather he was crazy about her, but she never let him think he could get anywhere with her. The guy must be nuts."

"And that's possible too," said Varallo equably, "but you can see it's just sense to take precautions. Can you take some time off your job?"

Hendrix said briefly, "The hell with the job. If they fire me I can always get another. I'm not going to let Francie out of my sight until you've got this bastard behind bars." They left him explaining to his immediate boss; he'd be going right home to stay with the girl.

Back at headquarters, they found O'Connor talking to the day watch commander, Lieutenant Gates, in his cubicle of an office behind the Traffic mustering room. "Damn it," Gates was saying, "we're spread damn thin as it is, with the rate up, we've only got so many squad men. Oh, I see it, I see it, the place had better be staked out. I'll have to divert a squad from somewhere else to cover that northwest section on all three shifts."

"Now look," said O'Connor, "this guy may be a little off his rocker, but he'll know a squad car when he sees one. Plant the black-and-white smack in front of that apartment, and if he ever lands here he'll take off like a rocket at one look."

"Teach your grandmother," said Gates rudely. "The men can use their own cars."

O'Connor looked at Varallo. "Is there a back entrance to that building?"

"Back door's off the kitchen," said Forbes, "at least in that place. Back stairs to the backyard."

"Hell," said O'Connor. "Then the stakeouts had better check on the Hendrixes every so often."

It was just past noon now, and the next Traffic shift would come on at four. "I'll work something out before the swing shift shows up for a briefing," said Gates. "There's no almighty rush about it, O'Connor. Orley couldn't be here yet, if he got away from Kansas sometime on Monday."

"We don't know, damn it," said O'Connor. "He could have pulled a heist right there that night and bought an airline ticket in the name of John Smith. He could be somewhere in this town right now."

"Well, they ought to be safe enough until four o'clock," said Gates dryly.

"Has anything turned up on that Barrios?" asked Varallo.

"Not a damn thing," said Gates. "He's vanished into the jungle."

They went upstairs to the communal office and found Joe Katz talking to a middle-aged couple, taking notes for a statement. Nobody else was in. By his tone of voice, Katz was making a little effort to be polite to the citizens. When they went out, about half an hour later, he flung himself back in his desk chair and said, "My God! People! Everybody ought to know how high the burglary rate is, there's been enough publicity about it, and that pair of damned fools go out to a movie last night and leave the sliding glass door open to the back porch so the cat can get out there to its litter box. I ask you. They're missing a big color TV, a movie camera, a lot of miscellaneous jewelry and a microwave oven, and they're mad at the police for not keeping the burglars off the street, and of course it's their own damned fault. Where've you been all day, doing any good?" He was interested to hear about Orley. "But you may have been wasting time, maybe he's already been picked up back there."

"Dawson would call back," said O'Connor. "The A.P.B.'s out from Lansing and he'd hear about it within fifteen minutes."

"Oh, and by the way," said Katz, "there was a rape went down. Delia went out on it."

The call had come in at eleven-twenty, and Delia had been the only detective in. The address was Cleveland Road, and it turned out to be a comfortable-looking old California bungalow with a well-manicured lawn in front and a bed of roses by the porch. The squad was parked in front, and she found Patrolman Morris talking to a woman in the living room. It was a pleasantly furnished room, the only sign of disorder a vacuum cleaner standing in the middle of the carpet.

"This is Mrs. Marion Ogden," said Morris. "Detective Riordan, ma'am. You can tell her all about it."

Mrs. Ogden was a nice-looking woman with dark hair, not young; at a guess, Delia put her down as in her forties. She was sitting on the edge of a chair looking dazed and distressed; her blue cotton housedress was torn at the neckline and she kept pressing the tear together with a slightly shaking hand. She looked at Delia and said, "Are you a detective? I thought detectives were always men. You read about it happening, but you never think it could happen to you. And broad daylight—ten-thirty in the morning! I didn't believe it was happening—getting raped! Right in the middle of cleaning the house. John's going to go right up in the air."

"So tell me what happened," said Delia, getting out her notebook.

Morris went out to get back on tour, and Mrs. Ogden said in automatic courtesy, "Sit down, won't you? I just didn't believe it was happening, and John's going to give me a lecture about locking doors, but for heaven's sake, the middle of the morning—and I was coming and going emptying wastebaskets, I'd started a load of laundry, the washer and dryer are in the garage—I wasn't going to lock and unlock the back door whenever I went out there for three minutes! We're having some people in for dinner, I was just cleaning up the place."

"You were here alone?" asked Delia, to get her started.

"Yes, of course, the children are both at school, they both go to Hoover High, and John—my husband—is at his office, he's with Holden and Lowe, the architects. I'd just started straightening the living room, emptied the wastebasket and dusted everything and so on, and I was just starting to run the vacuum when he jumped on me from behind—I nearly had a heart attack, not dreaming there was anybody near me. He must have got in the back door—"

This house was on a corner, and the separate garage faced the side street. "He could have noticed you when you went out to the garage and took a chance on trying the back door. Can you tell me what he looked like?"

"My heavens above," said Mrs. Ogden, "I can give you some idea but not much— It's a queer thing to say, but it all happened so fast I hardly had time to be frightened—and he raped me, but he didn't actually hurt me, I mean he didn't hit me or knock me down, anything like that. He just grabbed me from behind, I hadn't heard a thing because the vacuum cleaner was running, of course—and he was big and strong, he got me down on the floor and raped me—he tore my panties off and—well, he didn't waste any time, if you know what I mean. I tried to fight him but he was just too strong—and then he got up off me—I was still lying on the floor—and he said in such a funny, polite way, I'm sorry I had to do this—and he was gone before I could pick myself up. I couldn't believe it had happened."

The apologetic rapist again. "What did he look like?" asked Delia.

"Well, he was big, as I say—I'd say over six feet. He had dark blond hair down below his ears—I only got one look at him just before he ran out—he had a round sort of face—" She shook her head helplessly. "That's really all I could tell you. It was the queerest thing, his being so polite at the end. John's going to have a fit—"

"You'd better see your doctor, Mrs. Ogden," said Delia.

"Oh, I'm all right. It's not exactly as if I was a young girl. Of course it was an awful experience, but he didn't really hurt me." She looked at Delia more alertly and summoned up a small smile. "If you were thinking I might get pregnant, I had a hysterectomy last year."

Delia said bluntly, "I was thinking more of possible V.D., Mrs. Ogden."

"Oh, my heavens. Oh, yes, I see. I'd better call the doctor. Good heavens, that never entered my head, but one like that—you never know."

"Did he touch anything in here?"

"I don't think so, he just grabbed me." But he had probably got in through the unlocked back door. Delia used the phone to call the lab, and Rex Burt came up in the van, took Mrs. Ogden's prints, and dusted the solid back door. He raised a few good latents; but if the rapist's were among them it wouldn't be much help unless he was in somebody's records.

"Really, I'll be all right," said Mrs. Ogden. "You've been very kind. I expect I'd better call John, and I can just hear what he'll say. I certainly hope you can catch that man."

"So do we," said Delia. She had missed lunch again and stopped for a malt at the coffee shop down the block from the station. In the communal office she found O'Connor, Varallo, and Forbes talking while Katz and Poor were both busy typing reports. "What did you find out about the Hendrix girl?" she asked.

Varallo told her about that, about the arranged stakeout. "The more I think about it," said O'Connor uneasily, "the surer I am that Orley could be here by now. And Dawson said he'd be in touch, but—" He used Varallo's phone to put a call through to police headquarters in Lansing. Dawson was out of the office, but he got a Lieutenant Austin, who seemed to know all about it and told him there hadn't been a smell of Orley. "But I suppose," said O'Connor, "there've been some heists pulled around there since Monday night."

"Plenty of 'em," said Austin tersely. "On our beat and 'round about. We'd like to think we're just as smart as the California cops, you don't think we hadn't thought about that? So far as any information we've got goes, none of the heisters was Orley, by the descriptions. But of course there's a lot of country west of us, and we can't guess how far he might have got in forty-eight hours. I take it you've arranged to protect the girl."

"Yes, yes," said O'Connor. "We may still have some time before Orley gets here, if he ever does. You'll let me know if you hear any news." He put the phone down and massaged his bulldog jaw.

Delia told them briefly about the rape. "Two in four days," said Varallo. "He's not wasting any time, is he?"

"Just what Mrs. Ogden said," said Delia dryly. "But he may have left some prints this time. It's offbeat, all right, the polite apologies." She uncovered her typewriter and got out report forms.

Varallo sat back and lit a cigarette. "At least there was a little story about the minister on the second page of last night's *News-Press.* Hopefully, a lot of people saw it, and any female who did won't be trustfully opening her front door to take the missionary tracts."

The phone rang on Forbes's desk and he picked it up. "You've got a new body," said the dispatcher.

"My God, talk about a feast or a famine. Where? What? I will be damned. All right, we're on it." He looked at Varallo. "A body, up in the debris basin in Child's Canyon next to Brand Park. What next?"

Delia had taken time out for a cup of coffee from the machine down the hall and chatted desultorily with Katz about the rash of daylight burglaries. She had finished the report and had just decided it was probably too early to call and ask if Burt had made anything out of the prints from Mrs. Ogden's back door, when Lieutenant Gates came wandering in with a report in his hand. O'Connor, for once, was in his office, on the phone to somebody in Narco in Pasadena, and Boswell and Gonzales, having just brought in a suspect for questioning, were ensconced in one of the interrogation rooms. Only Delia, Katz, and Poor were in. Rosie had been sitting on Katz's lap having her ears scratched, and jumped down to greet another friend.

"Hello, Rosie," said Gates, bending to pat her. "Say, we've got something funny here. McLeon was telling me about it when the shift changed just now. I don't see that there's anything for anybody to do about it, but I suppose technically it could be called assault, and I thought I'd pass it on."

"Mmh?" said Delia vaguely, looking up from proofreading her report.

Gates sat down at Varallo's desk. "Well, it's a very funny little thing. McLeon was cruising down Central about an hour ago, when he got hailed by a couple of teenage girls on the street. One of them was about to have hysterics, he said. She'd had some of her hair cut off."

"What?"

"Hair," said Gates, gesturing around his balding head. "Damn long hair, McLeon said. You know how some of the girls wear it, hanging down their backs or in ponytails or in braids or something

—this girl had braids. Her name's Susan Alvarez, and she was blubbering all over the place about it, it seems she'd been growing it for years and was, you know, pretty damned proud of it. She had it in two long braids down to her waist, and this nut had cut one of 'em right off."

"Oh," said Delia suddenly. "There was something in a night report—what happened?"

"The two girls go to Hoover, and they'd come downtown after school to do some shopping. They'd been in a couple of shops over in the Galleria, and just come out to the parking lot—the Alvarez girl had borrowed her mother's car. Just as they were walking across the lot—it wasn't very crowded in the middle of the weekday—this nut came up behind 'em with a pair of scissors and snipped off the braid and ran off with it. All they could tell McLeon was that he ran back toward that big department store there, and they didn't get a good look at him. The other girl said he was tall and thin and had a silly grin on his face and waved the braid at them before he ran."

Katz laughed, but Delia said seriously, "The night watch had one like that just a couple of days ago. Well, it's funny, Joe, but not so very to that girl—and it's something like stealing underwear off the clothesline, it could be one of the earmarks of the sex freak just starting out."

"That crossed my mind," nodded Gates. "But there's no way to go hunting for him. I just thought I'd pass it on."

"Make a Xerox of the report," said Delia. "A little more paper cluttering up the office won't be noticed, and if we ever do catch up to him—or if he graduates to something bigger and we can tie him to that—it might be useful."

"Will do," said Gates cheerfully. "McLeon said he'd never seen anybody so upset, the girl wasn't fit to drive and the other one didn't have a license, they had to call that one's mother to come and take them home. All over a braid of hair." Thoughtfully he smoothed his growing bald spot. "Well, I can see how it'd be important to a young girl. Damn shame, I suppose she'll have to have the other braid cut off now and start growing hair again, she couldn't go around all lopsided. And of course the nut could be a real nut."

And there wasn't anything immediate to do about it, but it would be interesting to know who the nut was.

The body wasn't, strictly speaking, a body at all. When Varallo and Forbes got up to that rather desolate area north of the city, they found two big forklifts standing idle and some muscular men standing beside them, smoking: one of the city crews. The landfill area was one of several up in the hills where the accumulated trash of civilization was getting periodically buried and covered up to fill in canyons and old streambeds without cluttering up the land-scape. This one wasn't far above Brand Park, only a few blocks above Mountain Street, and they had to leave Varallo's car in the park and walk up there over rough terrain.

"Somebody called in a body," said Forbes.

"Listen," said one of the muscular men leaning against the near-est forklift, "you find a dead person, you're supposed to call the cops. And it's a dead person, isn't it? You can't deny that. Even if there isn't much left of it. We've been shifting stuff up here the last couple of days, getting ready to dump some more rubbish and get it covered up. You know the way we do, building up a landfill section." Varallo told him they both knew how landfill areas were handled. "And I'm shifting a load of dirt maybe forty minutes ago, and all of a sudden I see I turned up a dead person, and I know the rules—I got to call the cops. So I stop the rig and I find the nearest phone, down at the art library in the park, and I call in. What else would you want me to do? Nobody's touched it, we know better than that."

Varallo and Forbes looked at the dead person without enthusi-asm. You couldn't say that it had ever been a person; it wasn't much more than a skeleton, with a few shreds of desiccated, mum-mified flesh here and there. There seemed to be a few shreds of clothing, not much. "What the hell can anybody make out of that?" said Forbes.

"I suppose the doctors can tell us if it's male or female," said Varallo. "It could have been here for years. Or could it?" He looked at the forklift operator. "When was the last major work done up here, do you know? Around this particular spot?"

He shrugged. "Way last year sometime, I guess. We let every-thing lay about the last summer and winter, for the last load of stuff to settle in."

And last winter had been very wet. The rain, soaking through loosened soil, would have hurried on the decomposition; but whether the doctors could guess how long the body had been buried was another question.

"Not much to do but send it in to the morgue," said Varallo.

They had to go back to the library in the park for the nearest phone. Varallo called up a morgue wagon and then got hold of Dr. Goulding at Community Hospital and told him what they were sending him.

"You do come up with the offbeat ones sometimes," said Goulding amiably. "We'll have a look and see if we can tell you anything."

By that time there wasn't much left of the day, and Varallo dropped Forbes off at the parking lot behind the station and started home. Thank God, day after tomorrow was his day off; they'd been rather busy the past couple of months and he hadn't gotten around to pruning all his roses. Maybe he'd summon up the energy to finish that.

Patrolman Bill Watkins was interested to be handed a new assignment, a different job from cruising the beat in a squad from four until midnight and handing out a few traffic tickets, picking up drunks and dealing with the bar brawls and muggings. They weren't supposed to wear the uniform on this job, and after the briefing in the muster room he hurried home to change into ordinary clothes, and drove his own Chevy back to that corner. Graynold was a quiet street, and there were plenty of parking places on both sides. He parked the Chevy across the street from that apartment.

The hell of a thing, he thought, this nice girl's old boyfriend threatening to kill her and her husband. What got into people—well, he'd had a couple of steady girlfriends he'd thought a lot of, without wanting to get tied up in marriage, and maybe someday he'd meet a girl he could really fall for, so hard he might feel like killing anybody who took her away—but he couldn't quite imagine that.

He sat there and smoked a couple of cigarettes, and then he walked across the street. It was dark on Graynold, not many streetlights, but of course Glenoaks was a main drag and well lighted. He climbed the stairs to the second floor and rang the Hendrixes' bell.

"Who is it?" asked a male voice sharply.

"Police, Mr. Hendrix." The door opened cautiously on a chain and Watkins held out the badge. "Just letting you know we're watching out, sir. I'm right across the street, and somebody else'll take over at midnight."

"Okay, thanks," said Hendrix. "We appreciate it."

Watkins went back to the Chevy and settled down. At that, he thought, sitting lonely and bored on a stakeout wasn't going to be as interesting as cruising the beat and seeing a little action.

Unexpectedly, in the middle of the week, the night watch was kept busy. Of course it would be Rhys's night off. First, Hunter and Harvey got a call to a market out on Glenoaks Boulevard; it was a heist and something more. The market had been getting ready to close at nine o'clock, and there hadn't been any customers in, the manager bagging the day's take for the bank, only a couple of checkout girls and one box boy there. The manager and the girls were fairly good witnesses; they said there'd been two of them, both young and big and they'd both had guns. One of them had covered the girls, the other had gone for the manager at the back of the store. It looked as if it had been a well-planned caper, hit at closing time, and by the stories they had been cool and quick and slick.

"But Tony— Oh, my God, Tony—" The manager was James Bagby, an elderly fat man, and he was almost crying. Both the girls were weeping openly, both young, one blond and one dark. "Tony— Such a good boy, my God, he's only seventeen— An ambitious boy, one of the best I ever had, he's worked here after school for a year, he was saving up his money, wanted to be a doctor, such a good, smart boy— I ran out after them, I thought maybe I could get a look at what they were driving, and I did—it was a VW Rabbit, I think it was dark red, but the fluorescent lights change colors—but Tony—"

The box boy, Antonio Cordova, had been out in the parking lot collecting the wheeled market carts to bring back inside. The heisters had run him down, probably inadvertently as they roared out of the lot with their take. Bagby said he'd seen it; the Rabbit had been right outside one entrance and the boy pushing a load of carts toward the door. He'd been dragged, caught under the car; the mangled body was lying at the front of the lot, near one of the exits. "My good Christ," said Harvey, looking at it.

"But he was only seventeen," said Bagby. "Such a good boy—just a senseless thing— I don't know how much they got, what in hell does it matter beside Tony's life? No, I didn't get the plate number. When I saw the car hit Tony everything else went out of my head—"

The only thing about it was, if they ever caught up to the heisters, it would at least be a manslaughter charge. And if they did, and the charge stuck, how much time would they spend in the joint? With the state of the courts—

They didn't have time to write a report on it, after they had called the morgue wagon and done another job that cops came in for: breaking the bad news. The Cordovas were decent, good people, and the boy had been an only son; they both went to pieces and Hunter called some relatives for them. They hadn't been back at the office fifteen minutes when they got a call to another heist, at an all-night pharmacy on Colorado. That had been one man, by what the victim told them. He was a young man spelling the owner at night, and he said crisply, "I wasn't about to be a hero, if you get me. Mr. Grassley—he owns this place—always says, you get held up, hand over, it's only money and we're insured. This dude was high on something, I wouldn't say what, liquor or dope— he was waving a big gun around, I play like a good boy and cooperate. There'd have been maybe seventy bucks in the register, and checks, but he didn't take those—and he got me to put a lot of the uppers and downers in a bag for him. Well, he was about twenty-five, stocky, about five-seven or -eight, light brown hair— I might recognize a picture."

They asked him to come in to make a statement; all this would make some work for the day watch. They'd just gotten back to the office when they were called out again to a heist on the street. A young couple, Ruth and Bill Buck, had just left the Alex Theater after the last show when they were held up in the public parking lot behind the theater. They couldn't give any description—of course, it had been dark—and the heister had gotten about ten bucks and Buck's wristwatch.

By Thursday morning, nothing had been heard about the cop killer Barrios. Nothing had turned up on Frank Orley, supposedly heading west. The night watch had left them the hell of a lot of work, and Varallo and Forbes swore over the market heist, the other one. All those people would be coming in to make statements, and they would go hunting up the possible suspects, on the thankless job. "That poor damned kid," said Forbes. "And the worthless louts killing him by accident— Where's the sense to life, Vic?"

"It'd be nice to think there was some," said Varallo wryly.

The market manager came in, and the girls. Delia was talking to one of them when her phone rang; she picked it up. "I think," said Mary Champion, down in Juvenile, "you'd better hear about this.

I've just started to listen, and I can guess what it's about—my God, what a thing—but it's probably something for you as well as us. You'd better hear about it."

"All right, I'll be with you in a minute," said Delia. She turned the witness over to Gonzales, who was typing a report, and went downstairs to the Juvenile office. It was Ben Guernsey's day off and Mary was alone there, with a Negro couple and a little Negro girl about twelve or thirteen.

"Mr. and Mrs. Dakin," said Mary, "and Sandra."

CHAPTER FOUR

Dakin was a big, heavy-shouldered man about forty, his skin darker than his wife's or the girl's. Mrs. Dakin was a thin little woman, milk-chocolate color, with a round pleasant face and gold-rimmed glasses. The little girl was rather pretty, her black curly hair in two neat pigtails tied with pink bows; she was wearing a stiffly starched pink dress.

Mary said, "This is Miss Riordan, I'd like her to hear about this. Suppose you start over and fill in the background."

The man said, "Sure, anything you say, ma'am." He was looking angry. "As soon as Sandra told us about it last night we figured the police ought to hear about it. It's a dirty, evil thing. We've only been in California a couple of months, I got laid off the job at home, we're from Brownsburg, Indiana. Anna May's brother lives here, he wrote there was plenty of good jobs in construction here, so we come out, and I got a good job right off with a contractor here. And Sandra started school here as soon as we got settled. She liked the new school all right up to now."

Mrs. Dakin took up the tale when he paused. "And I got a job waiting on table at Denny's, I never worked since Sandra was born, a mother ought to be at home, but we've used up a lot of savings and Sandra's a real responsible child. I get home by five-thirty. But never mind about all that. Sandra, you just tell the ladies what happened. The school seemed all right, but now I just don't know." She was distressed. "But we knew the police ought to hear about it, you ought to arrest that woman. You just tell the ladies, Sandra."

The girl gave Delia a shy smile. "Well, it's like Mom says, I like the new school all right, I never have any trouble at school, I was in sixth grade back home, but they made me take a test of some kind and they let me skip a grade, I'm in seventh grade here—"

Her mother broke in. "Sandra's always been real good in school, one of the teachers back home told us she's got a real good brain, ought to go to college."

"I like school," said Sandra. "I haven't got to know many other kids here yet, just some in the same classes with me, and some at church that don't go to my school."

Mrs. Dakin said, "We go to the Baptist Church, and thank God Sandra's had a good, Christian raising and knows right from wrong. I shudder to think what might have happened. All right, honey, you just go on and tell."

"Well," said Sandra in her reedy little voice, "it was the gym teacher. I don't like gym much, I don't like playing games and all that, but everybody's got to take it. And the gym teacher, her name's Miss Lister, she asked me if I'd like to earn some money working after school. That was just yesterday, I have gym class right after lunch. She said I could earn five dollars if I wanted, and I thought she meant like doing housework or something like that, I could do that, and I thought it'd be nice if I could earn some, help pay for lunch at school and like that. She said some other girls at school worked for her. And I said I had to be home before Mom got home from work, and she said that was all right, and it'd only take about an hour. She said I should wait at the corner down from the school, at the corner of Glendale Avenue, and she'd pick me up in her car, right after school at three o'clock. And when I got there, there was three other girls, the only one I know was Doris Bloom, she's in my English class. I don't like her much," said Sandra thoughtfully, "she laughs too loud and sometimes she swears. And there was that foreign girl, she's Chinese or something, and another one that's Mexican, Teresa something. I asked Doris what kind of work we had to do, and she just laughed and said I'd find out, it was easy and lots of fun. And Miss Lister came and picked us up in her car and took us to this place. It was a photography place, it said Thorpe's Studio Portraits on the door. And it was all just— just awful." Sandra shivered, and for the first time looked embarrassed; she looked down at the floor. "There was a man there— Miss Lister called him Bob—and we went into a big room at the back of the place, there were some cameras there and funny big lights—and then some other men came—and Miss Lister told me to take my clothes off. Doris and the other girls were taking their clothes off, and I said I didn't want to do that, it's not right to take your clothes off in front of people you don't know—and men—and she was mad and said I wouldn't get paid if I didn't. But I didn't. But I couldn't help seeing what happened." Her head bent lower in embarrassment and misery.

Dakin said, "The work of the devil, and a schoolteacher, getting these kids into such a thing—"

"What happened, Sandra?" asked Delia.

She said in a low voice, "Well, they did awful things—with those men, things you're not supposed to do until you get married—you know. And other awful things. The other girls, and these men. And the man named Bob was taking pictures of them, movie pictures. I was just so scared, I wanted to get out of that place but I didn't know how to get home from there. I couldn't help crying, I asked Miss Lister to take me back to school, but she was mad—because I wouldn't take my clothes off and do all the awful things— she called me a silly baby. That Doris, she said I was crazy not to want to do all that, it was fun and easy, she said that when we were back in the car. Miss Lister took us back to school. And she said—Miss Lister, I mean—if I didn't want to earn easy money I could keep my damn mouth shut—but I had to tell Mom and Dad, and they said we had to tell the police."

"I should think so!" said Mrs. Dakin. "That wicked, wicked woman, and those men—such a thing!"

Delia looked at Mary. The child porno thing; there was a market for it in some segments of the population, and a dirty little thing it was. "I hope you're going to arrest those wicked people," said Mrs. Dakin.

"We'll certainly be doing that, Mrs. Dakin, and we're very glad you brought Sandra in to tell us about this," said Delia. "We won't ask you for a formal statement right now—maybe later." She added gently to Sandra, "It was brave of you to come in and tell."

Sandra blinked. "Mom and Dad said we had to, so you could do something to those men. But I'm sort of scared to go back to gym class again, what Miss Lister might do to me."

Mary said grimly, "You needn't worry, honey, she isn't going to be there long."

"Well," said Dakin heavily, "I guess we leave it up to the police from here."

They thanked them again for coming in, and the Dakins took Sandra out. "What a damned messy thing!" said Mary. "What's the best way to play it?"

Delia said, "We'll want some manpower. Let's go and consult Charles."

Upstairs they filled O'Connor and Varallo in on it and O'Connor barked out some choice epithets. "Contributing to the delinquency of the minors! And dealing in the hard-core porn—so they get shut down and charged, and what the hell kind of charge is it these days, they get the slap on the wrist and a fine and go right back in business! All right, all right, I see it, for God's sake, we've got to try to protect the innocent kids from this kind of thing— My God, those other kids already streetwise at twelve and thirteen, and probably they'll be cussing the Goddamned cops for cutting off their spending money—paying them five bucks a time, my good Christ—"

Varallo said sardonically, "Too late to salvage those, likely. At least we've got the name of the studio." He got the phone book out and looked it up. "Thorpe's Studio Portraits, it's on Magnolia over in Burbank."

"So we ask the cooperation," said O'Connor.

"That little caper Sandra described was yesterday afternoon," said Varallo. "The chances are he spent last night developing those negatives, and they could still be in the studio. Let's talk to Burbank," and he reached for the phone.

"And while you're on that," said Mary, "I think Delia and I'll go and have a heart-to-heart talk with Miss Lister at that junior high school." She was looking grimly pleased at the prospect.

Varallo talked to a Sergeant Serafino on the Burbank force who said, "Hell, you know as well as I do if we march in there without a search warrant and confiscate any relevant evidence, the charge'd never stick."

"It shouldn't take long to get a warrant," said Varallo. "We've got probable cause. But it's your territory, you'd better put it through."

"I'll get on it right away. With any luck, we'll have it in a couple of hours. I'll get back to you," said Serafino.

He called back at eleven-thirty and said the warrant had just come through, and he'd expect them any time. O'Connor and Varallo found him waiting for them in his small office in that smaller station, behind a scarred old desk; he was comfortably stout, middle-aged and balding. "This is the hell of a dirty business, it's bad enough when it's consenting adults, like they say, but when it comes to roping the kids into it—my God. Let's go and see what we can turn up."

Thorpe's Studio Portraits was housed in a small modern building in the middle of the block on Magnolia, nearly at the city line. They went into a small anteroom, and the opening of the door rang a bell somewhere. A cheerful voice called, "Be right with you," and a man came in from the rear premises. He was a handsome blond fellow about thirty, in expensively tailored sports clothes. He looked surprised to see three of them, but said genially, "What can I do for you?"

Serafino showed him the badge. "Police," he said flatly. "We've got a search warrant for this place. Are you Thorpe?"

"Oh, for Christ's sake," he said. "Yeah, I'm Thorpe. For Christ's sake." He cast one hopeless glance at the door leading off the anteroom, and they saw the thought pass through his mind: no chance to destroy evidence.

"I'll keep an eye on him," said Serafino. "You go and look."

They didn't have to look far. There was a big bare studio room at the back with several still cameras, one expensive movie camera. Off that was a well-equipped darkroom, and there were some strips of sixteen-millimeter movie film hanging up in front of a hot-air dryer. Varallo detached one from its hanger, flicked on one of the safety lights, and held it up. "Oh, yes, very hot," he said to O'Connor. "This is likely the footage he shot yesterday, you can make out the kids."

O'Connor took a look and said distastefully, "Goddamned dirt. Hot, you can say, and enough of the damned perverted creeps around who get a kick out of this stuff."

They took it all down for packaging as evidence. In a file cabinet in the studio, they found a couple of metal film cases, unlabeled, containing some more of the same blue movies, and took those, too. They went out to the anteroom. Thorpe was sitting smoking at a little desk there. Serafino said, "You picked up some evidence, good."

"As expected," said O'Connor.

Thorpe looked up at them. "And who the hell blew the whistle?" he asked wearily. "Don't tell me it was Carol, she likes the nice profit too good."

"That'd be Miss Lister?" asked Varallo. "Your girlfriend? How did you get her into this?"

Thorpe said cynically, "So you know some names. For Christ's sake. She's my half sister, for God's sake. It was partly her idea."

"Not as much as we'd like to know," said O'Connor. "Suppose you tell us who the other men are, the amateur actors in your little home movies."

"You can go to hell," said Thorpe bitterly.

"And the customers—who've you been peddling them to?"

"Go to hell."

But in the top drawer of the desk there was an address book; it contained some male names complete with addresses and phone numbers; it was at least likely that some of those would turn out to be the amateur actors, possibly a couple of the customers.

"Thanks very much for the backup," said Varallo to Serafino.

"Any time. I hope you can make a charge stick."

They ferried Thorpe over to the Glendale jail and booked him in; punctiliously, Varallo read him his rights. "I want to call a lawyer," said Thorpe.

"I just told you, you can call a lawyer as soon as you like." Back at the office, Varallo started the machinery on the arrest warrant. Neither of them had had any lunch, so then they went out to the coffee shop down the block for a sandwich.

Delia and Mary had considerably shocked the principal of that junior high school by asking for the Lister woman and telling him why. He said half a dozen times that he couldn't believe this; she had such excellent credentials, a most satisfactory record, seemed like such a nice woman, and the children all liked her. Delia cut short his dismayed protests and asked him to call her up to the office. He mopped his forehead and agreed weakly.

"But really I don't care to be present, this is the most shocking thing— I can hardly credit it—" That was fine with them. He took himself off somewhere and they waited for Carol Lister. She came in unconcernedly; she was a tall, strong-looking woman about thirty, with an untidy mop of blond hair and a homely face with a big nose and prominent jaw. She was wearing dark slacks and a dark pullover sweater. She looked at the badge in Delia's hand and her pale blue eyes went hard and cold.

"Don't tell me," she said in a hard voice. "That damned stupid black kid opened her mouth. Goddamn it, I was a fool to rope her in, but Bob wanted a new face and some of the customers like the blacks."

"We'll be bringing a charge of contributing to the delinquency of minors," said Mary coldly. "And maybe something else. You're under arrest as of now. And we know about Thorpe. What's your relationship with him, strictly business?"

She said bitterly, "He's my half brother. Goddamn it, why the damn cops have to be so goody-goody puritanical I'll never understand. What the hell is it to anybody how people get their kicks? Live and let live. Delinquency—for God's sake, most of these kids have played around plenty by the time they get into junior high, those other kids jumped at the chance to have a little fun and get paid for it. I thought that black kid was pretty dumb, she never talks much and seems kind of backward." But of course Carol Lister had only known Sandra in gym class; the other teachers could have told her about Sandra's brain.

"Just your bad luck," said Delia dryly. "We'll take you in now."

"Oh, hell," she said. "I left my bag and coat up at the gym—can I go get them? Goddamn it, you know what it'll come to, just a fine and probation, the courts don't hand out time in the joint for this kind of thing—and now I'll lose my teaching credentials and be stuck with a lousy job in an office or something—"

"You should have thought of that before you got mixed up in this. Come on."

They took her down to the jail, and Delia applied for the arrest warrant back at the office. Varallo and O'Connor had just taken off for Burbank then. Gonzales and Forbes were still talking to the witnesses of the three heists pulled the night before.

Boswell had taken the market manager, Bagby, to look at some mug shots. He looked in briefly just after noon to say that Bagby hadn't made any in their records and he was taking him to R. and I., downtown, to look at some more. Bagby seemed positive that he'd recognize one of the heisters, and with the box boy killed it would at least be a charge of manslaughter as well as robbery; they'd like to catch up to that pair.

The other witnesses had left by then, and Delia held down the office while Forbes and Gonzales went to lunch, and then went to lunch herself. She glanced into the Juvenile office, but Mary was talking to a weeping female and a teenage boy. She'd just gotten back, at half past two, when a call came in to a hit-run with a child dead, and Gonzales went out to look at it. When he came back, half an hour later, he said, "The usual damn messy thing, and nowhere to go on it. The kid was riding his bike, just left on the way home from school and this car came around the corner—there's only one witness, one of the nuns—it's a parochial school on Elk Street, she says the car turned off Glendale Avenue and never tried to brake, but the kid was on the wrong side and maybe the driver couldn't avoid him. She can't describe the car, and nobody else was around."

"I thought most schools aren't out until three o'clock," said Delia.

"He'd just come back after being home with the flu, told the sister he wasn't feeling too good and they let him leave. His name was Rudy Arrellano. Thirteen. Looks as if he was killed instantly. Hell of a thing, and nothing to do about it, of course."

Varallo and O'Connor weren't back yet when Boswell called in from downtown, and talked to Forbes. He said Bagby had made a mug shot from the books at R. and I.; he was positive on the identification; it was one of the heisters at the market. "It's a Dwight Gibson, he's got a little package with L.A.P.D., three counts of armed robbery, and he's just off parole. I've just been talking to his P.A. officer. He's supposed to have a job at a Shell station on Los Feliz in Atwater, and there's a home address, Harvard Street in Glendale. I'll check the station on the way back, but somebody might try the house."

Forbes passed that on to Delia and went out to look. Katz and Poor came in talking about that rash of daylight burglaries, and then Varallo and O'Connor came back and told her what had turned up on Thorpe, and she filled them in on Carol Lister.

"And that damned female is all too right," said O'Connor. As usual at this time of day he looked the complete tough, needing a shave, his tie rumpled. "What the hell will they get? We haven't checked records, but I'd have a guess it's a first count for both of them, one of the softheaded judges will hand them probation and a fine, and they won't spend a day in after a hearing. Granted, the Lister girl won't have such easy access to the innocent or not-so-innocent kids, but they'll be back in business again all too quick."

Varallo was looking over the address book from Thorpe's studio. "We'll have to chase up all these names."

"Oh, for the love of God," said O'Connor. "Just more of the same. Identify the amateur actors—the D.A.'s office can run off those films and spot them—and what the hell is that charge? Contributing to delinquency again, and probation. The customers— my good Christ, they wouldn't even come in for that charge, there's nothing the D.A. could land them with even if we find out who they are. And for God's sake, things shouldn't be set up that way, but we've got to look at the realities, there it is, and not one damn thing we can do about it."

"I know, I know," said Varallo ruefully, "but we have to go through the motions." And the phone rang in O'Connor's office; grumbling, he went to answer it, and ten seconds later called them in.

"Dawson," he said tersely, and punched the amplifier.

"Just a kind of confirmation that Orley's heading west," boomed out Dawson's voice suddenly. "No, we haven't got him—nobody's got him. But we got the word from N.C.I.C. half an hour ago. A fellow named Lowell walked into the police station in Durango, Colorado, and said Orley'd robbed him late this morning. Lowell'd been visiting his family in Denver, he's just a young guy—lives in Phoenix, a perfectly clean record, works at a Montgomery Ward warehouse. He was on his way back to Arizona. He says he picked up Orley just outside Salida, about 7 A.M. today, Orley was hitchhiking, and Lowell saw the uniform and wanted to help out one of our gallant servicemen."

"For God's sake, he's in uniform?" said O'Connor.

"Well, he was. Now we don't know. But what we've heard about him, that he's some dim-witted, seems to check out. He rode along with Lowell all the way to Durango, and he told him his right name, said he was on leave and trying to get back to California. Lowell says he felt sorry for the guy. Then, when they got to Durango, Lowell offered to buy him lunch, and they went someplace and ate and it was when they came back to the car Orley pulled a gun on him and took all the cash he had and took off in the car."

"So you've got a call out on the car," said O'Connor.

"Sure, it's a six-year-old Chevy sedan, Arizona plates. If he stays in it, and there's no reason he shouldn't, there's a good chance he'll be picked up pretty soon."

"At least he's still a little way off. Well, let us know any further news." O'Connor put the phone down and scrabbled for an Atlas in his bottom desk drawer. "Durango, Colorado—he's got all of Arizona to cross yet, and with the A.P.B. on the car he could be spotted any time."

Varallo wandered back to his desk and took up Thorpe's address book. "A couple of these names are right here in town, I think I'll do a little legwork on it."

"A damn waste of time," said O'Connor, but Varallo took the address book and went out. Only Katz and Poor were in, typing reports. When the phone rang on Varallo's desk ten minutes later, Delia answered it. The dispatcher told her a robbery had just been called in, added an address on Cumberland Road.

"Feast or famine," said Delia to herself. She went downstairs and headed for the rear entrance to the parking lot, but stopped to glance in at the lab. "Did you match any of those prints off the back door of the Ogden place?"

Burt looked up from the workbench. "There was only one good latent—besides the family's, that is. I chased Ray up there to get the rest of the family's for comparison. There was just this one that doesn't belong to anybody in the house. It's not in our records, I haven't got a kickback from downtown yet."

"Well, let us know," said Delia. She went out to her car and drove up to Cumberland Road. That was one of the better-class areas in town, with old and expensive houses on a quiet street. The squad was parked in front of a two-story stucco house with a wide lawn in front. The uniformed man was Stoner, and he let her in. "By what she says, it was that damned phoney minister again," he told Delia. "She's a Mrs. Florence Wagner."

Delia went in past a tiled entry hall to a big living room off to the right. "This is Detective Riordan, ma'am, you can tell her all about it."

Mrs. Wagner was an elderly fat woman with white hair. She looked at Delia in a little surprise and said, "Oh, yes. Well, as I told you it was such a surprise, I mean a minister, and he was so polite and respectful at first—"

"You just tell the detective about it, ma'am," Delia nodded at him and he started back for the squad. Mrs. Wagner transferred her attention to Delia. She was a placid-looking woman and her voice was unemphatic.

"I was just so surprised, he was so polite, and of course he looked quite respectable, he was wearing a nice dark suit and a clerical collar. He talked about some missionary society, and he said any donation would be appreciated, but anyway he'd like to leave me a brochure about it. It wasn't our church, we go to the Episcopal church, but I know all these missionary societies do a lot of good work, especially in all the backward countries—he mentioned Africa—and so I went to get my bag, I thought I'd give him a dollar or two. And then, when I opened the door, he came pushing right in, and all of a sudden he had a knife in his hand— I was really more surprised than frightened— I tried to hang onto my bag, but he sort of gave me a shove and got it away from me. And he took all the bills out of my wallet—"

"How much was in it, do you know?"

"Oh, I'm not sure to a dollar, but it wasn't more than about twenty dollars, I never carry much cash, my husband doesn't think it's safe. He's out playing golf," she added irrelevantly, "it was such a nice day. Since he's been retired he plays a lot of golf. He'll be annoyed about this, but really, how would anybody suspect a minister, and right in broad daylight in my own house?"

"Could you describe him?" asked Delia.

"Well, yes—" And she gave the same description, a tall man looking fairly young, dark hair and a little dark Vandyke beard. "No, I didn't see which way he went, he just went out the front door and down the sidewalk. I'd had time to feel frightened then —that knife—and that was silly when it was all over. No, I didn't see any car."

He could have parked around on the side street, these were short blocks, and gotten back to the car in two minutes.

"I'd just got back from the market," said Mrs. Wagner. "I was putting things away in the freezer when the bell rang."

Delia's interest quickened. That had been one feature of the other cases, the women just back from the market. She thought about it. Was that how he picked them? It was a possibility, that he had an eye out for older women grocery shopping and coming out to an expensive-looking car, and he followed them home. On the other hand, all the houses had been in the better areas of town. But the older women—more apt to be interested in the missionary societies, to respect an obvious minister. "Didn't you see the article in the *News-Press?*" she asked. "This man has robbed several women just the same way, Mrs. Wagner."

"Oh, no, I didn't, we don't take the *News-Press*, we take the *Times.*" So much for Vic's little idea, thought Delia.

"Well, at least he didn't hurt you. One woman was knocked down and had her arm broken."

"Oh, that's terrible, I'm sorry, but of course I hadn't any reason to suspect him."

"No, of course not. It's just lucky he didn't get a great deal of money." She noticed that Mrs. Wagner was wearing only a wedding ring. "He didn't ask you for jewelry?"

She shook her head. "He just took the money and went."

"Well, thank you," said Delia. "We'll hope to find him." That was a rather forlorn hope, with no more to go on than they had. She started back for the station, thinking she'd leave this report for the next day. It had been a fairly busy day, and she was still thinking more about the child porno thing. On the way back, something else occurred to her about that, and at the station she went into the Juvenile office. Mary was hunched over her typewriter, and looked up as she came in.

"The arrest warrant came through on Lister, and I suppose on Thorpe, too."

"Good," said Delia. "Mary, what about those girls? It's possible the D.A.'s office will want to talk to them. Sandra only knew one name, the Doris girl. I suppose something ought to be done about them."

"Our business," said Mary succinctly. "Ben's over at the school now." Ben Guernsey was the other ranking Juvenile officer. "We'll be locating them, the Doris girl will know who the others are, and we'll talk to them, see the parents. It's possible we might find there's been some neglect, but it's more likely the parents are perfectly O.K., just unaware. Too many of them don't know what goes on with some of the kids as young as these. Well, those girls—" She sighed and groped for cigarettes on her desk. "What can you do, when they're that wise that young? Fun, the Doris girl called it. My God! See what the parents look like, how they react. Yes, and that principal's going to have to find a new girls' gym teacher in the middle of the school year." She laughed. "What a thing!"

Delia went on upstairs, but she wouldn't be staying long; it was after five. O'Connor was alone in the office. He said, "I don't know where everybody's got to. And there's nothing else in on Orley. Of course there's a lot of wide space over there, not so many towns or lawmen around to spot that hot car. The A.P.B.'s still out on that Barrios, he's faded into the jungle somewhere. The L.A.P.D. boys will have been talking to all his known pals, any girlfriends."

"I suppose." Delia told him about the minister's new job.

"That one," said O'Connor, annoyed.

"None of the women thought they'd recognize a picture," said Delia, "and it's an offbeat enough M.O. that it ought to have turned up from L.A.'s computers if he's in Records."

"Too damned true," said O'Connor.

Mr. Beal looked in the door of the office. Rosie was curled up under Varallo's desk and came over obediently to have the leash snapped on. "The crooks keeping you busy?" asked Beal.

"Too damned busy," said O'Connor, scowling.

Delia left a few minutes early. It would be good to get home to the bright new place that would probably be home for a long time to come. She thought tonight she'd just sit and relax out on the balcony awhile, enjoying the view. There were things she could be doing: she hadn't finished putting all the books away yet; in a way, it had been foolish to buy the two-bedroom place, but she'd started to make a modest collection of books in the past couple of years and planned to make a little den out of the second, smaller bedroom, with bookcases and the TV, not that she ever watched TV much. The weekly cleaning and laundry she usually did on her day off. And she'd have to change the appointment at the beauty salon then, to an earlier time; Laura had asked her to dinner on Tuesday. But this had been a full day and she was tired, just wanted to relax.

There wasn't anybody in the lobby when she came in. She rode up in the elevator to the fourth floor, and as she stepped out there and came down the hall, she saw one of her neighbors, the middle-aged man with black-framed glasses, just going into the apartment next to hers. He didn't look very friendly the couple of times she'd seen him, but people in large apartment buildings didn't tend to fraternize, which was all right with her. She unlocked the door and heard Henry chattering busily to himself. "I like a little sugar in my tea. Yo-ho and a bottle of rum! Give us a kiss, dear—scratch Henry's head, please," he was saying in his loud, hoarse voice.

"Hello, Henry," she said, and he cocked his bright blue head at her and ruffled his wings. "Hello, Delia dear, you're a very pretty girl! Let's all have a little drink!"

He was rather an absurd character, Henry, but it was nice to have somebody to come home to.

At that gas station on Los Feliz in Atwater, Leo Boswell talked briefly to the owner. "Gibson?" said the owner, and spat disgustedly. "I'm good and damned fed up trying to be a nice guy and help the young dudes been in some trouble. Gibson's the second one I took on, guys on parole. I give him a steady job and maybe he'll straighten out, says the parole officer. Like hell. The other one skipped out on me as soon as he was off parole, and I figure Gibson did too. I haven't laid eyes on him for a week. That's the last time I'll hire an ex-con, believe me."

Boswell went back to the office, and Forbes told him he'd tried the place on Harvard and there was nobody home. "And look, we'd like to drop on him, but let the night watch check back. It's Joan's birthday and I'm taking her out to dinner, her sister's coming to baby-sit. I'm taking off, I've got to shower and shave again."

"All right with me," said Boswell. He'd be just as glad to get home himself. He'd recently halfway broken off with a girl he'd been going with, a nice girl, but she'd been getting pretty serious and he wasn't all that sure she was the one he'd like to settle down with forever. There was an old movie on TV he wanted to see.

Bill Watkins was already feeling damned bored on the stakeout. He took over from Neil Tracy at four o'clock, and dutifully checked with the Hendrixes. They were all right; he wondered if they were bored too, shut up there all the time. He checked the backyard; there was a chain on their back door. He sat in the car yawning; he couldn't even have the light on to read, of course. He hoped to God somebody would pick up this Orley pretty soon and let them get back to ordinary business.

Rhys got in first and found Forbes's note. When Harvey and Hunter came in, he said, "Sometimes the Lord's on our side, boys. That market manager made a mug shot, one of the heisters. Dwight Gibson, he's got a pedigree with L.A. and he's just off parole. The day boys didn't catch up to him, we're supposed to check the address."

"Thank God for that," said Harvey. "We see some things, but that poor kid last night, those poor damned parents—oh, you were off, you didn't know about it—"

Hearing about it, Rhys looked grim. "Let's go and see if he's home, but I'll take no bets."

The place on Harvard was an old, ramshackle single frame house with a little sparse grass in front. There was one dim light showing in a front room. Rhys and Hunter climbed broken steps to the front door and Rhys shoved the bell. After a minute a weak porch light was switched on and the door opened. A woman looked out at them and Hunter showed her the badge. "We're looking for Dwight Gibson, is he here?"

"Oh, my God, has he done something else?" she asked. She was an angular, gray-haired woman in a shabby green pantsuit and bedroom slippers. "I don't know why he has to go getting in trouble all the time. But I guess it's natural, he takes after his dad. I was a damn fool to marry up with that bum, and I got shut of him as soon as I wised up that he'd never be anything but a no-good drunk. What you want Dwight for?"

"Is he here?" asked Rhys.

"No, he's not. Sure he's been living here, I'm his ma, ain't I? But he cleared out this morning. I was just getting ready to go to work, when he comes out already dressed—I never knew him to get up that early unless he had to—and says him and Jack are taking off, maybe go over to Vegas or somewhere, and he don't know when he'll be back."

"Jack," said Rhys. "Jack who?"

"Jack Myers, he's about Dwight's best buddy."

"Were they going in Dwight's car, do you know?" There was an old Ford registered to Gibson; the day watch had put out an A.P.B. on it.

She yawned. "Oh, that old thing died on him a couple of weeks ago, it's not worth fixin' up. It's in the garage out back."

"Has Myers got a car? And do you know his address?" It was a fairly common name.

"Yeah, he's been living with his sister and her husband somewhere around, I think it's Milford Street. Yeah, he's got a car, they was taking that, Dwight said. No, I dunno what kind it is."

" 'Round the mulberry bush," said Hunter back in the car, annoyed. "But it figures. Whoever was on that caper with Gibson, they know they hit that poor kid. Any bets that Myers was the other one, and they've taken off for parts unknown because they're pretty sure they killed the kid?"

"No bets," said Rhys. They stopped at Communications and shot the inquiry up to the D.M.V. in Sacramento, and in five minutes the word came back on the teletype. Jack Myers had a car registered at the Milford Street address; it was an old VW Rabbit.

"Jackpot," said Hunter. They canceled the A.P.B. on Gibson's car and put a new one out on the Rabbit, covering eight states around. A lot of lawmen would be looking for that plate number.

They had just gotten back to the detective office when a new call went down. Rhys went out again resignedly with Harvey. It was an apartment up on Glenwood Road. The householders had just come home to discover they had had burglars.

"We're not usually out after dark, but it's our anniversary and we went out to dinner—" The woman was on the verge of tears. She wasn't bad-looking, tall and thin with red hair, and the husband was a weedy fellow with a receding hairline; they looked to be in their late twenties. "Just look at this mess—just look at it! Well, of course both the doors were locked, do you think we're idiots? We just got home and the door was still locked, I don't know how anybody got in—"

"Can you give us some idea what's missing?" asked Rhys patiently.

"Out of this mess?" The burglar had left the usual mess, drawers dumped out and pictures taken down, chair cushions on the floor.

"I'll tell you one thing that's gone," said the husband mournfully. "I thought of it right away and looked, I had a roll of old silver dollars under my handkerchiefs in the bedroom chest. They're gone."

"Well, we'd be obliged if you'd look and give us a list of what's missing," said Harvey. "The day men will want a statement about that. And if you've got a record of any serial numbers, cameras or small appliances taken—"

"The microwave oven!" she said suddenly, and ran to look in the kitchen. "It's gone! And it was only a month old. We'd saved up for it—the electric bill's so high and they say you can save so much money—"

"Serial number?" said the husband blankly. "I didn't know stuff like that had serial numbers. No, I don't have any record of anything like that." He added helpfully, "It's a Litton, that's the brand."

It was necessary to be polite to the citizens. They went looking and found that the burglar had used a jimmy on the back door. It didn't have a dead-bolt lock. "Well, if you'd come into the station sometime tomorrow," said Rhys, "and give us a list of what's missing, we'd be obliged."

They left them still bemoaning the burglary and went back to base. And ten minutes later they got another call, to an address on Kenneth Road. They chased out again, leaving Hunter to hold down the office.

As expectable at that address, the house was a big old place in that good area of town; the squad was parked in front. There was a bright porch light on and lights inside, and the squad-car man was waiting for them on the porch; it was Lopez. He said uneasily, "I hope I did the right thing and those females haven't messed up the scene for you. I figured you'd get here about as quick as a backup. The wife's having hysterics in there, I don't think she'd go near the body, but with females you never know."

"A body," said Rhys.

"Right inside the front door. I got something from the other one, she's the maid—they've got a regular live-in maid. She said he went to answer the door and somebody shot him right from the porch here. They both came running when the shots were fired and he was dead on the floor there. In the entry hall." Lopez gestured. "Whoever it was, fired right through the screen door."

There was a bright overhead light in the square entrance hall. The screen door had been a handsome aluminum one with fancy panels on each side; the screen was torn and gaping where the slugs had gone through it, one section hanging loose. The solid front door was wide open, and just inside it lay the body of a man. It was flat on its back; it was the body of a middle-aged to elderly man. He was wearing a navy blue suit and what had been a white shirt; that was stained in splotches with still wet blood, and there was more blood around him on the beige carpet. Somewhere nearby a woman was weeping loudly.

Rhys looked around the porch and spotted an empty flowerpot off at one side; he hooked the remnants of the screen door open and used the flowerpot to hold it there. Maybe it wasn't likely that the killer had touched either door, but you never knew, and the lab could be fussy about things like that. They went in, trying to edge around the blood, and had a closer look. The dead man had been rather good-looking, with a lean face, a high-bridged nose, a full head of silver-gray hair.

"Who is he?" asked Harvey. "Funny the neighbors didn't come piling out at the shots. Holy God, it must have been a cannon the way he's bled. Of course at that distance it wouldn't take a marksman, but he must have a few slugs in him, all in the chest."

"I don't know who he is, the maid just said the name's Turnbull," said Lopez. "I saw it was a job for you and called in."

"Well, you'd better call the lab," said Rhys. "I hope somebody's there. You can hang around until the van gets here, and then get back on tour."

"O.K., will do."

Rhys and Hunter looked around the porch, but they couldn't spot any ejected shell casings, so it would have been a revolver, not an automatic. The name Turnbull had rung a faint bell in Rhys's head, but for the moment he couldn't place it. They went past the body and found the living room a step down from the entry hall, a big, handsomely furnished room. There were two women there, one weeping on the couch and one just sitting looking a little dazed. Rhys said, "We're detectives, we'd like to ask a few questions if you feel up to it."

The weeping woman looked to be about the same age as the dead man, if anybody could ever judge a woman's age. She was a little too plump, in a fashionable black sheath dress and high-heeled shoes, and she had expertly dyed blond hair. They couldn't see her face, buried in a handkerchief. The other one was younger, with dark hair and a long, plain face. That one said in an unexpectedly stolid voice, "I don't figure the Missus can talk to you much, she's all upset and no wonder, him getting murdered practically before her eyes."

"Can we have your name, please?"

"Sure, I'm Muriel Buford. I work for them, general maid and cook. I've worked for them nearly ten years. It just don't seem possible anybody'd want to murder the judge. Oh, the Missus had said something about some nut threatened to kill him, but he hadn't been worried about it, said it was just foolishness."

"Judge?" said Rhys.

"That's right, Judge George Turnbull, he was a judge in the superior court right here in town."

"Well, tell us what happened."

"That's easy enough. They'd finished dinner about half an hour ago, they always have dinner late, about eight o'clock. And like always they went into the living room to have coffee. I have my dinner earlier so as to be free to clean up the kitchen and all. I'd just come in with the tray and poured their coffee, and the judge complimented me on dinner, said the roast had been done just right, when the doorbell rang, and he was kind of annoyed, but he went to answer it—"

The other woman lifted her face out of the handkerchief and wailed, "It was that terrible man! It must have been that terrible man on TV—he said George deserved to go to hell—" She was insipidly pretty, with a doll-like face, and her eye makeup had run down over her cheeks with the tears.

"And then we heard all the shots, it sounded like a cannon, honest to God, I was so shook I dropped the tray—" For the first time, they noticed that, the big silver tray lying on the floor beside the coffee table, with the coffeepot spilling over on its side, the silver cream and sugar jars overturned. "And we both ran to look, and there was the judge lying on the floor and bleeding all over the place—all that blood—no, I didn't see anybody or hear anybody running off—"

The house was on a corner, and possibly the neighbors next door were out or watching TV and hadn't heard the shots.

"And the Missus started screaming to call an ambulance, and I ran quick to call the cops. Then I came back and she was still yelling about an ambulance, but I could see he was dead, it wouldn't have been no use. I grew up on a farm, I know the look of dead things. And whoever'd want to murder the judge—unless it was that nut—it's awful— He was a nice, kind man." She added dispassionately, "But maybe you'd better call an ambulance for the Missus, she's in a state, and no wonder. They'd been married nearly forty years, they never had no family, she thought the world of him."

Lopez looked into the room diffidently and said, "The lab van's just pulling up."

"O.K.," said Rhys. They went out to brief the lab man, who

turned out to be Ray Taggart. And as Rhys edged past the body, all of a sudden the bell in his head rang loudly and he said to Harvey and Taggart just coming up on the porch, "By God, Turnbull! That judge—all that uproar a couple of weeks ago—that manslaughter charge—"

CHAPTER FIVE

That was waiting for them on Friday morning. It was Varallo's day off. O'Connor said forcefully, "Turnbull, my God! There was a hell of a fuss about it a couple of weeks ago, even the damned *Times* had an editorial, and there was that interview on the network TV news—what the hell was the guy's name—he got cited for contempt— Dangerfield, it was that heist job back in January sometime, you and Gil were on it, Jeff—"

Forbes said, "That's right, and we all did some cussing about that hearing a couple of weeks back. Another one of the damned bleeding-heart judges, that was an open and shut case, the bastard walked into that place to pull a heist, it was an all-night convenience dairy store out on Colorado—"

"Garcia," said Gonzales. "Juan Garcia, he had a string of arrests, a lot of petty thefts and a juvenile record, the typical lout, he'd been in and out of trouble since he was thirteen or so. It was a low-life family, the parents drunks, and there was a string of younger kids, a couple of them already piling up the juvenile records, using pot, snatching purses. Garcia was a little high on something when he pulled that heist, and for no reason at all he shot the manager dead. It was a senseless, random thing. Brian Dangerfield, the name just came back to me, he was just a young fellow, night manager there, only about twenty-five. We dropped on Garcia right off, there were three witnesses in the place, they gave us a good description and two of them identified a mug shot, picked him out at a lineup. Open and shut, you could say," and he stroked his little mustache absently. "And then that Goddamned judge—"

They were all remembering the case more clearly. Their job was just to catch up to the wild ones; when they turned them over to the courts it was out of their hands, and there was nothing they could do about it when the strict justice didn't prevail. With the state of the courts now, all they could do was the useless cussing when one of the wild ones got off with a slap on the wrist.

The courts were always backlogged, and Juan Garcia had just

come up before the bench for a hearing a couple of weeks ago, before Judge Turnbull in the superior court. "There was a plea bargain," said Forbes. "It was his second felony count, and that damned judge let him off with probation, handed down the decision that he'd spent nearly four months in jail since the charge had been brought and in view of his age he should be given opportunity for rehabilitation. My God in heaven!" Garcia was twenty-two. It had been a charge of voluntary manslaughter, and the plea bargain had gotten it reduced to involuntary.

There had been that scene in court, fully reported in the media. Young Dangerfield's father had been at the hearing, and after the sentence was handed down had jumped up and denounced the judge in some straightforward language. Told him he deserved to die and go straight to hell for turning a murderer loose, and said he'd be happy to do the job himself. He'd been found in contempt of court and given a suspended thirty-day sentence, and the network TV news had given him some prominent publicity in an interview that night, when he'd repeated what he'd said in court.

Forbes said, "So it looks as if maybe Dangerfield wasn't just blowing off steam. He made the threats, and maybe he did see to doing it himself."

"God knows he had the motive," said O'Connor. "He could have been brooding on it ever since, and finally decided to do it. He's the first one to look at. It's too early to ask the lab if they picked up anything, but we want to know about the gun pronto." He used the phone on Varallo's desk to call the morgue and talked to one of Goulding's assistants. "You haven't got to the autopsy, naturally, but we'll ask you to dig out those slugs and send them over to our lab soonest. And give us priority on the autopsy."

"And where do we find Dangerfield?" said Gonzales. "And do we go haul him in or wait for a make on the gun?"

"The hell with that," said Forbes. "The sooner we question him the better, before he has a chance to calm down some. I remember he was there when we talked to the victim's wife, a William Dangerfield—there was a wife and baby, they'd been living with the father, I don't remember the address."

"It'd be in the court records," said Delia, "or the newspapers, there was quite a lot in the papers about it. But more likely—" She got out the phone book. "Not that common a name, and here it is, William Dangerfield, it's Cameron Place."

"I think you're right, Jeff, we'd better haul him in right away," said Gonzales. "If he screwed himself up to murder the judge, he may be ready and willing to boast about 𝑖𝑡, tell the world."

"And," said Forbes, "the world might sympathize with him if he did, but that's something else. Come on, let's go and see if we can pick him up."

Delia hadn't written the report on the fake minister's latest job, and got down to that. O'Connor sat scowling into space and presently said, "I'd like to see a replay of that TV interview, hear exactly what Dangerfield said. It was covered in the *Times*, I wonder if the library would have back copies."

Before he had a chance to call and ask, Ben Guernsey came in, elderly and amiable, marking time until he'd be eligible for retirement, in a couple of years. He said, "We've just picked up a kid with a hell of a lot of stuff on him, good-quality pot and a lot of angel dust. He can't be over fourteen, but it looks as if he could have been peddling, with that much in his possession. The school principal called in, there was a little brawl on the playground, and he found the stuff on the kid. We thought you'd like to sit in on the questioning."

"And you thought damned right," said O'Connor. "The angel dust— Goddamn, a couple of forces around are running into a lot more of it than usual, and I'd like to know where the hell it's coming from." He followed Guernsey out.

A young couple came in and hesitated in the doorway. The man said, "Is this where we're supposed to come? The detective last night said to see a Sergeant Katz, we had a burglary last night—"

"That's right," said Delia. "Joe, you've got some visitors." Katz got up and beckoned them over to his desk.

Delia went on with the report. Ten minutes later, her phone rang and Burt was on the other end. "That latent off the Ogdens' back door," he said, "nobody's got a record of it here, sorry. Do you want me to send it to the Feds?"

The apologetic rapist. "You'd better," said Delia. Even if the polite rapist didn't have a record somewhere, the Feds had a lot of prints of the citizens with no criminal records, for various reasons. He might just be on file there. "Just in case."

"Okay, I'll shoot it out," said Burt.

The address on Cameron Place was a modest old stucco house with a detached garage. Gonzales pushed the doorbell and after a while the door opened halfway and a man's voice said, "What is it?"

"Police," said Forbes, and showed him the badge. "Are you William Dangerfield?"

"That's right, that's me," said the man. "What do the police want?"

"We'd like to ask you a few questions," said Forbes. "We'll take you downtown, Mr. Dangerfield."

"What the hell is this all about?" asked Dangerfield. He sounded genuinely surprised, but that didn't mean anything. He was a solid, stocky man about sixty, with a blunt-featured, square face and a pugnacious jaw. "I've had more than enough to do with the police," he said, "damn it. What's it about?"

"We'll talk downtown," said Gonzales.

He did some cussing, but they just waited, and finally he put on a jacket over his slacks and open-necked shirt, locked the front door, and got into Forbes's car. He didn't say a word on the ride downtown. There they put him in one of the tiny interrogation rooms and started to ask him questions.

"Where were you about nine o'clock last night?" asked Forbes.

"You think I've done something wrong? That's just crazy. I was at home, damn it, I was just at home, watching TV."

"Was anybody else there?" asked Gonzales.

"No, there wasn't anybody else there, I live alone."

"We understood, at the time your son was killed, back in January, he and his family were living with you."

Dangerfield's jaw thrust out and he said harshly, "That's right. They were. Lois and the kid, they'd still be with me, but they got to live, and I've only got the disability and the union pension. I had to take early retirement on account I've got a bad heart, you can't work at heavy construction with a bad heart. If I'd been an office man it'd be different. Lois had to get a job, Brian didn't have any insurance, they were just getting a start in life, and she couldn't get anything here. Besides, there's the baby, he's only seventeen months old, she had to have some place to leave him while she's at work. She went back to live with her mother in Monrovia, she's got a job at a Sears store and her mother looks after the baby. And just what business is it of yours?"

"So you're living alone and there isn't anybody can say you were at home last night," said Gonzales.

"What about it, what's this all about anyway?"

"You made some threats against Judge Turnbull," said Forbes. "You threatened to kill him. Well, he got himself shot last night and he's dead, Dangerfield."

"And we think maybe you knew that," said Forbes.

Dangerfield stared at them. "Now, is that a fact," he said slowly. "I can't say I'm sorry to hear it, but if you think I did it you're way off base. Sure I said I'd be glad to see him dead. Like Brian. One of these damnfool crazy judges turning the robbers and killers loose to hurt more innocent people. It just doesn't make any damned kind of sense. That guy who killed Brian, he's just a no-good bastard who'll never be anything else. Brian was a good man, ambitious and hard-working and straight as a die, and he was only twenty-five. He'd have got places, he was studying accounting, wanted to be a CPA. When it happened, well, I never thought I'd say I was glad Eleanor was dead, but I was then, the way she'd have felt if she knew about it. She died last year, it was cancer. We'd have liked more than one, but we were married ten years before we had Brian. He was the best son any man could have wanted, and he had his whole life in front of him— Lois and the baby—and this worthless bastard murders him for no reason, and that Goddamned judge turns him loose, probably to murder somebody else." His voice was shaking. "He deserved to get murdered himself, and I'm not sorry to hear he was, but I didn't have anything to do with it."

"Do you own a car?" asked Forbes.

"Yeah, I got a car, naturally. But I don't have a gun. You said he was shot. I don't know anything about it."

"Did you know where he lived?" asked Gonzales. The Turnbulls had an unlisted phone number.

"No, I didn't, how would I, I just saw him in court that day." But it would have been easy enough for him to have followed Turnbull home from the courthouse, spotted the address that way. They went on asking questions, and Dangerfield went on doggedly saying he didn't know anything about it. Before they'd gone to pick him up, Forbes had applied for a search warrant for the house. When they decided to let him go for the time being, it had just come through and they let him see it and drove him back there.

He said, "You can look anywhere you want, I've got nothing to hide." He sat in the little living room and didn't seem to pay much attention as they went through the house. It was a shabby old place, but neat and clean enough. There were three small bedrooms. They rummaged thoroughly through all the closets, looked in all the drawers, the pockets of all the clothes, the kitchen cupboards, without coming across anything suggestive, or a gun. They looked all through the garage and the old Ford sedan sitting there, the toolboxes on the workbench, the boxes half full of odds and ends. When they left, by the front door, Dangerfield said, "So you couldn't find a gun, I told you I didn't have one."

In Forbes's car Gonzales said, "It doesn't say a damn thing, Jeff. If he did it, he's smart enough to get rid of the gun, and it would have been a gun we probably can't tie up to him. Anybody can get hold of a gun under the counter without much trouble. Go down to Central beat downtown and try the first pawnshop. And he wouldn't bury it in the backyard after he'd done the shooting. Throw it off a bridge into the Wash."

"Probably," agreed Forbes. "Of course, he's the likeliest suspect for it, but without anything but the motive, the D.A. would never bring a charge. Unless the lab picked up something—and that's not likely, the way it was done, he just rang the doorbell and fired through the screen door from two feet away. He couldn't miss. No muss, no fuss. He'd have been back at the sidewalk before the two women got to the body."

"Well," said Gonzales, "we can't condone murder, but just between us I won't worry if he gets away with it. God knows he had a motive, and God knows we've got too many of the softheaded judges taking plea bargains and turning the violent ones loose to do it again."

Forbes started the engine. "You wonder what's in their minds. All the fancy legal education, and not one damn bit of common sense. Any ordinary mortal would know that one like Juan Garcia isn't going to turn into a useful citizen, ever."

"And I wonder what he's doing now. He'll be getting into more trouble if he hasn't already."

The Buford woman, the maid at the Turnbull house, came in in the middle of the afternoon to make a statement, as she'd been asked to do. Delia took it down and typed it, and she signed it. There wasn't anything new in it that hadn't been in Rhys's report. She sat in the chair beside Delia's desk and said in her flat voice, "It's terrible, the judge getting murdered like that. I don't expect that blood'll ever come out of the carpet. Did you know the Missus got took off to the hospital? The doctor said she was in shock. She'd said something about that guy threatened to kill the judge, I hadn't heard much about it, she said it'd been on TV but I hardly ever bother to look at TV. But today on the noon news they were talking about it, and they said that guy had really said he'd like to kill the judge, right out in public. Have you arrested him yet?"

"Not yet," said Delia.

"Well, I don't see why not, when he said right out he was going to kill the judge. I should think you'd have put him in jail already."

"We have to have evidence," said Delia, but of course that passed straight over her head. She went out, and ten minutes later the hospital called and said Mrs. Turnbull was anxious to talk to the police. By what they knew so far it wasn't likely that she had anything helpful to tell them, but Delia drove down to Memorial Hospital on the off chance.

Of course it was a waste of time. Mrs. Turnbull was a plump blonde with a vapidly pretty face, and she was sitting up in the hospital bed in a black lace negligee. All she wanted to tell the police was that it was all so terrible, George was the best and kindest husband a woman ever had, and that terrible man who threatened to kill him must be crazy. "Have you arrested him yet? Well, why not? You know who he is, I forget his name, but it was right on TV news that night, he looked just terribly fierce and dangerous, and he said George deserved to go to hell and he'd like to kill him and send him there— Oh, I was scared, I begged George to hire a bodyguard or something, but he wasn't scared at all, he said it was all foolishness— I knew that man was dangerous, I felt it in my bones, and now he's killed George just like he said he would, and I just don't understand why the police haven't arrested him—"

Delia listened to her politely for a little while and was rescued by the doctor coming in, telling her that she could go home, she was over the worst of the shock. Delia left her explaining vigorously that she'd never get over the shock of losing George, the best and dearest husband a woman ever had, and the fiend who'd killed him must be crazy and all the police dishonest because they hadn't arrested him.

Katz quite often felt disgruntled at the stupid citizens, and he figured philosophically that it was an occupational hazard of being on burglary detail. They went away and left windows open, and put off getting locks repaired, and were too cheap to leave lights on when they were out at night, and it was only about one in a thousand who kept records of serial numbers on any valuables. Even the sensible ones who took precautions got victimized occasionally, and it wasn't very often any of them got their property back or the bedeviled burglary detail caught up to the burglars. The professional burglars knew the fences, and the amateurs dropped off the loot at the nearest pawnshop, and even the honest pawnbrokers didn't pay that close attention to the hot list of stolen articles. But once in a while the job gave them a good laugh, and Katz had one that afternoon.

He and Poor had just come back from looking at another daylight break-in. The woman had been out only an hour, she said, grocery shopping. The daylight burglars were undoubtedly using the old and simple tactic of ringing doorbells to find out if anybody was at home. It was another middle-class place close in downtown, one side of an old duplex, and the burglar hadn't gotten much: a couple of small appliances, a little jewelry not worth much. Poor started to type the report on it; the paperwork went on forever. Then another call went down, and resignedly Katz went out to look.

Glendale had changed rather drastically in the last five years; there were all those high-rise office buildings north in town, the new shopping malls and now another of those getting built right downtown, and a lot of big apartment complexes and condominiums. The new burglary was in one of the big complexes, a building with three wings on the east side of town. The rents were probably lower than in a classier section, the tenants probably working people away most of the day. The apartment was on the fifth floor, and a young woman looked at the badge and let him in; the squad reporting to the call first would have gone back on tour.

She said her name was Eileen Collins. She was a pretty girl with reddish blonde hair and a nice figure, and she was seething with fury. There was a cute little blonde girl about three years old watching with solemn eyes. "I've never been so furious in my life!" said Eileen Collins. "And it was probably some of the kids who live here, there are a lot of teenagers in the building. Well, it's like everywhere, there are nice people and some not so good, and we don't really know anybody here, we're both busy working and all, oh, Terry's going to be mad, but he couldn't be as mad as I am! I just got home at three-thirty, Sally and me I mean—this is Sally—" The little girl gave Katz a wide smile.

"Excuse me, Mrs. Collins, how long were you out?"

"Well, since six o'clock this morning. I work at a day-care center here in town. It's nice because I can have Sally with me all day— we both leave at the same time, Terry and me, he doesn't have to be at work until seven-thirty, he works at the garage at the Chevrolet agency in San Marino so he's got farther to go—and he drops Sally and me off at the center, we've only got one car, and we take the bus home. He'll be in any minute— I have to be there at six-thirty to open up the place, see. And I came home and found all this upset— Terry says the locks here aren't too good, we'd meant to put a better one on but you have to get permission from the management—" The front door, with a rather flimsy lock, had been forced open with a chisel or some other sharp tool; there were marks on the jamb. "When I saw the door was open, I was mad—burglars, not that we've got much to steal—but when I went into the kitchen—"

"Have you any idea what's missing, Mrs. Collins?"

"Oh, not much really, just little stuff, why I say it must have been a kid or a couple of kids—the picture over the couch, and goodness knows that's not worth anything, and some costume jewelry from the bedroom, that's all except—oh, I was never so furious in my life!" She flounced out to the kitchen and Katz followed her. "Just look at that!" she said. On the kitchen counter a fat yellow cookie jar was standing empty with its lid beside it, and there was a big pile of cookies scattered all over the counter. "I've got a habit of dropping change in that, just saving up a little, I don't suppose there was more than five or six dollars there in small change—and I'd just baked those cookies last night, and they're the best I'd ever made, it's a new recipe—and the damned burglar never even ate one! I counted! They were just cool and I put them in the jar before we went to bed—and if there's one thing I'm proud of it's my cooking, I'm a very good cook, and those are the best cookies—and he never even took one! It's a kind of insult if you ask me, and I was so mad— Oh, there's Terry— Terry, we've had a burglar—"

Katz looked at the pile of cookies and started to laugh. You really never knew how the females were going to react to anything.

It was Varallo's day off, and a nice warm day but not too warm. When Laura had taken Ginevra to school and started for the market with Johnny, Varallo went out and did some work on his roses, pruning and feeding. He had quite a collection by now, some rare varieties, and in this warm April they were nearly all blooming beautifully. He got most of the pruning done by noon, when Laura called him in to lunch. She had the radio on for the twelve o'clock news, so they heard about Judge Turnbull.

"My God," said Varallo, "this is going to make some more work." But they both remembered that Garcia case, and Laura said vigorously, "That judge—the man whose son was murdered threatened to kill him, we both saw that interview on the network news. If it was that one who killed him, after he'd turned that killer loose, I don't blame him, Vic."

"He'll be the likeliest one all right, and what was his name—Dangerfield, that's it. I wonder if the office is turning up any evidence on him."

With the weekend coming up, business might be heavier for the night watch. It was Harvey's night off. There was a note from Forbes on Rhys's desk: He read it and said, "The morgue sent the slugs over and the lab tells us it was a .38 Colt. Common gun." They both remembered the Garcia case vividly, and Dangerfield.

"I wonder if any evidence showed up," said Hunter. "He's the obvious one."

Rhys was curious enough to call Forbes at home, and they heard about the dearth of evidence. "Of course we're ninety-nine percent sure it was Dangerfield who shot him," said Forbes. "But it doesn't look as if we'll ever be able to prove it, and he's never going to break down and confess. It isn't worth talking to the D.A.'s office about. Unless the lab turns up something else, we've got nowhere to go."

"I can see that," said Rhys. "I'm not going to lose any sleep over it."

They sat around discussing that for a while, and didn't get a call until nine o'clock. The location was one of the high-rise office buildings on North Brand, and the squad was pulled up in the middle of the big parking lot, bare and empty at night, only one other car there. The Traffic man was Weiss. He came up to them as they got out of Rhys's car and said, "Damn it, I called an ambulance fifteen minutes ago, where the hell is it? She doesn't look too good, she's been beaten up and she says she's been raped." He had the woman in the back of the squad. "Her name's Claire Sorenson."

The woman was huddled on the seat, clutching a light topcoat around her; it was stained with splotches of dirt. Under it she was wearing a blouse and skirt, and the blouse was torn and dirty, the skirt ripped up one side. Her face showed a couple of bloody welts. She was moaning a little as Rhys bent in the door. "The ambulance ought to be here soon, Mrs. Sorenson."

"Miss," she said faintly. "I think my arm's broken—he just kept on hitting me— I just managed to get up to the pay phone outside the rear entrance—called the police, and then I guess I fainted."

"Just take it easy," said Rhys. "You can tell us all the details later, when you're feeling better."

"No, I can tell you. I stayed late—to type that deposition, Mr. Colburn wanted it for tomorrow. I'm his secretary—he's a lawyer— I'd just come out to the rear door when this car drove into the lot—and the man jumped out and ran up and grabbed me—he wasn't very tall but he was awfully strong, I couldn't fight him—he started to beat me with his fists—got me down on the ground, and he tore my clothes—tore my panties off—raped me—and went on hitting me—" The fluorescent lights were still on in the lot, but they were high up and it was dark in places.

"Can you tell me what he looked like?"

She said in a fading voice, "No—tell you about his car—it was a white Mercedes sedan, a four-door— I saw it plain by the lights of the entrance—when it pulled in. I'm sure of that." The ambulance arrived just then, and when they helped her out of the squad she passed out, and the attendants got her on a gurney and took her off. Rhys and Hunter trailed the ambulance down to Memorial Hospital and hung around in Emergency for half an hour until they could talk to a doctor. He was a slight dark intern named Vargas, and he said, "She was raped, all right, and damned roughly too, and beaten. She's got a fractured arm and bruises all over her. We'll keep her overnight, and she'll be in bed a few days, I hope there's somebody to look after her."

Weiss had given Rhys her handbag, picked up alongside the pay phone. Hunter found the billfold in it, with a few bills and some small change, but the plastic slots held only a driver's license, a couple of credit cards. "Nobody listed to notify in emergency. Somebody ought to hear about her." The address was on Louise Street, and they went up there to find it was an apartment house. Hers was on the second floor and there wasn't any answer to the bell. Rhys tried the apartment next door and after an interval a young woman opened the door. Her head was wrapped up in a towel; evidently she'd just been washing her hair. She looked at the badge in alarm and asked, "What's wrong?"

"Nothing here. Do you know Miss Sorenson, in the next apartment?"

"I didn't even know her name was Sorenson."

"Then, you wouldn't know if anyone else in the building knows her?"

"I don't think so. People here don't mingle, we're all busy."

They thanked her and went back downstairs. "Well, she must

have a few friends around, relatives," said Hunter. "She'll probably be well enough tomorrow to call somebody to help her out for
a couple of days."

"At least this one wasn't the apologetic rapist," said Rhys. "Anything but. And there are a lot of Mercedes sedans around, but not
as many as some other makes. It'll give the day boys a hell of a lot of
legwork, but they may drop on him that way." They both knew
how the routine would go. Query the D.M.V. in Sacramento about
all the Mercedeses registered here, start with Glendale first, the
towns closest, and go and look at the owners. If that didn't turn up
a lead, spread the net wider for all the Mercedeses in the county,
and a hell of a job that would be. It was a tedious way to go at it, but
about the only way.

"My God," said Hunter suddenly on the way back to the station,
"that was a damnfool thing to do, Bob, both of us goofed on it. I just
thought, if he grabbed her handbag he might have left some prints
on it, and we've been pawing it all over."

"Oh, hell," said Rhys, "and we're both supposed to be the smart
trained detectives. You are so right. Well, prints are funny, they
can stay latent a long time, and if he did leave any they could be
anywhere on the bag." The handbag was made of shiny blue
plastic and would take prints easily. "Let's drop it off at the lab just
in case."

They'd been back at the office half an hour and Hunter had
typed the preliminary report on it when a heist went down at a bar
on Colorado and they both rolled on it.

It was a hole-in-the-wall place and there were only two customers in. The place was as dark as most bars, and neither the customers nor the bartender could give any kind of description of the
heister. "I couldn't even tell you if he was Negro or Mex, he could
have been either one, I think he had kind of a dark complexion but
not so very dark. You get me. He wasn't here two minutes. No, I
don't think he had an accent of any kind, he just said, 'Let's have
all the money,' the way any American might say it. Yeah, he had a
gun, I don't know what kind. Just a gun, and I wasn't about to
argue with it. I don't own this place, it isn't my money, he got
maybe forty bucks, business been slow all day."

So that just made more paperwork to do, and nobody would
catch up to this heister this time.

On Saturday morning all the detectives concerned held a little
conference about Dangerfield, kicked it around and came to defi-

nite conclusions. Varallo talked to Thomsen, in the lab, who said, "Ray didn't pick up any latents on either the screen door or the front door there. That didn't belong there, that is. There were a couple of Turnbull's on the front door, and one of the wife's—and my God, she put up a yell when I asked for her prints at the hospital yesterday—and a lot of smudges. Nothing on the front porch—it hasn't rained since February, no chance of footprints. What did you expect? Ray said by what you got the killer just fired through the screen door and went away. There were five slugs in him, at least that's what the morgue sent over."

The autopsy wouldn't tell them any more. "So that's that," said Varallo, passing a hand over his tawny blond crest of hair. "We can haul Dangerfield in again and try the old nice-cop / tough-cop routine on him, he might break."

"Not him," said Forbes. "He's not the type. It'd be a waste of time, we can try it if you want but I don't think we'd shake him."

"Well, for God's sake," said O'Connor roughly, "I'm not going to worry about it. Sure, he's probably the one who did it, we all know that, but he's not the pro likely to go out and kill somebody else. I'm the hell of a lot more concerned about all the foolish powder floating around killing the damnfool kids piecemeal, and the trigger-happy heisters, and the drunk drivers. My good Christ, that fourteen-year-old—he was carrying half a pound of angel dust and a hundred joints of high-grade pot, in a paper bag. He isn't one damn bit scared of cops, just mad that we took it away from him. Now he's one"—and O'Connor leaned back in the desk chair looking savage—"that a lot of cops are going to be seeing a lot of for a long time to come. He told us cool as bedamned that he doesn't go for that junk, he knows what it can do to you, but you can make the hell of a lot of easy money peddling it. He wouldn't give us the time of day about where he was getting it. And what happens to a fourteen-year-old? Probation, and he's back on the same stand the next day. His mother's divorced and she's got two counts of soliciting. He'll be wandering around all he likes, she couldn't care less. What the hell do we do with one like that?"

"Discouraging," agreed Varallo.

Delia sat up and lit a cigarette. "Like the girls roped into the porn movies. Mary's been talking to them. It seems that one of them, the one Sandra thought was Chinese, is Vietnamese and the parents don't speak English, they haven't been here long, and the girl had the vague idea that that was the kind of thing you were expected to do in an American school."

"Oh, for the love of God," said Gonzales.

"And the other two are mad as the devil at Sandra for blowing the whistle. I just hope they don't jump her and beat her up on the playground. Did you get anywhere with the amateur actors?"

"I found one yesterday," said Varallo. "One Barry Hancock. He's a very pretty boy, he has ambitions to make it big in TV or the movies, but meanwhile he's got to eat. He hasn't got much backbone and he caved in right away and admitted it. The others we've talked to out of Thorpe's address book aren't talking. And as Charles says, it's a handful of nothing. Another contributing-to-delinquency charge, and probation."

"And all too many kids like that ready to cooperate," said Forbes.

The phone rang on Varallo's desk and he picked it up and said his name. "About this skeleton," said Dr. Goulding. "We can tell you this and that about it but I'm afraid nothing very helpful. It's female, and she was probably under thirty-five. And she was killed, if you'll excuse the vernacular, by a bang on the head. Fractured skull. I wouldn't have a guess how that happened, whether it was murder or accident. She's been dead anywhere from two to four years. There weren't enough shreds of clothes to say anything, I suppose the lab could tell you what kind of material it was. That's about the gist of it."

"Teeth?"

"She had a full set of teeth, and I wish to God mine were as good," said Goulding. "No crowns or fillings. Even if you can get some idea who she might have been, no dentist is going to identify her."

"Helpful," said Varallo. "Well, thanks very much." He passed that on desultorily. "Just an anonymous female dropping out of things, maybe not even missed."

"And we could have a look at the missing reports all over the county, that far back," said Gonzales, blowing smoke at the ceiling, "and maybe spot a suggestive description, but when we never could prove it, what's the point?"

They all agreed. Anywhere in the country there were the anonymous young people roaming around, the runaways who'd lost all contact with families, the people without any families to start with, the drifters wandering in and out of relationships with the same kind, going from one cheap job to another or no jobs at all, the females living by prostitution and a lot of the males, too. The skeleton could have been one of those, dead of deliberate murder or accident all that time ago, and casually buried up in that big debris basin to be gotten out of sight. Nobody would ever know now.

The phone rang in O'Connor's office and he got up to answer it. In ten seconds the amplifier came on, and there was Dawson again, sounding very annoyed. "—State police found the damned car run off the road into a ditch just outside Scottsdale, Arizona. It's got a cracked radiator, it's not drivable. By now, of course, we've got Orley's prints from the Army, and he left quite a few in it. Yeah, Lowell's car. There's no telling how long it's been there, and of course there's no sign of Orley. It's a main highway and he could have picked up a ride right off. But Lowell had two suitcases full of clothes in the car, and they're both missing."

O'Connor uttered a few unprintable words. "So we're a hell of a lot worse off than we were, damn it. While he was in a known car, with the plate number on the air, there was a good chance that he'd be picked up. Now he's just another hitchhiker. Unless he's hopped another car. And if he has, we don't know which one. I suppose there've been plenty of cars stolen in and around Scottsdale in the last twenty-four hours or so, there'll be wants out on them, he might get picked up yet."

"Just keep your fingers crossed," said Dawson cynically. "I take it the girl and her husband are all right?"

"So far." Dawson hung up and O'Connor said, "But those stakeouts— Gates is getting mad about it, stealing three patrolmen off regular duty. By God, if Orley cracked up that car yesterday he could be here by now."

They sat thinking dispiritedly about the various things on hand. There hadn't been anything more to do about that hooker, Alicia Taylor, and that had got shoved into Pending, along with several of the anonymous heists. The A.P.B. on Jack Myers' VW Rabbit hadn't so far turned up Gibson and Myers. The cop killer Luis Barrios was still loose somewhere in the county—or out of it. And there was this new rape last night—not their apologetic rapist, but the violent one, the potential killer of women, and damn the head doctors' double-talk about how one like that got that way, it would be nice to know who he was and stash him in jail.

The first thing they had done this morning was to shoot that request up to the D.M.V. in Sacramento. Just in Glendale and environs, there would be quite a few Mercedes sedans, and when that information started to come in, it would make one hell of a lot of work. Of course, some of them would be registered to females, but he could have borrowed the car.

"Well—" Varallo stood up. "I'm just stubborn enough to want another go-'round with Dangerfield. Come on, Gil, let's go and pick him up and try to scare him."

Delia called the hospital and was told that Claire Sorenson had been released. She tried the apartment on Louise, and the door was opened by a friendly-looking redhead who looked at the badge interestedly and said, "You're a detective? It must be kind of interesting work." Delia thought about the noble career and didn't smile. "Yes, Claire's here. I'm her best friend, I'm Paula Scanlon, I guess Claire can talk to you, come in."

Claire Sorenson was somewhere around thirty, and ordinarily she'd have been fairly good-looking, with crisply curly dark hair, big dark eyes, a slender figure. At the moment she looked ill and miserable. She had one arm in a cast, her face was swollen with bruises and she had a black eye. She was lying on the couch in the living room, and she managed a small smile for Delia. "All the police last night were so kind."

"Aren't they supposed to be?" said Paula. "Of course they were. And if you'd had the sense to ask them to call me then, I'd have been at the hospital with you. You had to go and faint like an idiot." She looked at Delia. "There's just her mother back in Nebraska. It's just lucky I was home, I'm on vacation and I'd had some idea of going up to San Francisco to see my sister. When Claire called me of course I shot right over. Which I'd have done if I hadn't been on vacation," she added cheerfully. "I'm a legal secretary too, but my boss is a sentimental old dear and I've got him under my thumb. Claire's too conscientious. Staying overtime to type a deposition—you should have told him the days of slavery are over."

Claire had a small twinkle in her nice dark eyes. "But Mr. Colburn hasn't much sense of humor, he'd just have looked at me blankly and said, 'I'm quite aware of that, my dear, but what has it to do with Mrs. Willoughby's deposition?' It took longer than I expected, because I had to put in a new typewriter ribbon."

"And why you don't make him buy you a good word processor—"

"Well, never mind," said Claire. She looked at Delia. "I couldn't tell the other officers much last night—"

"That's what I want to ask you. Now you're feeling a little better, can you tell me anything more about the man? You said he was driving a Mercedes, and he wasn't very tall but strong."

"I've been thinking about it," said Claire. "Sort of living it over—" She gave a small shudder. "It was dark, it was right at the rear entrance to the building, you know, and I couldn't see him clearly— I couldn't even tell you what clothes he was wearing— but there is one thing. He— sort of talked to me."

"Oh? What did he say?"

"When he first got hold of me, he said, 'Come on, baby, don't make no big thing of it'—and then, when he was hitting me—before and after he raped me—he kept saying, 'You don't know why I got to do this,' and he called me some dirty names—but the thing is," said Claire, "he had an accent. Just from that much I could tell."

"An accent—as if he were Mexican, or what?"

"No, a sort of southern accent," said Claire. "Not like deep South. I've been trying to place it, and it came to me just a little while ago. Last year, Mr. Colburn had to put a will through probate, and the heir was from Texas, there was a lot of property to straighten out and he came into the office quite a lot. And the man last night, he sounded just like him, just a sort of hint of a drawl."

"A Texas accent," said Delia. "Well, that could be a big help, Miss Sorenson. When you feel up to it, we'll want a formal statement from you."

"She'll be fine," said Paula briskly. "I'm feeding her good nourishing soups."

"And you can say what you like about Mr. Colburn," said Claire. "He was nice about it. He said to take however long I needed, and he was so sorry about it."

"Which cost him nothing."

"I'll come in on Monday and give you the statement," said Claire.

"That'll be fine." A Texas accent, thought Delia. It was a little something more to go on.

Sometimes, Saturday night could be hot and heavy, and later on in the year it probably would be, as the unbearable summer heat built up. Tonight the night watch sat around with the radio tuned to police frequency and nothing happened for them until ninethirty. There was a pileup on the Ventura freeway, Highway Patrol business. The only call they had the whole night was to a heist. It was a liquor store on Glenoaks, and the heisters had hit just before it closed; the owner had been alone in the place. "There were two of them," he said excitedly, "just two young punks, couldn't have been more than seventeen, one of 'em had a gun and the other one had a knife—but they didn't get much, I'd bagged the day's take for the bank and it was in the trunk of my car— I went out after them, thought I might spot a car, and they took off on a motorcycle out of the parking lot out there—"

"That pair again," said Rhys. Just another report to write.

On Sunday afternoon at about two o'clock, Patrolman Colin McLeon got a call, unknown trouble, to an address on Tamarlane Drive. That was a nice residential area, a street off Verdugo Road. It was a classy-looking house on a corner lot, a stucco place painted gray with white trim. There was a citizen waiting for him, the one who'd called in. He was a good-looking man about forty-five, very sprucely dressed in tailored sports clothes. There was a year-old Caddy parked in front of the house and he was standing beside it. He came up as McLeon got out of the squad, and said, "Thank God, they were very prompt at sending you— I don't know anything's wrong, but I'm terribly afraid—"

"What's the trouble, sir?"

"I'm Arthur Ferguson." As if automatically, the man handed him a card. It said ARTHUR FERGUSON, FERGUSON REALTORS, an address on Chandler Boulevard in North Hollywood. "It's my stepmother, this is her house, and I haven't been able to reach her on the phone for several days, she's not a young woman and we've been afraid, my wife and I, that something could be wrong, she could have had a fall or been taken ill—a stroke—and I haven't a key to the house. I've asked the neighbors but they haven't seen her in the last day or so—and I didn't know what to do, how to get in— I thought if I called the police—"

"Well, if you authorize us to break in, Mr. Ferguson—"

"Yes, yes, anything, just to find out if anything's happened to her —she's sixty-five, anything could have happened—"

CHAPTER SIX

The list of all the local Mercedeses had come in and everybody in the office had been roped in to work that. Nobody was in but Varallo and Delia when the call came in to a new body, and they went up to Tamarlane Drive in Varallo's car. McLeon and another man were waiting beside the squad in front of a house on a corner, an attractive stucco house in this affluent area of town.

"This is Mr. Ferguson," said McLeon. "It's his stepmother dead in there." The other man was looking distressed and agitated.

"We were afraid something was wrong, I usually talk to her a couple of times a week on the phone, and I hadn't been able to reach her for several days. That was unusual. She isn't out much, lives a quiet kind of life, she'd just be going to the market or the library a couple of times a week and she isn't often out at night. We were afraid—my wife and I—that something was wrong, she could have had a fall, a stroke—but we never thought of anything like this!" He got out a handkerchief and wiped his forehead. He was a very solid-looking citizen, good clothes, a good-looking stocky big man about forty-five. "My God, it's terrible to think of, her getting murdered— The officer here said that's what it looks like— We never dreamed it could be anything as bad as that— I hadn't a key to the house, the officer broke in— I thought it would be best to call the police—"

McLeon said, "The place was pretty secure, good locks, I broke a back window to get in, but as soon as I took a look I knew it was a job for you, I didn't touch anything, just called in. I had to handle the inside of the front door to let you in, that's all. There's one of those little nibs you push inside so when the door shuts it locks automatically."

"He wouldn't let me go in there," said Ferguson agitatedly. "How was she killed? What could have happened? Nobody would have had any reason to kill Edith— I don't understand it, it couldn't have been a burglar when the house was all locked up—"

"Just let us have a look, sir," said Varallo.

McLeon had left the front door open, and they went in to a small square tiled entry hall. "It's in the living room," said McLeon. That was off to the right; this wasn't a large house, but in an expensive area and well furnished, with neat landscaping, obviously a house where someone lived who had more than sufficient money. The living room was tastefully furnished all in Early American maple; there was a small upholstered couch, a few chairs, a pair of ceramic lamps on end tables, a standard lamp in one corner.

The body was hunched up near the coffee table in front of the couch, the body of a small elderly woman. She had gray hair cut short and curly about a thin, wrinkled face, and she was wearing a brightly printed pink cotton housecoat; one of her black velvet house slippers had fallen off, and there was a pair of plastic-framed glasses lying beside her. Beside the glasses were two little folded brochures. Varallo bent and picked them up. "Those won't take prints," he said, "any more than the others." The first one was a double-folded page with a picture of some African children on the front, and the printing below said, "Salesian Missionary Society, devoted to Christian work throughout the world." The other one was a tract about a Baptist missionary school in Asia. "Our phoney minister," said Varallo softly. There was a handbag gaping open on the couch. "She tried to fight him when he pulled the knife, and he knocked her down. He hasn't used the knife, it's just been a threat."

"But he hit that other woman," said Delia, "and broke her arm. It looks as if she could have hit her head on the coffee table, it's got pretty sharp edges, Vic. He wouldn't have meant to kill her, and maybe he panicked when he saw he had, to leave those brochures."

Varallo agreed. "But he shut the front door after himself, maybe automatically, and just maybe he's left some prints."

"It could be."

They went back outside. Ferguson was leaning against his Cadillac smoking nervously. "Can you tell us her name?" asked Varallo.

"Edith Ferguson, she's my stepmother but really more like my own mother, she and my father were married when I was just a kid, this is a terrible shock, how was she killed, who could have killed her? I don't understand it—"

"When did you talk to her last, Mr. Ferguson?"

"It was last Monday night, she was just fine then."

"She lived here alone?"

"Yes, my father's been dead nearly ten years. Edith was sixty-five but she was a very strong woman, she got along fine alone, she had her own car of course, but she didn't go out much, she lived a very quiet life— Of course she had her own friends— My father had left her very well off, of course— I came in for the realty business but there was a separate estate— I can't get over this, Edith getting murdered! Who could have had any reason to murder Edith? She never hurt anybody in her life, she was a good woman—"

"We don't know too much yet, Mr. Ferguson," said Varallo, "but it could have been the accidental thing, not intended. Would you know any of her friends we could contact?" The doctors would give them the approximate time of death, but if they could narrow it down, discover who might have talked to her last, it would be helpful.

"Yes, of course," he said numbly. "Beatrice Radford, and Bernice Crosswell— I can't think of any others at the moment, but there'll be names in her address book—"

"Did she have any particular day for going to the market?" asked Delia.

He looked surprised. "Oh, I don't think so—she'd probably be shopping a couple of times a week— I don't know."

"Well, thanks," said Varallo. "We'll be in touch with you—if you'll give me your address—" Ferguson gave him a card. "You understand there'll have to be an autopsy. You'll be informed when you can claim the body, I don't think there's any more you can do here right now."

"Yes, I see," said Ferguson. "This has been a terrible shock, it'll be a shock to my wife—we thought a good deal of Edith. My God, I hope you can find whoever killed her, it doesn't seem possible she's dead— Yes, I suppose you have your own routine, but you'll let us know—whatever you find out—"

"We'll be in touch," said Varallo. Ferguson got into his Cadillac and drove off.

Varallo used the radio in the squad to call the lab. They waited for the mobile van and Delia said reflectively, "You know, Vic, he sounds like a small-time operator, everything we've heard about him, the con-man type. The pitch about the missionary societies, the clerical collar, the respectable front. He hasn't actually offered violence to any of the women, the broken arm was just an accident when that woman was knocked down. He might be just the type to panic and run when he saw that this woman was dead. If he'd taken those brochures away, we'd never have connected him, it might have looked as if she'd tripped and fallen, and got put down as an accident."

"That's so," said Varallo.

"And the fact that the M.O. hasn't shown in records, he might not have any pedigree at all, half an amateur. Just his bad luck that she fell against the table, if we ever find him it'll be a manslaughter charge in one degree or another."

The mobile van arrived presently and Burt and Thomsen got out of it. "Try the front door for latents first," said Varallo. "And then give the living room the works. And the body."

"O.K.," said Burt. He glanced at Delia. "By the way, we got the kickback from the Feds on that print from the Ogdens' back door. It's not on file."

"Well, it was just a chance," said Delia.

There wasn't any point in watching the lab men work, but they followed them in and waited while Thomsen dusted the handbag and had a look inside. There was a bunch of keys, and Varallo took those. The billfold just held some small change. "He'd probably already grabbed the bills," said Delia, "when he realized she was dead. I suppose something ought to be done about that broken window, Ferguson won't want a burglar on top of this."

"He can get new glass put in tomorrow, the lab won't take long. I'll call him when they're finished." And it would be a little while before the lab could tell them about any prints—they'd have to get the corpse's for comparison—or about anything else they turned up here. Varallo and Delia left them to get on with it and went back to the station.

Everybody else was out looking for the Mercedes owners. There'd be a preliminary report to write on Edith Ferguson, and Delia started that while Varallo joined the other hunt. They'd divided up a list of Mercedes registrations. The day wore on and at least nothing new went down. When the day crew came trailing in, one by one, after five o'clock, nobody had turned up anything suggestive on the Mercedes owners. All they had to go on was the fact that, according to the Sorenson woman, the rapist was fairly uncultured of speech and had that Texas accent. None of them had run across a Texas accent among the owners, and so far none of the owners had admitted to lending the car to anybody else. For the moment, the detectives were skipping the female owners.

It had been a good deal warmer today and the legwork had been tiring; they'd all be glad to get home.

Delia was enjoying her balcony even more than she had expected to. It turned cooler after dark, and she had a couple of new novels from the library, but she sat out on the balcony for quite a while, with the brilliant panorama of city lights spread out below, while Henry chattered and whistled to himself in the living room. After five months she'd gotten used to tuning Henry out automatically. She'd found a new shawl for his cage, to match the colors in the living room; the only way to shut Henry up was to cover the cage, which sent him to sleep. She had just decided she'd better go in and get undressed, do a little reading, when the phone rang. Somewhat to her surprise, it was Katharine O'Connor. Sometimes Katharine joined her and Laura for lunch, for shopping, but she wasn't as close a friend as Laura. She was asking Delia to dinner on Friday. "Now you're living right in town," she said in her warm contralto voice, "we really ought to see more of each other. And I know you must be tired, all the upset of moving. Do come, Delia, you can come straight from the office, no special occasion."

"Well, I'd like to," said Delia.

"Fine, we'll look forward to it."

Monday was Colin McLeon's day off and he had a date with his girl. Her name was June Fletcher, and they had just gotten engaged last month, were going to be married when his vacation came around, in August. They were both working and didn't get together for dates very often. She was a nurse at Community Hospital and last month she'd gotten transferred to night duty; he worried about her driving alone so late, but she was a sensible girl, careful about keeping the car doors locked.

McLeon would have liked to go down to the beach or somewhere like that, but there was a movie June wanted to see playing at the Alex Theater, a new musical. He wasn't much for movies, but he was in love with June and wanted to please her. They'd decided to make the first show and then spend the late afternoon going back to her place to listen to records, or going up to Brand Park to watch the Little Leaguers practicing baseball— June was crazy about kids, especially little boys, and they planned to have at least two.

McLeon put on a pair of new slacks, a casual shirt and a sports jacket, and picked her up at twelve-fifteen. The theater opened at twelve-thirty. He parked in the big public lot behind the theater and they walked around, and he bought tickets at the booth in front. There wasn't anybody in the lobby but an usher, and when they went into the auditorium there weren't more than fifteen people there. What with the old and new movies on TV, the big movie theaters weren't doing the business they used to. The curtain wasn't up yet, the house lights still on; the show wouldn't start until one o'clock. As they started down the aisle, McLeon noticed a man sitting in an aisle seat as they passed, a man slouched down with his head tilted back looking idly up at the ceiling. His heart gave a small extra thud, and he took June's arm and propelled her back up the aisle to the lobby. "What's the matter?" she asked.

McLeon said in a low voice, "That's Barrios in there—that cop killer. And we're going to play it cool and easy, see." He hadn't been riding around in the squad for ten days with that ugly mug posted in front of him for nothing. He asked the usher for the manager and was directed to an office at one end of the lobby. The manager was a fat little man named Ginsberg, and he didn't lose his head; he was steady and cooperative. At McLeon's advice he went out and closed the ticket booth. McLeon called in and explained to the dispatcher, and asked for the backup. He left June sitting safely in the manager's office and waited in the lobby. He wondered what the hell Barrios was doing in a movie house in Glendale, but there he was. And all peace officers were supposed to go armed at all times, but he felt a little naked without the businesslike Colt Police Positive .38; all he had on him was the snub-nosed .32 in the shoulder holster.

The backup arrived in a hurry in ten minutes—Stoner, Tracy, Whalen and Morris—and they came into the lobby looking all excited.

McLeon said, "He's on the left side of the center aisle, in an aisle seat. The manager's holding up the show, the lights are still on."

"O.K.," said Tracy, "let's make it quick and clean." They all went down the aisle together, and Barrios was still there, sitting back looking at the ceiling. They all had their guns out; this wasn't one to take chances with. Tracy stepped into the row behind him and Morris stepped in front of him; Barrios drew back his feet to let him pass, and Morris leaned down and got a grip on him by both arms. "O.K., Barrios," said Tracy, "there are four guns on you. Get up and walk out nice and quiet."

Barrios stared up at Morris' face within inches of his own. Tracy's gun was against the back of his head. He said in naked surprise, "How the hell did you know I was here?"

"We've all got ESP," said Tracy. "Up, and let's go out nice and easy." They surrounded him in a body as he went up the aisle, and

in the lobby they put the cuffs on him and went over him. He was
carrying a gun, probably the same one he'd used to shoot Sergeant
Hollister.

"It was damned lucky you spotted him," said Stoner to McLeon.
"But why the hell were you spending your day off at a movie, of all
places?"

"You can thank my girl," said McLeon; "she wanted to see the
show."

L.A.P.D. received the news with heartfelt thanks, and four men
shot over from Hollywood to ferry Barrios down to the Central jail.
Gates went up to the detective office to pass on the news; only
O'Connor was in.

"Well, that's a step in the right direction," he said. "Now, if
somebody would just pick up Orley—"

Gates said, "I only hope to God somebody does. Tying up all
those patrolmen on the stakeout—and last night, damn it, Hendrix
asked Watkins to stay with his wife while he went out grocery
shopping, they were running out of supplies. The men are all fed
up with it, bored as hell, and I should think the Hendrixes would
be damned bored too, shut up there."

O'Connor gave him his sharklike grin, "Don't take any bets,
they're newlyweds."

"If you ask me, Orley's never going to show, he's given up the
idea."

"From what they heard from his pals back there, I don't think
so," said O'Connor seriously. "I think he'll show eventually."

There had been a lot of local agitation over Turnbull, and it
wasn't doing the police any good. The ordinary muddleheaded
citizen didn't know anything about rules of legal evidence, and it
looked to most of them like an open-and-shut case. William Dangerfield had threatened to kill Turnbull, and Turnbull had been
killed. Why wasn't Dangerfield arrested and locked up? It had
been reported in the local papers that he'd been questioned and
released without being charged. There was a TV call-in show on
the local network that enjoyed some popularity, and on last night's
program half the time had been spent on Turnbull and Dangerfield, with most of the callers voluble on labeling the police either
stupid or corrupt and a few, more sensible ones trying to defend
the system. And the public memory was short; in all the furor over
Turnbull only a few people seemed to remember Juan Garcia and
the original reason Dangerfield had made the threat.

O'Connor sat in his office after Gates had gone out and did some swearing to himself. The noble career, he thought, the knights in shining armor and everything black or white, no shades of gray. It was always a damned dirty thankless job, and sometimes it looked as if they couldn't win— It was damned if you do, damned if you don't.

On Tuesday morning about eleven o'clock, Varallo located another Mercedes owner, and as he talked to him thought maybe he'd hit the jackpot. His name was Douglas Murphy, and he worked at a plumbing and heating shop on Olive Avenue in Burbank. He was about thirty, stocky and muscular-looking, with no pretention to good looks, and as he talked to Varallo there was a little drawl in his voice, a faint soft slurring of vowels. Texas accent? thought Varallo. "We're just making a routine check, Mr. Murphy, if you haven't done anything wrong you've got nothing to worry about. Can you tell me where you were between eight and nine o'clock last Friday night?"

Murphy was a little belligerent. "Cops!" he said. "Why should I? Well, for God's sake, I was at my mother-in-law's. My wife works nights, she's a waitress at Damon's, and she asked me to take some stuff over to her sister, some stuff she'd been sewing for her. Her sister still lives at home, just her and my wife's mother. I went over there after dinner and we played cards awhile, I guess I was there till around ten."

Varallo was just enough interested in him that he wanted to check the alibi, and he got the address, Raleigh Street. It was a modest frame house on an old, tired block, and the mother-in-law was home. She looked uneasy to find a cop on her front porch. She was a fat woman with hennaed hair and shallow blue eyes; her name was Hopkins. She said, "Why you asking about Doug? Yeah, he was here Friday night, he was here with me and my other girl, Debby. I guess he left around ten."

The girl worked at a beauty salon in the Galleria, and Varallo went over there to talk to her. She was in her early twenties, and in time to come was going to resemble her mother. She was flustered at being called away from a client to talk to a cop, and she said nervously, "Well, that's right, Doug was with us last Friday night. Up to about ten, I guess. Why are the police asking?"

"Just checking," said Varallo. That put Murphy out of the picture; for a while, he'd thought he had something. That rape hadn't been a planned thing. It looked as if the driver of the Mercedes had just happened to be passing that public lot when he'd seen the woman come out alone, and the lot empty, nobody around. It had been a spur-of-the-moment deal. They hadn't had a violent rape in a while, and of course it was all up in the air, he could be somebody living here or somebody living in Santa Monica or San Fernando who'd had some reason to be on North Brand in Glendale at that particular time. But it wasn't on the cards that one like that would be satisfied to pull one rape; he'd either done it before or he'd do it again. Would it be any good to talk to forces around, see if they'd heard anything about a violent rapist with a Mercedes and a Texas accent? Varallo decided it might, and back at the station he spent most of the afternoon talking with men in Pasadena, Hollywood, Valley Division, Highland Park, and he asked R. and I., downtown, to put it up to the computers. Nothing at all conclusive turned up.

Delia was slightly annoyed with Laura. When she landed at the Varallos' house, on Hillcroft Road, Laura had said brightly, "Slight change in plans. I was just starting to put the roast in when Audrey Butler came over, our newest neighbors, you know, and they're having a cookout in the patio—and she said the more the merrier, we should bring you. They're nice people, you'll like them, they've got a girl a bit younger than Ginevra and a boy about the same age as Johnny."

Delia would have preferred a quiet evening with them alone, but it was arranged. The Butlers had a big paved patio with lights and a barbecue pit, an electric grill, and they weren't the kind of people she'd ever want as bosom friends: Bob Butler a little too hearty and telling childish jokes, Audrey a little too bright and winsome. The children got rather boisterous until they were hustled off to bed. There was another man, a Don something, Audrey's brother. They had drinks and Butler grilled hamburgers and there was a lot of inane talk. The other man was a deadly bore; he worked at a bank and all he could talk about was stocks and bonds and money-market funds. Delia made an excuse to get away as soon as she could, using the old plea of a headache and being tired after a busy day. It was a relief to get home, to Henry's chatter and the view from the balcony. She sat out there awhile before coming in to get undressed for bed. She said good night to Henry and draped the shawl over the cage, and Henry subsided into silence and presumably went to sleep. By then she was too tired to sit up reading, and went to bed.

The night watch mercifully didn't leave them anything new to work. The computers downtown hadn't turned up anything suggestive on the violent rapist, and there were still a good many Mercedes owners to talk to. It was Wallace's day off, so they were shorthanded. Katz and Poor had a couple of new burglaries to work.

Varallo came back to the station after lunch to compare notes with Forbes, Gonzales and Boswell, and none of them had come across any possibles for the rapist. Rosie had been lonesome with all the men out on the legwork, and came to sit on Varallo's lap. She liked Delia well enough, but in Rosie's small world only men belonged in a police station, and she was pleased to have proper company again.

"This is the long way around to go," said Forbes. "He may not be the world's greatest brain, but even if we think we've spotted him, all he has to do is deny it, and we've got no evidence, the woman admits she couldn't identify him."

Gonzales said lazily, "Wait until he does it again and maybe there'll be more evidence."

"Now, that's a negative attitude if there ever was one," said Varallo. "And for God's sake don't come out with things like that where the general public could hear you. We're coming in for enough adverse publicity over this damned Turnbull thing." They had brought Dangerfield in and grilled him again and gotten nothing out of him; they never would. As Forbes said, he wasn't the type to break down and confess.

At least nothing new had gone down today so far. They were still sitting there when a uniformed man came in and looked at them diffidently. He was a new rookie, and they didn't know him. He said, "Lieutenant Gates said I'd better tell you about it. It was a funny enough thing, I didn't know just what to do about it, and I didn't want to start off on the wrong foot, if you get me. I've only been on the job a month." And he'd have been through the police academy, all that rigorous training, but he looked very young and innocent to the detectives; he couldn't be over twenty-one.

Varallo said genially, "Well, what's it about? Should we know your name?"

"I'm Farley, sir. Well, it was like this, I'm on a beat down in the south part of town, and about an hour ago I was on Adams just below Chevy Chase, and just as I got to the intersection there was a woman hailed me, at the corner outside the drugstore there. She was waving her arms around and yelling, so I stopped and got out of the squad. She was just a young woman, and all upset, crying and carrying on. And she said some nut had cut off her hair. There was a man there too, he was the pharmacist, he said he'd just been about to call the police when they saw the squad coming up."

Varallo laughed. "That one again. My God."

"Lieutenant Gates said there'd been other cases like that. At first I thought I'd just put in a report at the end of shift like usual, but the more I thought about it the funnier it seemed. I didn't know it had happened before, of course. I came back to the station to tell the lieutenant about it, and he said I should tell you. Her name's Teresa Ortiz, and she works at that drugstore. She said she was busy restocking some shelves, and there weren't any customers in—and the pharmacist was in the back and the only other employee out to lunch—and she never heard anybody behind her, but all of a sudden she felt a kind of tug on her hair, and she turned around and there was this nut grinning at her and waving a pair of scissors around and he'd cut off some of her hair."

"Long hair?" asked Gonzales.

"Well, pretty long. Pretty hair too, she's a good-looking girl and she's got a nice head of hair, black and wavy, down past her shoulders. He'd cut a great big piece of it out, you could see. And she screamed, and he just went running out. She can't give much of a description, just that he was young and thin and had a sort of silly grin on his face."

"Well, that is one for the books," said Varallo. "But it's true enough that it may not be anything to laugh at, the sex freaks start out with that sort of thing and sometimes graduate to something more serious. All right, Farley, get it down in your report, and thanks for letting us know."

As Farley went out, the phone rang and he picked it up. "Varallo."

Sergeant Bill Dick, on the desk downstairs, said, "I've got a call from Placerville, it's a sergeant named Cardoza up there. He wants a detective."

"So put him through."

Sergeant Cardoza sounded brisk and efficient. "You're the boys put out an A.P.B. on a red VW Rabbit registered to a Jack Myers, address down on your beat, the occupants wanted for homicide—"

"Don't tell me you've got them?" said Varallo.

"That's just what. The car died on them outside town about an hour ago, and they were damn fools enough to hail a Highway Patrol squad and asked the driver to call in for a tow." Varallo started to laugh. "Naturally he spotted the plate number, called the backup and put the arm on them. Yep, that's right, two of 'em, Gibson and Myers, they're both carrying I.D. We've got them in the town jail. What do you want to do about it, will somebody come up to fetch them?"

Varallo considered. It was quite a way up to Placerville, he thought. "Is there any way to fly, have you got an airport?"

"What the hell," said Cardoza indignantly, "you think we're a bunch of rubes out in the boondocks? There's a shuttle flight to San Francisco three or four times a day."

"Well, so somebody'll be up to fetch them," said Varallo. "Thanks very much, Cardoza. We'll be in touch, let you know when to expect an escort." Putting the phone down, he passed on that news. "Who'd like a plane ride up there? And on second thought, two of us ought to go to shepherd them both." It was a little break in the monotony of routine.

Gonzales volunteered and Boswell said, "Come to think, I've never been to Placerville. That's the old frontier Hangtown, you know. I wonder what the hell Gibson and Myers were doing up there."

"You can ask them when you see them," said Varallo. He looked up airlines and asked questions. There was a flight to San Francisco at 8 A.M., and it was only about an hour's flying time. They could probably get to Placerville and back by the middle of the afternoon. And there was a flight down at two something and another at 4 P.M. "Extra day off for both of you," said Varallo. "And that clears another one up, thank God. Though of course there's Turnbull—"

"What?" said Boswell.

Varallo looked at his cigarette ruefully. "Judge Turnbull may have gone to his reward, whatever it's going to be, but God knows we've still got enough judges of the same kind. That pair, Gibson and Myers—killing the bright, ambitious seventeen-year-old. By what that market manager says, and he's mad enough at them, it wasn't deliberate, it was an accident—he just got in the way when they were skipping out after the heist. They've both got previous convictions"—they'd turned up a count of assault for Myers—"but you know it'll be a charge of involuntary manslaughter, and what might they get?"

Forbes shut his eyes and leaned back in his chair. "A one-to-three suspended, and probation. They won't spend a day in."

"The lady with the blindfold," said Gonzales, "isn't always so

impartial. As we all said, we can see Dangerfield's point of view.
There ought to be some kind of moral judgment in the legal
system to separate the wheat from the chaff. Balance a Brian
Dangerfield against Juan Garcia—the bright seventeen-year-old
against Gibson and Myers."

"There's a source that says eventually justice gets handed out,"
said Varallo.

Gonzales gave a sharp laugh. "And I once believed it, back when
I was an altar boy."

Varallo stabbed out his cigarette. "I suppose we'll find out eventually. I wonder where Delia's got to?"

Nobody knew.

Delia had been sitting at her desk smoking and thinking about
the minister after getting back from lunch. They had heard something from the lab, and it was probably all they were going to get.
There hadn't been any liftable prints on Mrs. Edith Ferguson's
front door or anywhere in her living room, a few of hers elsewhere
in the house. The cheap paper of the missionary tracts wouldn't
take prints. There ought to be an autopsy report today or tomorrow, and they could guess what it was going to say: fractured skull
where she'd fallen against that coffee table.

And none of that pointed out any way to locate the fake minister. There hadn't been anything in the news about Edith Ferguson; Varallo had asked the press to keep it quiet. If the minister
knew they'd connected him with the homicide, he might just
vanish and never be heard of again. He'd know she was dead, but
it was possible he didn't realize he'd left the missionary tracts
there. But they hadn't a single lead on him; it was a dead end. Of
course if they ever did drop on him, the other women could
identify him; they'd declined to look at mug shots, and privately
Delia thought he wouldn't be in any records anyway, but seeing
him face to face in a lineup would be a different matter.

She was startled when the voice spoke from the door, and
jumped and looked up. She was alone in the office except for Rosie,
who was sitting on Varallo's desk chair looking lonesome. There
was a man in the doorway of the office, a small man with a round,
fresh-complexioned face and thin brown hair brushed carefully
over a bald spot. He looked about forty. He was wearing a neat
gray suit, a white shirt and a discreet dark tie, and gold-framed
glasses. He gave a little cough and said, "The man downstairs said I
should come up here and talk to a detective. Are you a detective?"

"That's right," said Delia. "Come in and sit down, tell me what it's about."

He advanced into the office. "My, what a cute little dog," he said to Rosie. He sat down in the chair beside Delia's desk. "My name is Oliver Carpenter, miss. I'm afraid I've been rather foolish, but I'm not a suspicious man and I really had great faith in the woman. You see, I've always been interested in all the various aspects of parapsychology—" He looked at her doubtfully as if he thought she might not know what he meant. "Er, psychics, ESP, and especially in faith healing. There's a very definite power there, you know. I often consult psychics, really some of them are quite uncanny, what they can see with the inner eye, or in the tarot cards. Business advice and so on, not that I've ever been greatly interested in that, I'm not a man to risk money except on certainties, not that I've ever had a great deal of money to invest. Perhaps I should say that I work at a furniture store, the Plaza Furniture Store in Eagle Rock."

"Yes, Mr. Carpenter," said Delia patiently.

He sighed. "As I say, I often consult the psychics. And not so much to obtain predictions for myself, but as a study. It's a most interesting subject, you know. And I had gone to see this one several times. I suppose you could say it's my greatest interest in life, I'm a bachelor and live alone, and I do a great deal of reading on the subject. She has a studio in her own home here, where she gives readings and does horoscopes. Her professional name is Sister Star, and I considered her a very talented medium. Several times she has told me that I had great potential as a faith healer, if I studied and meditated under her guidance I might achieve great powers. I was quite excited about it, and I agreed to embark on whatever course she suggested." He sighed again and took off the gold-framed glasses to polish them on his handkerchief.

"Yes," said Delia.

"She instructed me to read a certain list of books, and certain Bible passages, and to meditate at least two hours a day, concentrating on gaining absolute perfect faith in the ultimate power, that is, God. I had been doing so for the last three months." Regarding him, Delia thought that honest, simple Mr. Carpenter must surely be the ideal mark. If it hadn't been the psychics, it would have been the lost gold mine or a share in a legendary fortune.

"Yes?" she said.

"Well, you know, I really felt I was attaining a new, higher level of faith, just as Sister Star said I would. I could actually feel the power growing within me, it was quite exciting to feel that I might be able to help mankind—for we're all brothers and sisters and must consciously love and help one another—as so many great faith healers have done and are doing. And then last Sunday night, when I had my regular weekly meeting with her, Sister Star told me that my feeling was true, I was very nearly at the level of faith where I might achieve great powers. There was only one more test I had to pass before reaching my goal. You see," and his expression was devoutly earnest, "it's necessary to clear the mind and spirit of all materialities, all thought of material things and especially of money. She told me that if I wanted to achieve perfect faith and harmony with God, I should take all my money, everything I'd saved, and I was to bring it to her to bless and pray over, and then I must cast it into the sea. And then I'd be free forever of all the worldly chains binding down my spiritual powers. So I did. That is, I took out all my savings and turned it into cash, it was nearly two thousand dollars, and I did what Sister Star said. I put it all in a big manila envelope, and I took it to her on Monday evening, and she lit her ceremonial candles and blessed it, and we sang some hymns. And then she said I should meditate while she prayed over the evil symbol of materialism. So I did that, and she gave me back the envelope. I had had to puzzle quite a time before I saw just how I could cast it into the sea, and then it came to me. There is an excursion boat sails to Catalina Island every day. So I drove down to Long Beach yesterday—I had made inquiries and that's where it sails from—and it left about noon, and it was such a pleasant day, I was really enjoying the experience. And I thought when the boat was well out to sea, I would cast the envelope overboard. Only," he sighed, "as the saying goes, the spirit is willing but the flesh is weak. I'd taken a long time to save up that money, miss. A long time. And I thought—well, it was very weak of me, but I thought I'd just look at it again before—before—"

"You cast it into the sea?" said Delia.

He blinked at her. "Well, yes. And when I opened the envelope, why, all that was in it was a lot of strips of newspaper, it wasn't my money at all. I was simply astonished, I couldn't think what had happened. But I remembered what Mr. Cohen often said to me— he's my employer, he owns the furniture store—and he's a very fine man though he is a complete skeptic, and he's often told me I shouldn't trust these people who call themselves psychics. That's how he talks, he doesn't believe at all. And I'd had absolute faith in

Sister Star, she seems so very spiritual-minded, but I remembered what he said, and I don't know, perhaps he's right about her, though I very much dislike to think so." His eyes were mournful. "At any rate, this morning I told him what had happened, and he got a most peculiar look on his face, and had a terrible coughing spell, and then he said didn't I tell you so, and I should go to the police. The police here, because she lives here in Glendale."

"Mr. Carpenter, just where does Sister Star live?" asked Delia gently.

He blinked again. "Oh, it's a little house on Kenilworth Street. Not a very nice house, but she always says she's above the soulless materialities."

Delia regarded him in some fascination. But the citizens did come all shapes and sizes.

It certainly wasn't a pretentious house: an old frame bungalow in need of a paint job, with brown grass in front and a crack in one of the front windows. When she went up onto the porch, she glanced at the old black metal mailbox: there wasn't any name on it. She pushed the bell. She was feeling quite curious as to what Sister Star might look like, but whatever image her imagination could conjure up, it wasn't that of the woman who opened the door, a little thin dried-up-looking woman with mousy hair and a long nose, wearing a shapeless brown dress and a long rope of carnelian beads.

"Sister Star?" inquired Delia. She felt a little foolish pronouncing the name.

"Oh, I'm sorry, she's not here now. Would you like to make an appointment?" The woman's voice was thin and high.

"Well—" said Delia. "When do you expect her back?"

"She said she'd be back on Sunday, she hadn't any appointments till then, but of course she'd never disappoint Mrs. Rockford, or Mr. Carpenter—she was quite exhausted, you see, she takes so much out of herself with the sittings. She's simply a wonderful psychic—I'm her sister and I know. I expect you want a reading, it's your first time, isn't it? I can make an appointment for you sometime on Monday. Would you like a card reading too?" Unexpectedly businesslike, she added, "It's ten dollars for a regular reading and five dollars extra for the tarot."

Delia was well aware of the nature of entrapment as regarded by the present judicial system. She said cautiously, "Well, I'd like to see Sister Star."

"That's right, dear, you can make up your mind later." She let Delia into a shabby crowded small living room and took up a large plastic notebook from a table, opened it. "Two o'clock is free, is that all right? Then, I'll put you down. Oh, you mustn't give a name at first, dear, then, if Sister saw something true about you, you might suspect that she was dishonest, had looked you up somehow. We're very careful about that, so many people have nasty suspicious minds, and that way you'll know that whatever Sister tells you she gets from her psychic power." The little woman was chatty now. "I mustn't ask you if you saw the advertisement in the paper or if one of the other clients recommended Sister, but I expect she'll know as soon as she sees you. She takes so much out of herself, it's a shame, and she was simply exhausted, she said she had to get away for a few days and just rest. She didn't say, but one of her dear friends, an old client, has a charming beach cottage near San Diego and I expect that's where she is. I do hope she'll be rested up when she gets home. Ordinary people don't have any idea how hard a good psychic has to work, you know. Well, we'll see you on Monday, then, dear, and Sister's always pleased to have a new client."

On that Delia would take a bet. She thought there wasn't any hurry about it. It would give them time to get the formal statement from Oliver Carpenter and apply for the arrest warrant: the straightforward charge of fraud and robbery. The sociologists, often as muddleheaded as the ordinary citizens, or the liberal judges, were fond of proclaiming that the state of mankind was improving by leaps and bounds, civilization reaching its zenith and now reaching out hopefully into space. But cops had to deal with realities, and the ordinary mortals didn't seem to change much from one century to another. Very likely, shortly after the colonies got established on Jupiter or Mars, they would include the Sister Stars pulling the old gypsy switch, and the heist men and the wanton murderers and all the rest of motley humanity—and the easy, gullible marks like Mr. Carpenter.

Mr. Joseph Cobb was a teetotaler and nonsmoker. It wasn't from religious convictions, but physical ones: Mr. Cobb was something of a physical-fitness buff. He was fifty-five, but he exercised regularly, consumed all the recommended vitamins, was careful of his diet, and watched his weight. As a result, he was fond of telling everybody, he was as fit as a man half his age. He never mentioned, if he ever thought of it, that his grandfather and father had lived to be ninety-five and ninety-seven respectively, that both of them had smoked like chimneys and consumed as much good whiskey as they could come by.

But his personal convictions had nothing to do with his business instincts, and he was the owner of a large and prosperous liquor store on Broadway. As he told his wife, it wasn't anything to do with him if people chose to poison themselves, and it was a profitable business.

He was just getting ready to close the store at ten minutes of nine that night. His one clerk had already left, and he was busy putting all the day's receipts into the bag for the night deposit at the bank, when the two holdup men came in the back door from the parking lot. Mr. Cobb had never been held up before, and he was both frightened and furious. The bigger holdup man had a gun, and he looked to be only about eighteen years old. The other one was even younger, and he had a big knife. The first one brandished the gun at Mr. Cobb and said brusquely, "O.K., buster, hand it all over." Reluctantly, Mr. Cobb shoved over the bag of money—all that beautiful money. "That's fine, bud," said the holdup man. "Now you just stand there and don't call the cops for five minutes, see." Then they both went out the back door.

Mr. Cobb's fury overcame his fright by a small margin, and ten seconds later he followed them out. If he could describe their car to the police—maybe even memorize a license-plate number— As he came out the back door, he heard the roar of an engine, and he saw a motorcycle take off out of the lot with the two holdup men on it. The one riding behind the driver was holding the white cotton bank bag. Futilely, he ran across the lot after the motorcycle, saw it turn out into Broadway and accelerate up toward the intersection. Dumbly, he stood and watched while the accident happened.

The traffic light was red on Broadway, but the motorcycle didn't seem to notice it. The motorcycle didn't even slow down; it flashed into the intersection just as a big Ford pickup truck was in the middle, and hit it broadside.

Mr. Cobb ran back into his store to call the police.

Hunter and Harvey waited in Emergency for what the doctors could tell them. It was, of course, Rhys's night off. The intern who finally talked to them briefly passed on some I.D.: a driver's license issued to Derek Angard; there wasn't anything to say who the other one was. "They're not in too good shape," said the intern.

"One of them, probably the operator of the cycle, has internal injuries and a compound fracture of the leg, concussion. The other one's not so bad, simple concussion. You could probably talk to them sometime tomorrow or next day."

At least they'd caught up to that pair of heisters, by the fluke of an accident.

CHAPTER SEVEN

Gonzales and Boswell would be starting north on Thursday morning. As the rest of the men came in, they heard the news about the heisters and laughed about Sister Star and Mr. Carpenter. They were still looking at the Mercedes owners.

Varallo was just about to leave the office when he got a call from one of the assistant D.A.'s, one Canfield, on the child porno thing. "We'd like to have a full investigation on this," Canfield said, "and make a charge on everyone concerned. I realize it probably won't result in any kind of sentence, but the District Attorney feels that we should make an example, and try to crack down on this sort of thing. If the police can identify everyone concerned, we intend to bring full charges on all the principals."

Varallo said, "We haven't identified all the other men, those probably employed by Thorpe to appear in the films." He could guess what was coming. "There are a lot of names in Thorpe's address book, of course."

"That's fortunate," said Canfield. "There shouldn't be any difficulty if you've got names and addresses. We'll ask a couple of you to view the films so you can identify the, um, actors." Varallo suppressed a groan. It was going to be one damn bore to sit through the blue movies, and a waste of time to go looking for those men and arrest them. They'd all get bail, which Thorpe and Carol Lister had already gotten, and sometime later come up before the bench for a hearing. There'd be a fine and a suspended sentence, and not much would have been accomplished. Thorpe might be a little more cautious in the future, that was all. "If you can see your way to being in my office say at ten o'clock, we can run them off and have that much out of the way."

Varallo agreed and roped Lew Wallace in on it. "Oh, for God's sake," said Wallace disgustedly, "the things we have to do. Watching porn movies at ten o'clock in the morning yet."

Delia had been on the phone too. She said, "I've been talking to R. and I., downtown, and Sister Star's got a little pedigree. Her real name's Agnes Dooley. She did six months in jail for another count of fraud and robbery, she was operating in Hollywood then as a Spiritualist minister."

"People," said Varallo, and went out with Wallace. Delia had Mr. Carpenter coming in to make the formal statement. When she'd typed it and he'd signed it, she would make the application for the arrest warrant.

He looked at her mournfully as she stapled the pages. "I suppose you're going to arrest her."

"Well, she did steal your money, Mr. Carpenter, and she's done this kind of thing before."

"Oh, really? I didn't know that. I really thought she was the most gifted psychic. Really, this kind of thing is upsetting. It brings such doubt and suspicion on the whole field, the genuine honest psychics. Well, I suppose I was gullible to trust her, but as I say I'm not a suspicious man, I expect I tend to believe the best of my fellow creatures, and Mr. Cohen says that's always a mistake."

Delia sent in the application for the arrest warrant. It was John Poor's day off, and Katz came in about eleven o'clock grumbling about the stupid citizens. There'd been another burglary overnight. "And talk about bricks without straw," he said. "I sent Rex up to print the place, but you know he won't get a damn thing, it looks like a pro job and he won't have left any prints." He started to type the report.

Delia went out to lunch with Mary Champion, and when she got back, Jeff Forbes had just come in. "I want to get hold of Vic," he said. "I think I've run across a possible for that rapist. I've just been talking to an insurance salesman who drives a Mercedes and has a Texas accent you could cut with a knife. I'd like to bring him in and lean on him some." Delia told him where Varallo and Wallace were and he swore.

"Oh, hell. Is Charles in?" But O'Connor was down in Juvenile since ten minutes ago, talking to a kid from Hoover High who'd been picked up holding some angel dust.

Forbes sat down at his desk and Rosie jumped into his lap, and his phone rang. He picked it up, listened, and said again, "Oh, hell. All right, somebody'll be over. The hospital," he said to Delia. "One of these heisters is conscious, I suppose we ought to hear a few answers, but it's no big deal, they had the loot on them, there's just the paperwork left to do. But they've pulled off quite a few heists in the last couple of months if we read it right, and if we can get them to admit it—"

Delia said absently, "By all the descriptions they're probably minors."

"So they'll get probation," said Forbes. "I know, I know. Well, I might as well talk to this one anyway." He went out. Ten minutes later, a young woman came in hesitantly and said, "Is this the detective office? The guy downstairs said to see the detectives."

"That's right," said Delia. "What can we do for you?"

She came farther in and on invitation sat down beside Delia's desk. She was a plump dark girl in her early twenties, and she looked unhappy and nervous. "Can I have your name?" asked Delia.

"I'm Sharon Morley. Say, look, I don't like to be a tattletale, but I've been thinking it over, and I told Debby she ought to come clean about it. But the way she dithers around, she's a good kid but she's just not so long on the brains, see. She comes out with all this to me and I tell her it's not such a smart idea to tell lies to the cops, and she says they were just thinking of Maureen, but she got nervous when a cop came around asking, because if it was just what he said why were cops coming to ask, and I told her she ought to come clean about it. But she dithers, and she'll probably be mad at me for blowing the whistle, but you know, I think she's sort of scared of the guy and I figure if he's done anything, the cops ought to know."

Delia said, "If you'll just tell me what you're talking about, Miss Morley—Debby who?"

"It's Mrs.," she said. "Debby Hopkins, we both work at the Fashion Coiffure Shop in the Galleria. She's a good kid but she's not long on brains, like I say. It was on our coffee break yesterday, she's telling me about it, she's awful worried about it and says she doesn't know what to do. See, her sister's married to this guy named Murphy, her sister works nights, and it was this guy asks Debby and her mother—she lives at home with her mother—to give him an alibi for some night last week, how I make it out. If anybody came asking, they were supposed to say that he'd been there all evening. But they hadn't expected it to be cops asking, and it sort of scared them, and now Debby's sorry they said it, told the lies to the cops, but they don't know what to do about it. They don't like this Murphy guy so good. I think Debby's sort of scared of him for some reason, but he's a relative, and like she said, they're thinking about Maureen, that's the sister, I guess they don't want to see any trouble between them. Debby got the idea he'd been with another girl and maybe it's her husband or boyfriend might come asking, and it shook them when it was a cop. And if I know Debby, she'd go dithering around about it from now on and never do anything, and I figure if the cops heard about it and talked to her, she'd be kind of glad to get it off her chest and come clean."

Delia didn't know anything about this, but it sounded interesting. She took down the names and thanked the girl for coming in. "Maybe," said Sharon Morley, "she won't know it was me blew the whistle. I figure if the cops just ask her again she'd come apart."

"Well, thanks very much for the information," said Delia.

"And I got to get back, I've got a client at two-thirty and I'm late already." She went out as if she was glad to go, and ten minutes later Varallo and Wallace came in.

Wallace was grumbling, "I feel as if I need a bath, all that God-damned hard porn, and now we've got to waste more time hunting up all the amateur actors, when all they'll get is a slap on the wrist—"

Delia said, "Vic, do you know anything about a Debby Hopkins?" She told them what Sharon Morley had said and Varallo looked surprised.

"For God's sake," he said, "I'd written that one off. Murphy? By God, I thought when I was talking to him I might have hit the jackpot, and then those two women alibied him and I forgot about it. By God, Lew, we might have something here, let's go and talk to this girl."

The boy propped up in the hospital bed was thin and dark with a pale beardless face and sad dark eyes. He'd told Forbes his name was Jason Angard. His head was bandaged and he had one arm in a cast.

"You've pulled quite a few heists around town with your brother," said Forbes. "You're ready to admit that? How old are you, Jason?"

"I'm sixteen. Derek's eighteen. Yeah, that's right, I didn't want to but he made me, they both made me do it." He had a high thin voice, and he sounded listless, as if it was too much trouble to talk, to tell about it. "I never wanted to do like that, it isn't right. I was awful sorry when we had to go back to live with Ma— I guess that's an awful thing to say, because she's my own mother, but it's the truth, I got to tell you the truth. See, she got in some trouble, she got arrested for stealing some money where she worked, and our dad's up in Folsom, and Derek and me, we got sent to different

foster homes. It was about a year ago or some more. I got put with
Mrs. Edwards, and I liked it real good, see." He moved restlessly in
the bed. "Mr. and Mrs. Edwards, they're awful nice, they treated
me real good, and I liked their house. It's clean all the time, and
Mrs. Edwards' a real good cook, we had nice things to eat. And she
kept my clothes clean, and we went to church on Sunday. I'd
never been to a church before and I liked it, I liked Mr. Went-
worth, he's the minister there, it's the Grace Christian Church. I
learned an awful lot in church. But then Ma got out of jail and we
got sent back to live with her. Derek, he didn't like the foster
home he was in, he said they were too damned strict, and he was
glad to be back with Ma, but I wasn't. Derek, he hasn't got no use
for school, he dropped out a couple of years ago, but I never
minded school, I'd sort of like to go back and maybe graduate.
Only, Ma said that didn't matter none. And she said it was about
time we started to earn our keep and bring in some bread, with
Dad up in the pen it wasn't so easy to get along, and she got fired
from that job at a dress shop last month. We had to have money for
the rent and all like that. So Derek said we'd do some heists, and I
didn't want to but he made me. He made me carry that knife, and
he got the gun from a friend of our dad's lives over in Hollywood.
And he made me go with him to do the heists." He was staring out
the window now; his bed was by the window in this three-bed
room.

Forbes asked, "You couldn't get out of it?" The boy seemed a
little immature for sixteen, and maybe that was understandable.

He said miserably, "No way, you don't talk back to Derek or Ma.
And Ma was awful pleased about it, she said Derek took after our
dad, a real good provider. We got a lot of money, but Derek didn't
give me any, he split it with Ma. I didn't really want any of it
anyways, because I know now that's a wrong thing to do. I never
thought about it before, but now I know, since I been to church
and know about them things. And I'm kind of glad about the
accident, so you'll stop Derek stealing money like that. I suppose
we'll both go to jail for it. I guess we ought to."

Forbes felt a small pang of sympathy for this forlorn waif; it was a
sorry tale. He said, "I don't think you'll be going to jail, Jason. We'll
have to see." The social welfare departments, the courts, could be
careless and cold-blooded, but there might be a chance that Jason
could end up back in the nice, clean, orderly foster home.

The brother had had a driver's license on him; the address was
on Garfield Avenue in an old and shabby part of town. Forbes went

down there to see if Ma was home. It was an ancient apartment building. Angard was listed in a rear upstairs unit. He pushed the bell and in a minute the door opened and he took a look at Ma. She might be any age, her puffy face raddled with makeup and long unwashed, her old bathrobe grimy, her feet bare; her bleached hair was in a tangle, and she was more than half drunk. She peered at him and asked in a slurred voice what he wanted. Forbes wondered whether she'd noticed that the two boys hadn't come home last night. He said, "Nothing," and turned away. She slammed the door after him.

Forbes felt tired. The things they saw on this job! He went back to the station and talked to R. and I. downtown. Rita Angard had four counts of soliciting and one of grand theft, and had gotten out from serving a year's sentence on that four months ago. Richard Angard was currently serving his third term for armed robbery. It might be a little help to Jason if the report going to the D.A.'s office could spell out some names and facts. Forbes got on the phone again to various social-service departments, got handed around some, but finally managed to track down the foster parents. The latest time Rita Angard had been arrested, she'd been living in Hollywood, and both the foster homes had been there. It wasn't any part of a cop's job to follow up after an arrest, but he got hold of the Edwardses and told them about Jason.

Mrs. Edwards sounded motherly and concerned. "That boy's not a bad boy," she said. "He's got good instincts. I'm sorry to hear about this, Mr. Forbes. What's going to happen to him?"

"He's still a minor. He won't be tried as an adult. There's a possibility that he'd be held in Juvenile Hall until he's eighteen, but the court might very well put him on probation and send him to a foster home."

"Well, we'd be glad to take him back if that should happen. He's really a good boy, he just got off to a bad start with that unfortunate background."

That you could say in spades, thought Forbes.

Debby Hopkins stared at Varallo and Wallace, there in the little gaily furnished anteroom of the fashionable beauty salon in the big shopping mall, and burst into loud tears. There was a client waiting, an elderly woman leafing through a magazine, who looked at them curiously. Varallo said, "You'd rather talk to us in private, Miss Hopkins," and they led her out to his car in the lot. She wept all the way, and she didn't do any talking immediately; she sat in the back seat and sobbed and hiccuped. Wallace lost patience with her after three minutes and said abruptly, "Come on and tell us about it. You told a lie to Sergeant Varallo, didn't you? About your brother-in-law being with you and your mother last Friday night?"

She sat up and mopped her eyes with a crumpled tissue. "Yes, I did," she said thickly, "Mother and I both did. But he said it wasn't anything important, he just didn't want Maureen to know, was all."

"Your brother-in-law, Douglas Murphy?" said Varallo.

She nodded and hiccuped. "He came to the house about ten that night, last Friday night, and he said he'd been at a bar and there was a fight and the cops got called—and he didn't want Maureen to know—he used to drink a lot and Maureen got him to go to that thing— Alcoholics—"

"Alcoholics Anonymous?"

"Yes, that was it, and he got so he didn't get drunk so much, so he said he didn't want her to know he'd been at a bar, and if anybody came asking we should say he was with us all evening, and we said we would. And I didn't say so to Mother, but I wondered if maybe it hadn't been that at all, if maybe he'd been with another girl and he was afraid her boyfriend or husband— I never said so to Maureen, but I never liked Doug so good. There's just something about him I don't like, a kind of funny look in his eyes. And then you came and asked, with the badge and all, and I got scared there was something wrong about it, a cop, why should a cop be asking about Doug? But by then we'd both said it, we told you he was there, and I could see Mother was a little scared about it too, but it was too late."

"Well, you've told us now," said Varallo, "so it's all right." He wasn't going to flurry her further by asking for a statement right now, and at this stage they didn't know whether they'd need one. "You've got it off your conscience, so you needn't worry about it any more."

"Has Doug done something? Something bad?"

"We don't know, Miss Hopkins."

Maybe they'd find out. It was getting on for four o'clock. She started back to the beauty shop, still sniffling into the tissue, and Varallo said to Wallace, "Let's go talk to him."

They didn't talk to him on the way in. They had found him repairing an old hot water heater at the shop where he worked.

They took him down to the station, planted him in one of the interrogation rooms, and began to ask questions.

"Just why did you think it was important enough to arrange that fake alibi for last Friday night, Murphy?" asked Varallo. "We've heard all about it, you know. Debby's conscience got to bothering her and she told us about it."

"You weren't with her and your mother-in-law that night," Wallace took it up. "Where were you? By any chance, were you beating and raping that woman in a parking lot on North Brand?"

Murphy sat with his head bent across the tiny table, his heavy shoulders hunched. He didn't say anything for a while, and they asked the same questions over again. Finally he said in a tired voice, "Don't you try to tell me that about those damned women. Women, they're always makin' trouble, one kind or another. I should have had better sense than to ask them to say that. I wasn't using my head, but I was kind of nervous. That's how you know, isn't it? That squad-car man saw me when I drove out of the lot, saw my car. There's an awful bright light right there. You probably got me by the car, and there was that customer in this afternoon, I bet he was that squad-car man in plain clothes, and he reckanized me. So you went to the women and got them to say it wasn't so, I wasn't with them that night."

"So you were in that parking lot instead," said Varallo, "beating and raping the woman." He wondered which squad had passed that lot just then, with no reason at all for the patrolman to take any notice of a car leaving a public lot, he wouldn't have thought twice about it, but of course Murphy had been nervous. In fact, it had probably been the squad sent to Claire Sorenson a few minutes later.

"Well, you know it was me," said Murphy despondently.

"You saw her come out of the rear door of the building?"

"I'd just been driving around, I was feeling kind of jumpy that night. Maureen asked me to take that stuff to her sister, and I did, and then I was just driving around. I thought about maybe lookin' for a hooker, but I had kind of a bad time with the last hooker I picked up, and I changed my mind." His voice was dull. "I was just passing that lot when I saw that woman come out, and there wasn't nobody around, and before I hardly knew I was goin' to do it, I pulled in the lot and got out and grabbed her."

"Why did you have to beat her up?" asked Wallace. "Wasn't it enough to rape her?"

He sat staring at the table. "Can I have a cigarette? I'm all out."

Varallo gave him one and lit it for him. "I tell you how it is," said Murphy and took a long drag. "I tell you— Maureen, my wife, she don't like the sex thing no way, she hardly ever lets me. And I—it's like something kind of getting ready to explode in me, I don't mean just the sex, it's like something in my head—and the last couple of times she's yelling I hurt her real bad. And it was a damned awful funny thing, but the time after that I picked up a hooker she changed right in front of my eyes, she changed into Maureen, see. She was a blond and Maureen's a redhead, but she changed into Maureen. And for God's sake, the hookers don't care what you do to 'em but I guess I beat on her some too. And ever since, every time I been with the hookers it's like that, all of a sudden they changed into Maureen. And I got to hurt Maureen as bad as I can."

Varallo exchanged a glance with Wallace. "Did the woman in the parking lot change?"

"Oh, yeah, I couldn't see her too good, it was dark that side of the lot, but she did, I could feel she did, and I beat her up good. But then when I was driving out of the lot I saw that squad car, and I got nervous the guy had noticed me—that woman, she'd call cops and that guy'd remember the car there at the right time—"

"So you arranged the alibi," said Varallo.

"Yeah, that's why. I made up some story for Debby and the old lady— I thought they believed me—and that woman, she'd fought me and scratched me some on one arm, but I told Maureen I had a little accident at work, and she don't pay much attention to me anyways. I tell you," said Murphy suddenly, "I think there's something wrong in my head. It isn't natural, those women all of a sudden changing into Maureen."

Varallo said, "We'll be arranging for you to see a doctor about it, Murphy. Right now you're going to jail."

"I figured," he said dully.

Wallace took him over to book him in, and Varallo sent in the application for the warrant. It was after six and the night watch was drifting in. He should have called Laura but there hadn't been a chance. He went out to the parking lot and Wallace was just coming back.

"Left my jacket up there," he said. "I suppose you had the same thought I did, Vic. He could be the john who killed the Taylor woman."

"Oh, yes," said Varallo, "it crossed my mind. But we'd never prove it and there's no point in bringing it up. They'll send him for psychiatric evaluation and he'll probably end up in Atascadero, for a while anyway. They didn't use to let them out of there very soon, but I understand they're crowded these days, he may get out fairly quick."

"And go looking for more females to rape," said Wallace.

Varallo got into the car. "Well, I don't know, Lew. Once he's away from the frustrating Maureen, maybe not. Or he may go back to being a drunk."

"Anyway," said Wallace philosophically, "it's out of our hands."

Delia had forgotten to replenish Henry's supply of sunflower seeds on Tuesday, and the nearest place she could get properly germinated ones was at an exotic-bird store in Burbank. In the previous five months she'd found out quite a lot about the correct diet for parrots. It was seven-thirty when she got home, and she shared the elevator with the man who lived in the next apartment, the tall dark one. They didn't exchange a word and she wished she could think why he seemed vaguely familiar.

Gonzales and Boswell had had a long day. Sergeant Cardoza might not think Placerville was in the boondocks, but to the city men it seemed away off the beaten path. There wasn't any difficulty about getting to San Francisco, but there they had to wait three hours for a flight to Placerville, and once they got there, another three hours for a flight back. Cardoza was cordial and took them out to lunch, but he seemed to be nearly as busy as a city cop. They wandered around town a little, and at four o'clock collected Gibson and Myers at the jail and got a flight back to 'Frisco. There they had to wait until six-forty for a flight to L.A. They landed at the Hollywood-Burbank airport at seven-fifty and had to take a cab to deliver Gibson and Myers to the Glendale jail.

Both the prisoners were complaining loudly of starving to death, and Boswell said irritably, "And how the hell do you think we feel? We haven't had any dinner either."

"Yeah," said Gibson bitterly, "but you can go some place and buy some. And the jail chow got passed around a couple hours ago." They would both know; they'd been in before. They hadn't done much talking on the way down, except to cuss the damned bad luck of getting dropped on, and Gonzales asked now, "What the hell were you doing up there in the wilds?"

"Oh, for God's sake," said Gibson wearily, "we'd been over in Vegas and neither of us did no good at anything, the slot machines or blackjack or roulette, we was heading up for Reno to see if we could do any better there when the Goddamned car died on us."

"Simple when you know," said Boswell as they came out of the jail.

"For God's sake," said Gonzales, "let's head for the nearest restaurant, I could eat a horse."

In the middle of the week, business was usually slow, and the night watch didn't get a call until nine-thirty. The dispatcher said it was reported as a shooting, and Rhys and Hunter went out expecting to see a body. Instead they found Lopez in the small living room of a little house on Ethel Street, a homey-looking room, acting as a nurse to an elderly man lying on the couch. A little white-haired old lady was sitting in a rocking chair with her hands folded in her lap, rocking steadily and staring at the opposite wall.

"You ought to see a doctor, Mr. Dolan," Lopez was saying. The old man's shirt was lying across the foot of the couch, stained with blood, and Lopez was mopping with a wet towel at a flesh wound in the man's left upper arm.

The old man said placidly, "It'll be all right, son. The bullet didn't stay in, did it?"

"No, sir." Lopez looked at the detectives rather helplessly. "I've got it." He came over to Rhys and Hunter and beckoned them out to the front porch. "Look," he said, "I don't know how you want to play this. The old lady took a shot at him. I took the gun away from her, she was waving it around and giving him a hell of a tongue-lashing when I got here, she was the one who called in, she wants you to take him to jail."

"Take him?" said Rhys. "Why did she shoot him?"

Lopez started to laugh. He handed over the gun, which was a little peashooter of a Colt .22, and the slug. "It went right through his arm, I dug it out of the wall for you. She's a cute little old lady, I don't think you'll want to take her to jail, but it's up to you."

They went back into the living room and Rhys asked her, "What's your name, ma'am?"

She said in a bitter voice, rocking back and forth, "For my sins, the same as his. Dolan, Emily Dolan. And after being married to this wicked, sinful man for fifty-four years I finally lost patience with him." She looked up at Rhys fiercely and her blue eyes were snapping. She was at least seventy-five and maybe older. "Wouldn't you think that by the time a man gets to be eighty years old he'd forget about chasing women and start thinking about what's in store for him in the next world? But not Pat Dolan, oh, no." She rocked harder. "Sit up in his coffin to make eyes at anything female! I knew he was down the block visiting that Parker hussy, and her seventy if she's a day and plastered all over with makeup like a Jezebel— Going up to the corner for cigarettes, a likely story, and staying away two hours! It's disgraceful at his age, and I made up my mind to teach him a lesson."

The old man cackled from the couch. "It isn't every man can say a female shot him for love when he's eighty years old. Now, Emily, you'd've been right sorry if you'd killed me, who'd you have to argue with? So what if I like to pass the time of day with Ruth Parker—"

"And those chits of saucy waitresses at that restaurant up on the Boulevard, and old Miss Wills next door, her simpering at you like a silly old fool, and every other woman you lay eyes on! He's had a roving eye ever since I've known him," she informed Rhys, "and I've stood all I'm going to. I should have shot him in the leg, keep him tied down to the house awhile at least."

He cackled again and gave the other men a roguish look. "Life in the old dog yet, that's all, no harm in it. Now, you don't want to pay any attention to Emily, boys, she seems to think you could put me in jail for flirting, but I don't expect you can. Yes, sir, that's my pistol, I keep it in case of burglars. Emily just flew off the handle for a minute, but she's always been good at that. First time I ever tried to kiss her, she took a broom handle to me, and I still got the scar where she threw the iron at me, that was some years back. I'm not hurt, just lost a little blood." They both looked like very hale and hearty old folk. "I don't want to prefer any charges, if that's how you say it. You all just go away and she'll calm down, she always does."

They were all trying not to laugh. "You'd better have a doctor look at your arm, Mr. Dolan," said Hunter.

"So I'll call Jim," said the old man comfortably. "That's our youngest, and he's a doctor. Youngest of twelve if you'll believe me, Jim is, and we got twenty grand-kids and eleven great-grand-kids. Now the cops are going away, Emily, you go and make yourself a cup of tea and simmer down."

Out on the sidewalk they all began laughing, and Rhys said, "My mother after me to find a nice girl and get married— Not on your life! I might get one like Emily. It's a risky business, marriage."

Bill Watkins had never been so bored in his life. It could be monotonous, tooling the squad around the beat, spotting traffic violations, handing out tickets, occasionally dealing with brawls and drunks and accidents and dead bodies, but at least it was action, and he was damned fed up with sitting on this stakeout. After all this time, he figured it was a false alarm; this Orley was never going to show up. He's changed his mind about wanting to murder the girl and her husband, and he might be in New York or Miami by now.

He hoped to God the front-office boys would come to the same conclusion and call off the stakeout, let them get back to the regular job. For one thing, sitting motionless in the dark like this, night after night, it was hard to keep awake, keep his mind alert. He sighed and pulled back the cuff of his jacket to take a look at his watch with the pencil flash. Hell, only ten o'clock. Two hours before Dempsey showed up to relieve him.

He stretched and tried to get into a more comfortable position. Then he saw a car turn down Graynold Avenue from Glenoaks. He looked at it idly at first; this was a quiet block, but every night he'd been planted here, a few cars had passed, people going home to the single houses, another apartment house farther down the street. This car was moving very slowly, and it slid in to the curb and parked right outside the apartment building across the street. Watkins sat up. He'd never seen any of the other tenants there come home as late as this. The manageress seemed to stay in all the time, and the other apartments were occupied by older people who didn't go out much at night.

After what seemed a long time, the driver's door opened and a figure got out. In the darkness, Watkins could see only that it was a tall thin person, and it moved slowly. It went uncertainly around the car and crossed the sidewalk to the narrow porch at the apartment entrance. Watkins eased his door open silently and got out. The front door to the little lobby was left open for tenants, and he heard it open. He counted twenty and crossed the street; the door was ajar and he peered cautiously in. There was a dim overhead light, and now he could see that the figure was a man, just starting up the steep cement stairs.

Watkins started after him, moving as quietly as he could. He didn't know whether this was a legitimate tenant or a visitor, or Orley. The man ahead of him was climbing the stairs with painful slowness, hauling himself up by the handrail, and Watkins could hear hoarse breathing. On the first landing he staggered against the wall, caught himself, and started up the second flight of stairs. Watkins decided that, whoever he was, he was drunk. Then, as the man got to the top of the stairs, he turned to the right down the hall, and by the dim overhead light there Watkins saw that he had a gun in his right hand.

He took the rest of the steps in a rush and caught up with the man just outside the Hendrix apartment and tackled him from the side. He had his own gun out. "All right, buddy, this is the end of the line," he snapped.

The man didn't make any effort to fight back, and he didn't say a word. He sagged under Watkins' grip on his arm. "Drop the gun," barked Watkins, and heard the faint thud on the carpet as the order was obeyed. "Now, up against the wall and put your hands on your head—move!"

That order didn't get obeyed. The man sagged limply down and slithered out of Watkins' grasp and folded up on the floor. Passed out cold, or playing possum? Watkins bent over him. He didn't smell of liquor, but he was dead out. Watkins pushed the bell of the Hendrixes' apartment, keeping an eye on his captive, and when the door opened on the chain he said, "It's me— Watkins. Will you both come out here, please."

In a moment, the Hendrixes came out to the hall, both in bathrobes, the pretty blonde and the good-looking young husband. "Is this Orley?" asked Watkins. The man was lying sprawled out on his back, what light there was directly on him. Now Watkins noticed that he looked filthy and ragged; there was several days' growth of beard on his long, narrow face, the upturned shoes had soles completely worn through, and he was wearing a dirty gray suit too small for him, and a dirty blue shirt.

"That's Frank Orley," said Frances Hendrix. "He did come— But what's the matter with him, did you knock him out? Did he have a gun?"

Watkins picked up the gun from the floor. It was a big Colt revolver. "No, I thought he was drunk but—" He stooped over Orley and felt his chest, listened to his breathing. He straightened up and said in astonishment, "I'll be damned—he's sound asleep."

When the backup he called for arrived, Steiner in the squad, they couldn't rouse Orley at all, he just lay and snored and breathed hoarsely. Watkins didn't like the sound of that breathing, and they called an ambulance and followed it down to the emergency wing at Memorial Hospital. The Hendrixes had told Demp-

sey about it when he showed, and he was down there before
Watkins had talked to a doctor.

It was half-past twelve before a doctor came out to them, an
older, bald man, not an intern, and Watkins asked, "Is he all right?
Why did he pass out like that?"

The doctor said perplexedly, "What in hell's been happening to
that man? No, he's not in very good shape. He's filthy all over, and
his feet are in a bad state, it looks as if he's been walking for miles
with no soles to his shoes. He's got a heavy cold and I wouldn't be
surprised if it turned into pneumonia. We're getting antibiotics
down him and cleaning him up. He's running a damned high fever
and I don't think he's had much to eat in a while. How did he get
into this shape?"

"We couldn't tell you, Doctor. Can somebody talk to him very
soon?"

"Don't count on it," said the doctor. "On top of everything else,
I think the poor devil's starved for sleep, and he's pretty well
dehydrated. Is he under arrest?"

"Technically speaking," said Watkins. "We don't want him for
anything, but the Army does, he's AWOL. We'll have a guard on
him."

"He's not going anywhere soon," said the doctor dryly.

They left Dempsey holding down an uncomfortable chair outside the cubicle where the nurses had parked Orley, and Watkins
went back to the station to leave a note about it for the day crew;
the night watch had already left.

Friday was Varallo's day off, but the rest of them heard about
Orley with interest. The car he'd left outside the apartment had a
want on it; it had been stolen in San Bernardino the day before
from a public lot. O'Connor got on the phone to Dawson. "We
can't tell you anything else, it's the Goddamnest thing. We
checked back with the hospital this morning, and he's still unconscious. He's got pneumonia, the doctor says. Oh, they'll pull him
through all right, with all the antibiotics and intravenous feeding,
but it may be a while before he's sitting up and taking notice.
There's no hurry about the Army sending the MP's to get him."

"I'll be damned," said Dawson. "Where the hell do you suppose
he's been?"

"God knows. He had the gun on him, and he was trying for the
Hendrixes' apartment when our man jumped him. They were all

cussing about the stakeout, but as it turns out it was just as well we set it up."

"Well, I'll let his commanding officer know. I'll give you his number and extension, Lieutenant Duvall, you might let him know when Orley can be moved."

"We'll do that."

"And if he ever comes to enough to tell you what happened to him, I'll be interested to know."

"So will we," said O'Connor genially. "They say we can probably talk to him in two or three days, I'll let you know."

Delia was telling Boswell and Gonzales about Sister Star—they'd missed that one—when her phone rang and she picked it up. "Delia," said Mary Champion urgently, "I need you. Rather, your Spanish. I've got a poor old soul here trying to tell me something, and she's got about six words of English."

"I'll be right with you."

In the Juvenile office, she found Mary and Ben Guernsey looking concernedly at an old woman in the chair beside Mary's desk. "She came into the lobby about ten minutes ago," said Guernsey, "and all Bill could make out was that she was saying some girl is gone."

"Sí, " said the old lady, understanding that much. She waved her arms. "Gone. Not home. *Malemente.* " She was a thin, bent old lady in a shabby black dress and old flat-heeled black shoes. She clutched a big black handbag on her lap.

Delia found a chair and said in Spanish, "Tell me about the girl. What's your name?"

She turned in vast relief at the familiar language. She began to pour out voluble information. She was a Mrs. Elisa Estrada. "Oh, never have I understood better how my Marco used to say, Mama, you should learn English! But there is never any need, I am home with the children, at the shops nearby are those who speak Spanish, you understand. And so it goes on—all the children, they are smart children, they speak English well, and they are at me too, Mama, you should learn, but by now I am too old, you understand. We have been in North America for forty-five, forty-seven years—Marco and I, we came across the border, all very legal, to make a better life, we became citizens, the children are all born here." Delia was trying to follow the rush of words. "Marco, my husband, he was very smart too, first we lived in San Diego and he had a good job in a market. Then we saved up our money and we came to Los Angeles and Marco opened a nice shoe store, and had a steady trade. We weren't millionaires, but we lived well. But our two sons, Marco and Eduardo, they don't like the city, they want land and farms, and they both worked hard and saved money, they each have a big farm up north—nice farms, good land, near a place called San Luis Obispo. They wanted me to come there when my Marco died, five years ago, but I have lived in the city too long, and it isn't good for two women to be in one house, they both have good wives, nice children. Marco bought the house here when Los Angeles began to have so many criminals running in the streets, we have lived here twenty years now. And when Marco died we had saved up enough money, enough for me to live on until I die, but the boys send me something every month too."

"The girl," said Delia patiently.

She began to cry gently. "Anita is a good girl, she would never run off or do what is wrong. We go to Mass every Sunday, she has been brought up well, she's a good, modest girl. My granddaughter, Anita Reyes. You understand, my only daughter, my Teresa, she stayed here and married a very good man, Juan Reyes, he had a good job selling insurance. They had only the one child, Anita. And two years ago, only the good God knows why such things happen, they were killed in an automobile accident— And Anita was only fifteen, so she came to live with me. There was not much money left for her, Juan was not a saving man. And she didn't want to go to her uncles' farms. She stays with me, and she's a good girl, a smart girl, she has one more year of school, and then she will study to be a hair stylist, that is her ambition."

"Where does she go to school?"

"Glendale High School. We live on Cabrillo Drive." That was an old and good area of town; Marco Estrada must have bought the house when real estate prices were low. Delia had wondered fleetingly why none of Mrs. Estrada's English-speaking neighbors had come with her to interpret, but probably in that area the neighbors wouldn't speak Spanish. "And she didn't come home from school yesterday. Always, always, she comes home straight from school, to study. Anita is a very serious girl."

"Has she a boyfriend?" asked Delia.

She waved an arm. "There is a boy, an Anglo, Dudley Newton, he has taken her to school dances and the moving pictures, but it is nothing serious with Anita, she likes him but there is no romance. He is a nice boy, very respectful and polite. But there is another, Anita is afraid of him. She has said so. He is a very wicked boy, no, he is not a boy but a young man, he used to go to the high school but no longer, and he runs with a pack of wolves, one of these street gangs where all the members use drugs and become drunk and commit many violences—oh, Guerreros, that's the name. His name I do not know, I don't think Anita knows, but she says he is always meeting her on the street when she leaves the school, when she waits for the bus, and he says he is in love with her, and Anita is afraid of him— And when she didn't come home from school I was frightened, I waited and waited and she didn't come—and I telephoned her best friend, that is Inez Mederos, and she said that Anita had left the school at three o'clock, usually they go together, but Inez had to look for a book at the school library and she was late. And all night Anita didn't come, and I was more and more frightened, and early this morning I called my son Marco, and he is frightened too and angry at me, he says I should have called the police last night—and so I have come— And the police will look for Anita? I am afraid that bad young man has abducted her—"

Delia said involuntarily, "My God," and she felt frightened for Anita Reyes, too. One of the Guerreros, that vicious gang of street toughs, one of them taking a fancy to the modest, well-brought-up girl.

"What's she saying?" asked Mary impatiently. "What's it all about?"

"Nothing very nice," said Delia, "and just what we can do about it I don't know."

Katz had just finished a report on the latest burglary, after lunch, and was feeling piously thankful that tomorrow was his day off, when a new call came in, and he swore and went out on it. It was an address on Grandview Avenue, and when he got there McLeon was waiting for him beside the squad. He grinned at Katz. "Sometimes we cuss the stupid citizens, Sergeant, but sometimes they come through for us too. I think you'll like to meet Miss Dorothy Webber."

"Oh, yes?" said Katz.

"It's the left front apartment upstairs."

The apartment was an old eight-unit place. The front door of that apartment was open, and Miss Webber was sitting in a chair in the living room with a chenille bathrobe clutched around her. She was about twenty-five, with brown hair and a rather plain face, and at the moment she wasn't looking her best; she had an obviously bad cold, and she was sneezing and blowing her nose, and her eyes were red and swollen and her voice hoarse. She said, "I was never so surprised in my life. I've got this terrible cold, I've been feeling lousy, and I've been off work two days. I work at Pacific Savings and Loan—my brother lives here too, it's cheaper to share an apartment, but of course he's at work, he works at Sears in the personnel department—and I thought I heard the bell but I was half asleep, I'm full of aspirin, and the first I knew about it was when I heard a thud in the living room, and I realized there was somebody in here, and I got up and looked, and there was this man just unplugging the new portable TV—"

The daylight burglar, or one of them. "Can you describe him?" asked Katz rather hopelessly.

She coughed and sneezed. "Oh, I've got him for you," she said. "He was more scared than I was. I was so mad— Bob had saved up for that TV— The little man was just petrified, he looked at me as if I was a snake, and of course he was standing just by the hall closet, so I just pushed him in and locked the door. There's a lock on it because Bob keeps his shotgun there, on account of burglars, and he keeps it loaded, and sometimes our sister comes with her little girl."

"He's in the closet?" said Katz.

"That's right. He's just a funny little man."

They let the burglar out, and he was quite subdued and docile. Katz took him back to headquarters to question; when he ran the name through records he found that this particular burglar had two other counts on him.

Delia, O'Connor, and Forbes had discussed the possible abduction, and O'Connor had done a good deal of cussing about it. He and Forbes had gone out to haul in some of those gang members and grill them, and Delia and Gonzales were the sole occupants of the office at two o'clock except for Rosie, who was sitting on Gonzales' lap having her ears scratched, when a man came in and said politely, "The desk sergeant said the detective office was up here. Are you any of the detectives who had anything to do with Judge Turnbull's murder?"

Gonzales stood up. "Yes, sir, that's right."

"Well, I've come in to tell you that it was me who did it," said the man simply. "I don't want Mr. Dangerfield to suffer for something he didn't do. I shot Judge Turnbull, and I've come to tell you about it." He reached into his pocket and drew out a gun and put it on Delia's desk. "That's what I did it with. I'd better tell you all about it."

CHAPTER EIGHT

He was a man about thirty-five, tall and well built, with a square, plain, clean-shaven face and a pleasant deep voice. He was wearing well-tailored sports clothes. Wallace said, "May we have your name, sir?" O'Connor came in and at Delia's glance sat down silently in Varallo's desk chair.

The man said, "I'm Howard Chesney," and he added an address on South Street. He sat down in the chair beside Delia's desk. "There's been all this talk about Mr. Dangerfield, how he threatened the judge and must have been the one who shot him, and evidently you haven't arrested him yet, but I was afraid you would, and I don't want him to pay for what I did. I've come in to tell you all about it."

The gun was a Colt .38. "Yes, Mr. Chesney," said Wallace. "What about it?"

"You could say," said Chesney remotely, "that it was the same sort of motive for killing him that Dangerfield had, but it wasn't quite the same at that. It was our little girl, Kathleen. I don't know if any of the police would remember it, it was more than a year ago. We were very happy up till then, Marcia and I were married more than five years before Kathleen was born, and we loved her so much, she was such a lovely little girl. I have a good job, I'm in the trust department at the Security-Pacific Bank, and we were buying a house, everything was fine. And then a year ago last February that man took Kathleen and raped her and beat her. She was just out in our backyard, and Marcia couldn't stop blaming herself. She hadn't any reason to do that, she was a good mother, she always kept a close watch on Kathleen, took good care of her. Kathleen was only five, I don't know if you remember."

O'Connor nodded just once. He said in his deep voice, "Kathleen Chesney. Yes, I remember it."

Chesney said, "She was just out in the backyard playing in her sandbox, it was a nice warm day. Marcia had checked on her not ten minutes before, and then she was gone, Marcia couldn't find her, and she called me and we called the police. The police found her about an hour later, in the backyard of the house next door. Those people had just moved in, we didn't know them. Kathleen had been raped and beaten, and it was the next day the police arrested the man, he was the brother of the man next door, and he'd done that kind of thing before, the police found that out, he'd raped another little girl over in Pasadena. Kathleen was hurt very badly, she was in the hospital a long time, and then the doctors told us she'd had a lot of brain damage from the beating and she'd be like a vegetable all her life, she was blind and she'd never be able to think or learn anything even if she lived very long. And Marcia kept thinking it was all her fault, she hadn't kept a close enough watch on her. But Kathleen was a friendly child, when that man spoke to her over the fence she'd have gone right over to him, it wouldn't have taken ten seconds. And how could Marcia have known there was one like that next door?" He brought out a pack of cigarettes, and lit one carefully. "Of course she couldn't. It was a long time before the man came up for trial, and by then Marcia was in the sanitarium. She'd got into a deep depression and our doctor had sent her to a psychiatrist and he put her in the sanitarium. She'd gone on blaming herself, you see, she couldn't stop thinking about Kathleen. Well, the man came up for trial—"

"Jonathan Draper," said O'Connor suddenly. "I remember the case."

"Yes, that was his name. It wasn't a real trial, just a hearing before a judge. Judge Turnbull. And the judge sentenced him to a year in jail and then suspended the sentence and ordered him to see a psychiatrist. That was all. He never went to prison. When Marcia knew about it, it set her back a good deal, she was pretty bitter about it and so was I," said Chesney. "But she seemed to be getting better, feeling more like herself again, and in January they let her come home. And then in February Kathleen died. The hospital bills had been astronomical, but that doesn't matter. She died. She'd had damage to her liver and kidneys from the beating, and she died. Marcia took it pretty well, we both agreed that when she couldn't live a normal life it was better she should go. Marcia was still having fits of depression, and I was afraid she'd have to go back to the sanitarium. And then there was that business about three weeks ago, about Dangerfield threatening the judge because he'd released that other one, the one who killed Dangerfield's son. It was in the papers, and on TV, and Marcia saw it. It just brought everything back to her as if it'd happened yesterday, and she couldn't stop talking about Kathleen, she couldn't stop thinking about it. Blaming herself all over again, I couldn't do anything with her. I tried to get her to see the psychiatrist again, but she said he was a fool and didn't know anything about how she felt, and his office said he was out of town. I was worried about her, but I never thought she'd kill herself, she'd never threatened to do that, she was just bitter and resentful about that judge, and depressed. But she did, you see. A week ago Monday night." And Delia vaguely remembered the night report, the autopsy report, the straightforward suicide, just the report to write. "I came home and found her, she'd slashed her wrists and she was dead. So it was all finished," said Chesney with a vague gesture. "Everything. And of course the one to blame was that Draper, who'd killed Kathleen— Because he did kill her, she died of what he did to her. But I couldn't get at him, I'd have killed him if I'd known where he was, that would have made a little more sense, I know. But as it was, you could say the other one responsible was the judge. You could say he killed Marcia. He let that man go without serving a day in prison, and when Marcia saw about the other one—Dangerfield— it put it all in her mind again, brought it all back, and that's why she killed herself. The day she was buried, everything was finished, you see. The funeral was in the morning, and maybe I wasn't very sane myself then— I don't know, maybe a psychiatrist would say I was crazy, but I didn't feel as if I was insane, it just seemed to me that somebody ought to pay for all the heartbreak and misery. Do you see what I mean? And the only one I could get at was that judge. That judge who kept turning the criminals loose. I didn't particularly care whether I got caught for killing him, but I thought if I tried to kill him at the courthouse, in public, there'd be people around who might be able to stop me."

O'Connor asked, "Did you have the gun?"

"No, I'd never owned a gun. But that was the quick, sure way. It was queer how I knew what to do. I've never done anything against the law in my life," said Chesney. He put out his cigarette and lit another. "I went down to Los Angeles, to the worst part of the old city—it was somewhere down on Alameda—and I went to a pawnshop and I told the man I'd pay him whatever he asked if he'd sell me a gun and some ammunition right away, with no questions asked. I paid him five hundred dollars for that loaded gun." It was the Colt .38 the lab had spotted. "And then I came back here and I waited in the courthouse parking lot. There was a parking slot with his name on it, I got a place where I could watch it. When he came out I followed him, and he went up to a big house on Kenneth Road. But it was still light. I don't know why I wanted to wait until it was dark, but I did. I drove around a little, and I went back home and looked at Marcia's things in the closet and wondered what I'd better do with them. Neither of us has any relatives left. But I'd made up my mind to kill the judge, and after a while I went back to that house—and you know how I did it. I said I didn't care if I was caught, but I didn't see how you could know I'd done it. Only then there was all the fuss about Danger-field, and I was afraid you'd arrest him and he'd pay for what I did. So I thought I'd better come and tell you."

O'Connor said, "You know you're under arrest as of now, Mr. Chesney. We'll want a formal statement from you if you're willing to give us one, and I'll have to tell you all your rights."

Chesney said tiredly, "That's all right. Whatever you say."

"You'll want an attorney," said Wallace quietly.

"I don't know any lawyers," said Chesney. "I suppose I'll have to have one. I haven't been sleeping very well, I'd just like to go somewhere and lie down."

Wallace took him over to the jail to book him in.

Delia said to O'Connor, "Can we really lay the blame and be sure it's in the right place? You can't even talk about confused values."

"For God's sweet sake," said O'Connor. "No. There's three lives gone to waste, four if you count the judge, and more than that, the people victimized by the ones he turned loose. There's Chesney, the upright productive citizen just going off the rails once, and these Goddamned worthless louts Jeff and I have been out chasing, who'll just go on making trouble as long as they live."

Delia said broodingly, "That Reyes girl." She lit a cigarette. "Just between us, Charles, I'm a little sorry Chesney was honest enough to come in and talk. Which is a damned stupid thing to say, I know. We're supposed to be committed to law and order, right against wrong."

"So we are," said O'Connor sardonically. "But as Gil was saying the other day, the lady with the blindfold isn't always so God-damned impartial." Neither of them felt like starting to type the formal statement for Chesney to sign.

They were still sitting there when Forbes came in, looking tired and grim. O'Connor was slouched in Varallo's desk chair, his collar rumpled and tie crooked as usual, the bulge of the .357 Magnum prominent. "Those Goddamned punks," said Forbes. "What are you looking so sad about?"

O'Connor told him briefly, and Forbes exclaimed profanely. "I will be damned, that's a nice surprise. Yes, you can feel sorry for the poor devil but he gets us off the hook, all the screaming the media's been doing, and thank God for that."

"I think I'll call the *Times* and spread the word in time to get it on the six o'clock news," said O'Connor, and went up to his office.

"Did you get anything from the gang members?" asked Delia, and Forbes leaned back and shut his eyes.

"The snot-nosed mindless kids, doing what comes naturally. We picked up half a dozen of them at one of their usual hang-outs, a garage out on Colorado. Do they give us the time of day? They don't know nothin' about no girl named Anita, they don't know nothin' about nothin'! But we frisked them and a couple of them were holding—the pot and a little angel dust—so we stashed them in jail to think it over. Maybe when we talk to them again in the morning they might have remembered something, but I wouldn't bet on it. There's never much honor among thieves, and that bunch runs in a pack, sure, but what you heard from the old lady, it's possible that this could be just a lone caper by one of the gang. He's got a yen for this girl, he gets hold of her somehow for his private satisfaction. Or something else could have happened to her. You checked with Emergency, she wasn't involved in an accident of any kind."

Delia said, "I don't see what else could have happened to her, Jeff. I went up to the school this morning and talked to some of the girls in her last class, and two of them saw her leaving the school grounds. Inez Mederos says she was just her usual self, they'd arranged to do some homework together on Saturday, and she was intending to go straight home. She'd have waited for the bus on the corner. This—well, lout—and I wish Mrs. Estrada knew his name—would probably have known what time she'd be there, and if he had a car he could have snatched her right there. Waited until there weren't any other kids around, a lot of them have their own cars and some of them would have been staying after school, at band practice and athletics or whatever. I don't like it, Jeff. That poor girl could be anywhere."

Forbes said, "We'll have another go at the louts tomorrow. But if this one just fancied the girl for himself, would any of the other gang members know about it?"

"There is that," said Delia. That was one feature of the gangs: most of the girlfriends were held in common.

"Well, there's not much more we can do about it at the moment," said Forbes.

"I passed it on to Gates, her general description and the clothes she was wearing—for the four o'clock briefing. The squads will be on the lookout for her, but if she's being held somewhere—"

O'Connor came back and said, "And the damned D.A. agitating about the amateur actors in that porn ring, getting Vic and Lew to watch the dirty movies. They haven't rounded all of them up yet, and there are the customers, damn it. There's nothing in it, damn it. And the weekend coming up, I'll lay you there'll be some more heists to work."

Forbes said, "It's a noble career, Charles."

Katharine had said no special occasion, but if Delia had known there'd be another guest she'd have gone home and put on something more festive. Katharine said, "Nonsense, you look just fine, navy always suits you. And you'll like Dr. Farren, he's a dear. I was never so grateful to anyone in my life—it was back in February when Charles was in New York to pick up that ex-con, he put his car in for a tune-up, and my battery was down, and there was Vince with a temperature of a hundred and three at nine o'clock at night— I was at my wits' end—and I called the answering service just as a last chance, and the dear man actually came to the house—"

"Talking about me?" said Dr. Farren, coming into the kitchen with O'Connor to superintend drinks. "I've got a reputation to live up to, taking over my father's practice. He was the kind of old-fashioned practitioner who took house calls for granted." He smiled at Katharine.

"And you'd only seen us once before, too. You remember, Delia, it was just a light case of measles and Vince bounced right back—"

Vince was bouncing now, getting in everyone's way and obviously delighted to see the doctor, and Maisie, the outsized Afghan hound, was bouncing too. Maisie loved company, and her long legs were going in all directions. "Charles, for heaven's sake put her out," said Katharine. "And you're going to bed, young man, so we can have some peace. Now, you all relax over your drinks, I'll just get him settled and be with you in ten minutes. Everything's ready, just enjoy your drinks."

It hadn't taken Delia ten seconds to see through Katharine's

little ploy, and she was amused and slightly annoyed. So, find a
nice eligible man for Delia. The doctor seemed to be unattached.
And she liked Dr. Farren; he was an attractive man with a warm
personality, but of course she was much too old and staid to be
interested in acquiring a man at this late date. All that had been
put behind her nearly five years before, and the rest of her life was
settled and planned, and it was a good life with an interesting job
to do if not always a pleasant one.

She still had Howard Chesney at the back of her mind and
wasn't feeling much like bright conversation, but the doctor was a
good talker. She saw with some amusement that he and Charles
got on well, admiring each other probably for different reasons.
And of course Charles had to talk about Chesney, and the doctor
was interested from a clinical point of view.

He was a very nice man and she liked him. She didn't suppose
for a minute that he had succumbed sufficiently to her feminine
charms that he'd be phoning her to ask for a date, but perversely
she decided that if he ever did she'd turn him down. It was really
rather impertinent of Katharine to try to interfere in her life. It
was a life she was perfectly satisfied with. She would go on living in
the comfortable modern apartment for a long time to come, with
Henry—parrots lived a long time—and at the end of the career
there'd be the pension and security for the potential old age. And
the years went fast.

She enjoyed the evening moderately, but she was just as glad to
get home at eleven o'clock, with Henry greeting her brightly:
"Hello, Delia dear! You're a very pretty girl, dear, give us a kiss!
Scratch Henry's head! Henry wants an orange!" She draped the
shawl over his cage and went to bed, wondering if the night watch
was going to be leaving them anything.

It was Harvey's night off, and it started out quietly with no calls.
The first summons they had was at nine o'clock, and it struck Rhys
as a queer location, one of the shops over in the Galleria. "I
thought everything there closed at six, except for the restaurants."

"Well, let's go and see what it is," said Hunter. They'd have had
quite a time finding it in that maze of shops, but the Traffic man,
Weiss, was waiting for them at the Central Avenue entrance to the
big parking lot and guided them back down the ground floor
corridors past dark store fronts. Tansy's Fine Gifts occupied one of
the smaller shop premises, with a modest single front window.

There was a woman standing in front of the little shop, and Weiss said, "Mrs. Tansy, these are the detectives."

"Oh, yes," she said in an unnaturally calm voice. She wasn't a young woman, perhaps in her fifties, her pale face innocent of any makeup, with a shapeless figure and gray hair. The lights were on in the shop and they could see her clearly. She said, "I'm afraid my husband has been robbed and murdered. I was worried, you see, when he didn't come home. He called me about ten minutes to six, he said he was going to stay a little late to work on the books, he'd be home about eight. He closed the shop at six except for Saturday nights, when he stayed open until nine. And he'd just said that when he said he had to hang up, there was a customer just coming in. But when he didn't come home I began to get worried, and finally I came down here. Martin's always been perfectly well, but he's fifty-seven and something could have happened— And I found him, he's dead and it must have been a robber—"

"Now, take it easy, Mrs. Tansy," said Rhys. "We'll want to talk to you a little later, but you'd better sit down and wait while we have a look." There was one of the benches for the convenience of shoppers in front of the next store, and she went to it unsteadily and sat down.

Weiss said, "That's what it looks like, a heist. He's been shot, and there was evidently a struggle. It might have been that late customer coming in, I take it the door would have been locked after six and it was wide open. It could be he resisted the heister, broke away to his office in the back, maybe after a gun. He's holding a gun."

Rhys and Hunter went in. There were glass-topped cases on either side of the little shop, displaying glittering costume jewelry, shelves behind holding ceramic figurines, clocks, a miscellany of decorative items. At the rear of the shop was a smaller display case, and its glass top had been savagely shattered; there were shards of glass all over the floor and over the green velvet lining of the case, only a single gold bracelet left there. A small hand-lettered sign lay crookedly across that: It said *All jewelry 14K.* "The better stuff," said Hunter. "Pawnable."

Past a narrow curtained doorway they came into a little office about ten feet square. Beyond it was the door to a tiny lavatory. The only furniture was an old desk and desk chair. The body was lying on one side in front of the desk, the body of a rather plump small man in a brown suit and white shirt. There was a bullet wound in the forehead which had bled only slightly. He was on his left side with his right arm flung out, and his right hand held a gun. Rhys bent and looked. "S. and W. .32," he said.

"It looks as if some shots were fired," said Weiss. "You can see where the slugs hit the wall behind the desk." There were three marks on the plastered wall, looking fresh; if there were slugs there the lab would dig them out.

Rhys, still looking at the body, said, "Look here, Dick. He's had some kind of fight, his right hand's marked up." Tansy the shop-keeper, the salesman, had had carefully manicured hands, plump and soft, the hands of a man unused to manual labor. The one holding the gun had its knuckles bruised, the skin cracked badly. "Educated guess," said Rhys, "the heister put the gun on him and the little man had the guts to fight back. A damn fool thing to do, but he took a swing at him. And there are heisters and heisters, a lot of them only use a gun as a threat, hesitate to pull the trigger. It wasn't until Tansy ran back here that the heister followed him and took some shots at him. And look at this." On Tansy's other hand, just visible at his left side, was another red mark which had bled a drop or two, on the left ring finger. "He had a ring on that finger and the heister tore it off. Smashed the case out there to get at the good jewelry."

"Well, we'd better get the lab out," said Hunter. They went back outside and Rhys went over to the woman on the bench.

"Mrs. Tansy, there isn't anything you can do here," he said gently. "I'd just like to ask you, did your husband keep a gun at the shop?"

She looked up at him wonderingly. "Why, no, he didn't. He didn't like guns."

"Did he wear a ring on his left hand?"

"Yes. Yes, he did. He's had it for years, it's a diamond ring, the stone's one carat. Is it—gone?"

"Do you feel well enough to drive home?"

"I'm all right," she said. "It was just a terrible shock, finding Martin dead like that. But of course I'd better go home and call our son. I'll be all right." Rhys got the address in La Crescenta, and Weiss escorted her back to her car.

Rhys used the radio in the squad to call the lab. As they waited for it, Hunter said, "Funny about the gun. Unless he had one and she didn't know it. Could it be the heister's? He got it away from him after he'd been shot?"

"Head wounds can be queer," said Rhys. "He might not have

died right away. And the general signs—the shots into the wall—it could have been an amateur heister."

Ray Taggart showed up in the van, and Rhys said to him, "You might pick up some latents here. Give it the works anyway. I suppose Mrs. Tansy's may be around, she'd have used the phone to call in, somebody'd better get her prints tomorrow for comparison. You can call the morgue wagon when you're finished."

"Check," said Taggart, and opened his black case containing all the tools for dusting.

There wasn't anything else for Rhys and Hunter to do, and they went back to the station. Rhys settled down to do an initial report on Tansy, with the radio humming on police frequency in the background. There was a pileup on the Golden State Freeway for the Highway Patrol to sort out. The clock worked its way around to a quarter to eleven, and then another call went down. The address was California Street, and Weiss was waiting for them.

"Busy night," he said. "You've got a rape now. It's the upper right apartment."

The building was one of the old four-family places. They climbed thinly carpeted stairs to the upper hall, and the door to that apartment was standing open. They went in. A young woman was sitting on the couch smoking a cigarette, with a glass in her other hand. She was a good-looking girl with a lot of black hair, a high-cheekboned face, and a good figure; she had a fuzzy blue robe belted around her slim middle. "The officer said some detectives would want to talk to me," she said, looking at them. "Excuse me, I don't want you to think I'm a lush, but I was pretty shook, I thought a drink might help."

"Yes, ma'am," said Hunter. "Can we have your name?"

"Dolores Castillo," she said. "I got my maiden name back after the divorce. I've had this and that happen to me, but I've never been raped before. I don't recommend it. Sit down, won't you?" They found chairs.

"Tell us what happened, Miss Castillo," said Rhys.

"Well, I got home late, I work at Horne and Weeks, you know the brokerage firm, I'm a bookkeeper there. I had some shopping to do for my mother's birthday, so I took myself out to dinner and went up to Robinson's, they're open till nine Friday nights. I got home about eight-thirty, and I watched some TV, and I was just getting ready to go to bed when the doorbell went, and of course I went to answer it. My God, your bell rings, you answer it, no? I thought it was probably Mrs. Amberg, across the hall, she's a great one for running out of coffee or milk or something overnight and asking to borrow, and you can't start feuds with neighbors. So I opened the door and there he was, and I had my mouth open to ask him what he wanted when he pushed me back inside and shut the door. And the next thing I knew he had me down on the floor. He didn't waste his time, five minutes later, I'd been raped. Sure I tried to fight him, but it wasn't any use, he was pretty strong."

"Can you describe him?" asked Rhys.

"For what it's worth to you. He was about six feet, he wasn't bad-looking—a kind of round face—yes, he was a white man, he had blond hair down past his ears, and he was dressed all neat and clean in brown sports clothes." She took a sip of her drink. "But I haven't told you the really weird part of it. After he'd raped me, he got up and he said he was sorry to do that to me and I was a nice girl. Can you tie that one? But there was more to come. You see that?" She gestured, and they looked. Lying on top of the TV was a guitar. It was a rather fancy guitar, with gold and silver fittings. "I'm fairly good on it," said Dolores Castillo. "I belong to a sort of amateur combo, we do country rock. Well, this creep spotted it, and he got a kind of happy look on his face and said did I play it, and I said I did, and he said he'd bet I couldn't play it as well as him, and he picked it up and sat down on the ottoman and he started to play and sing." She finished her drink.

"What?" said Rhys.

"That's right. And brother, he plays one mean guitar, he's damned good. He didn't have a bad voice, either, kind of a husky tenor. He sang 'You Are My Sunshine' and 'The Yellow Rose of Texas' and 'Green Grow the Lilacs,' and as an encore he gave me 'The Last Roundup.' "

"I will be damned," said Rhys. Hunter laughed. "This one is the end."

"Oh, has he done it before?" she asked acutely. "I tell you, I was shook. It was weird. And then he put the guitar down and said if I practiced a lot I might get to be as good as him, and then he said, all polite and nice, thank you and good night, and out he went."

"I will be good and Goddamned," said Rhys. "This is an offbeat one all right."

And Hunter said, "Damn it, if he shut the door—there might be prints, and Ray'll still be fussing around that heist at the gift shop."

"Use whatever brains you're supposed to have," said Rhys. "He handled the guitar. Have you touched it since he left, Miss Castillo?"

"Listen," said Dolores Castillo, "I haven't exactly been feeling like practicing the guitar in the last half hour. I can't speak for other girls, but it's definitely not my idea of therapy after getting raped."

"No, I suppose not," said Rhys. "Well, don't. We'll ask you to stay home tomorrow morning and somebody will come up to get your prints."

"That's fine with me," she said. "Somehow I don't think I'll feel like going out anywhere anyway. You know, I think I'll have another drink. What a night! I hope you can catch up to that creep, he must be a nut of some kind."

By then it was nearly the end of shift. Rhys left a note for the day crew; let one of them do the initial report on it and chase a lab man up to dust that guitar. And maddeningly, ever since they'd left Miss Castillo mixing herself another drink, "You Are My Sunshine" had been running around his head; he couldn't get rid of it. He had never been particularly partial to the country-western stuff, and of all the inane and silly songs, that one took the prize. The damned thing was still singing itself in his head as he got home and went in to find his mother sitting up with one of her prize Cairn terriers, who had a digestive upset.

On Saturday morning, Varallo heard all about Chesney with some astonishment. "I think I'll agree with Delia, it's a damn shame he's an honest man and decided to tell us about it. But— shades of Judge Turnbull—he may not spend much time in at that. Conceivably the D.A. could call it voluntary manslaughter, and he's got no previous convictions, he could get a one-to-three and be out in a year. Conceivably, a psychiatrist would say he was temporarily insane and he'd never serve any time at all."

"But what's it going to mean to him?" asked Delia soberly. "He really hasn't much to his life at all now."

Varallo shook his head. "Yes, there is that. But after all, he's not that old— Life could open out for him again, you never know."

He and Wallace were still on the legwork, chasing up those amateur actors and looking for the possible customers for the blue movies. They started out on that again.

The rest of them passed around the night report and laughed about the apologetic rapist; Forbes called the lab and sent Burt up to Dolores Castillo's apartment to dust the guitar. "Of all the Goddamned queer things," said O'Connor, "that's about the queerest we've had in a while. Raping the girl and then singing at her. 'The Last Roundup,' my God."

Forbes said, "Damn it, Charles, it's funny, but it's another thing like the nut cutting off the women's hair. He could be a genuine nut, the sex freak who'll graduate to something worse."

"Well, he's damned well bound to have left some prints on that guitar," said O'Connor forcefully, "and maybe he's on record with somebody."

"There was that print on Mrs. Ogden's back door," Delia reminded him. "Nobody had it on file."

"Oh, hell, that's right," said Forbes. "And here's this damn new homicide to work, and it's too early to ask the lab what they turned up at the scene. Has anybody checked the hospital to ask about Orley?" Delia called to ask, and after an interval talked to one of the doctors. Orley's condition was improved, but he was still too ill to be talked to. Possibly later today or tomorrow, said the doctor vaguely.

There were still a few heist suspects to look for out of Records, and the rest of them went out on that legwork. It was Katz's day off; he could forget about the burglars for a while.

Burt wandered in about ten o'clock with a little box in his hand. "I got some pretty good latents off that guitar. I'm just about to have a closer look at them. Say, this is the stuff off that homicide victim last night—contents of his pockets. To be handed over to the relatives." Delia glanced at the little miscellany: a billfold, some loose change, a used handkerchief, a bunch of keys. From Rhys's report on it, that one would make some work, unless of course the lab turned up some known prints. And a small gift shop in the Galleria— It didn't sound like the obvious choice for the heister who knew where there was likely to be some valuable loot. The report had said some good jewelry, probably not a great deal. And the man, little Mr. Tansy, had tried to fight back and gotten himself shot. A vague picture formed in her mind by all the details in the report, the nervous amateur heister, the shots fired, dropping the gun and running with the handful of loot, after Tansy had taken a swing at him.

She looked down at the box. One little thing to clear out of the way. She looked up the address in La Crescenta and drove up there to hand over the personal effects.

It was an old frame bungalow on a quiet street, and Mrs. Tansy had relatives giving her moral support; a sister-in-law, a nice-looking son about thirty, and his wife. She thanked Delia listlessly, turned over the small objects in the box. "Do you think the police can track down who did it?" asked the son bluntly.

"It's early to say, Mr. Tansy. We're waiting to see if our laboratory can pick up any prints. Mrs. Tansy, we'll need your fingerprints for comparison. I suppose you had been to the shop fairly often?"

"Well, no, not really. When Martin first had his own business, that was twenty years ago, I used to work there too— It was a jewelry shop on South Central, Martin always loved jewelry and knew a lot about it, all the stones and where they come from and about jewelry design— But with the retail prices up so high, and there's always a very high markup on jewelry, you know, the sales fell off, and he thought if he went into the costume line and giftware he might do better. It was a chance he took, leasing that place in the Galleria, the rent was pretty high, and I know he'd been worried about the sales going down after Christmas. You want to take my fingerprints?"

"It's just a formality," said Delia. "Will you be at home all day?"

"Oh, yes. But we'd like to know . . . what to do about the funeral—"

"Now, Mother, Susan and I'll see to all that, I talked to the Reverend Fallow last night."

"Yes, Jim, but I'd like to choose the hymns. Martin would want 'Rock of Ages' and 'Lead, Kindly Light'—"

"You do understand that there has to be an autopsy," Delia explained. "We'll let you know when you can claim the body." Mrs. Tansy burst into tears, and the other two women rallied around. The son followed Delia to the door.

"If you don't mind, I'd like to ask some questions. All Mother can tell us is that some bastard tried to rob him and ended up killing him. How the hell could it happen? Dad—just about to close up, he said—and this bastard walking in on him— Is that what happened?"

"Well, from all the evidence," said Delia carefully, "it seems possible that he may have tried to put up a fight, Mr. Tansy."

He was a rather good-looking, stocky, fair young man. Unexpectedly he gave her a slow mirthless grin. "And wouldn't that have been just like him, at that. He'd worked hard for everything he'd got, and he had some pretty rigid notions about honesty. It'd have galled him to the soul to have one of these casual thieves scoop up something that belonged to him. But if he'd just stood still for it, he wouldn't be dead." There were sudden tears in his eyes and he got out a handkerchief unashamedly. "He was a damned good man, Dad was. A brave man."

"I'm sure he was," said Delia gently.

The press had had the news about Chesney last night, and if the morning *Times* was any example, would be going all out on it. Chesney was now under formal arrest, but they wouldn't be hearing until sometime next week what charge the D.A. would decide on, and if he was sent for psychiatric evaluation, maybe not then. There would be more editorials and passionate opinions spread around, and just as it had been with William Dangerfield, most of the opinions would center around Judge Turnbull; as Juan Garcia had been, in a sense, lost in the shuffle, everybody would forget about Jonathan Draper and Kathleen and the motive Chesney had had for aiming the gun. The lady with the blindfold, thought Delia on her way back to the station, sometimes got lost in the shuffle too.

She had just gotten back to the office and was thinking of going out for an early lunch, and O'Connor was sitting in Varallo's desk chair scratching Rosie's ears, when a new call came in: of all things at that time of day, a heist. They were the only ones in, and both went out on it.

It was a shabby-looking small shop on South Brand, and the sign over the door said ARKOUDIAN'S NUMISMATICS. There was another sign in the front window, COINS BOUGHT AND SOLD. The Traffic man was Neil Tracy, and he was poring over a display of gold coins in a display case interestedly. Mr. Reuben Arkoudian was a fat dark man with a hooked nose and an unexpected Brooklyn accent.

"And I know the cops do their best," he greeted O'Connor and Delia as though they were in the middle of a conversation, "but there are just so many of you and so damned many of them, the damned robbers who won't work for a living, just want theirs from the do-right people. And it doesn't much matter what kind of damn business you're in, if you're in business at all there'll be cash in the register, but the business I'm in—" He gave a vast shrug. "Well, I'm dealing with negotiables, and rare coins or new ones, they don't carry serial numbers. If you ever drop on this pair, and they still got the stuff on them, what the hell is there to say it was the stuff they got from me? Krugerrands yet. British sovereigns. Brother." He sat down in a sagging old chair beside the cash register on the counter at the back of the store, brought out a fat cigar, bit the end off and placed it carefully in an ashtray, and lit the cigar.

"It was two men who held you up?" asked O'Connor.

"Yeah, a pair. It's the first time I've been held up," said Arkoudian, and added, "in California. I got so damned tired of getting heisted back in New York, I came West, I got a sister living here. So I'm in business six months and I get hit again. Almost I'm ready to say the hell with it and take a job selling shoes or something."

"Can you describe them?"

"Sure, for what it's worth. They were both black, maybe in the twenties, one about six feet and the other one shorter. The bigger one had the gun. They made me open the safe in back."

"Can you tell us what's missing?" asked Delia.

Arkoudian cast his eyes to the ceiling. "Oh, brother. The negotiables. Lady, you get anywhere in business, you know your stock. They got away with my last roll of Krugerrands, in case you don't know they're a solid Troy ounce each, and a lot of British sovereigns, they're gold too, naturally, and a whole mess of uncirculated silver dollars. But one thing I can tell you, they were smart enough to pick me and steal the solid real stuff, instead of hitting a liquor store or something for worthless paper, but they don't know anything about numismatic values. The rarities, the collectibles, you know? They passed up a lot of stuff in the safe, the rarities worth a hell of a lot."

"Did they touch anything?" asked O'Connor.

"They touched the safe," said Arkoudian. "No, I'm not being funny, they got me to open it, like I say, and then the short one pawed through it while the other one held the gun on me." That sounded promising; the heist men were seldom very smart. O'Connor called the lab, and Burt came out to print the safe.

"Hope I can do you some good here," he said. "I haven't done you any good at all on that Castillo girl's guitar. Oh, there were some latents on it besides hers, but as soon as I got one of 'em under the scope I recognized it, it was the same print I picked up on that back door the other day."

"At least we know it belongs to the polite rapist," said Delia. But nobody had had it on record. They left Burt dusting the safe. Back at the station, Delia collected Mary Champion and they went to the coffee shop down the block for lunch.

Tracy was cruising slowly on the beat down on Glendale Avenue, about one-thirty, and at the city line went around a block to head back in the other direction. At random, after a few blocks, he turned down a side street to head over for Brand, and in the middle of the next block hit the brake when a girl came staggering out into the street. She waved at him frantically, and Tracy got out. "What's the trouble, miss?" Then he saw that she was almost naked under a short topcoat clutched around her and there was a discolored bruise on her jaw and her black hair was wild.

"Please, can you help me, mister? They raped me—and tied me up— I just got away—"

"My God," said Tracy.

"And I want somebody—please—to call my grandmother, because she'll be awfully worried— They wouldn't give me anything to eat and I'm so hungry and thirsty—" She leaned against Tracy's broad chest and started to cry weakly, and she said, "My name's Anita Reyes—and my grandmother'll be just awfully worried—" And then she passed out on him.

He got her into the back seat of the squad and called an ambulance, and then he called into the station to tell the detectives.

When that word came up from the desk, O'Connor was on the phone to somebody in Narco down in Central, and Delia was the only other one in. She drove down to Memorial Hospital in a hurry and asked questions, but it was half an hour before a young Japanese intern came out and said, "You're the policewoman asking about the girl just brought in?"

"Detective," said Delia before she could stop herself. She'd worked damned hard for the title and resented having her rank lowered even through ignorance. "How is she, Doctor? Can I talk to her?"

He smoothed his cap of black hair. "It's a police matter, then— I assumed it might be when I had a look at her. Well, she's been raped repeatedly and knocked around a little, and she tells us she hasn't had anything to eat or drink for a couple of days. But she's conscious and very anxious to tell the police about it. You can talk to her for ten minutes, and then we'll get her cleaned up and feed her and put her to sleep for a while. She was a virgin prior to the rape, by the way." He led her down the corridor past the admittal desk and indicated one of the curtained cubicles. "Ten minutes— I'll time you."

Anita Reyes was a very pretty girl indeed, even with her curly black hair disordered and a dark bruise on one side of her jaw. She was propped up in the hospital bed avidly sipping a glass of water. Delia introduced herself and Anita gave her a shy, grateful smile. "Please, could you call my grandmother— Mrs. Elisa Estrada— she'll be just terribly worried—when I didn't come home—but she doesn't speak much English, I don't know if any of the police speak Spanish—"

"Yes, I do. I talked to your grandmother, and of course she was worried, she'll be so glad to know you're all right. I'll call her." The girl's English was without any accent, she was third generation and fully American. "Can you tell me what happened to you?"

"Oh, yes," and her eyes filled with tears, "when they raped me —but it wasn't my fault, I couldn't fight them—"

"Of course not. What happened?"

"I'll tell you so you can arrest them. It was this fellow, he was in school up to last year and then he dropped out— I don't know his last name, his first name's Tony. He was always after me for dates, but I never went out with him, he can't even talk good English and then somebody told me he belonged to that gang, and I was scared of him after that. He used to come up to me on the street, when I was leaving school, and, you know, say dirty things to me and— well, how he wanted to make love to me. I was scared of him, but there was usually somebody else around, he didn't do anything— until last Thursday. I guess this is Saturday, isn't it? I sort of lost track. I was waiting for the bus on the corner, and there wasn't anybody else there, and he came up in a car— There was another boy driving it. And this Tony, he got out and grabbed me and threw me into the car, and I guess he knocked me out—" She felt her jaw tenderly. "When I came to I was in this place— I didn't know where it was then but I do now—and Tony, he, oh, he raped me and he hurt me awful bad, and then he said that wasn't any fun, I was no good, and, and the other one should do it too, and he did. And when they went away they left me all tied up with ropes, like clothesline. They didn't give me anything to eat, and I got so thirsty—and some other boys came, I heard them all talking in the next room. It was a funny place, just a little tiny room. They were all talking about making some kind of dope, something called angel dust. And Tony and the other one, they raped me again— that was last night—but this morning when they were there I think they'd been taking some kind of dope, they were acting all wild and silly and laughing, and when they went away I guess they forgot to tie me up, or maybe they didn't care if I got away—

They'd taken my clothes off, there was just my school coat there, and I got out into the next room—it was just a funny little house, only three rooms, and I'd been in a bedroom—and when I went to find a door to get out, the next room looked like some kind of—of —oh, like the chemistry laboratory at school, there was a sink and a lot of bottles and things— I guess it was the kitchen of the house— And I got out to the street, there wasn't anybody there—"

And how O'Connor was going to love this, thought Delia a little excitedly. "You said you knew where the house is?"

Anita said, "Sure, I do now. When I got out to the street, I felt pretty weak but I got up to the corner and there was a sign that said Chestnut Street. And I'd know the house—there's a big house in front and a funny little one behind it, and they're both painted green, and there was a black dog tied up in the yard next door."

The doctor looked in and said, "Your time's up. We're going to make you more comfortable, young lady, if the detective"—and he emphasized the word—"will stop pestering you."

"Oh, but isn't that just a Goddamned beautiful thing!" said O'Connor. "Like a chemistry lab— My good Christ, these stupid punks, it's a wonder they haven't blown themselves to hell, that stuff's very tricky— And good riddance if they had. Oh, it's the answer to a Goddamned prayer—"

"And you'll have to get a search warrant," said Delia practically, "before you can go and look at it."

"Damn it, I know that." O'Connor charged out, presumably to identify the house and then apply for the warrant, and Delia called Mrs. Estrada to tell her about Anita. The flood of Spanish kept her on the phone some time, and ten minutes after she'd put the phone down, Sergeant Bill Dick, on the desk downstairs, called up.

"I've just had a call from a Traffic man, McLeon," he said. "He's got your phony minister. It seems the minister tackled this woman not knowing her husband was home—McLeon got a kick out of it —the husband's an ex-pro heavyweight, and he belted him one, he'd seen the story in the paper about it, and he called in and the minister's just come to and McLeon's got him in cuffs, he's bringing him in."

CHAPTER NINE

McLeon had just brought the prisoner in when Varallo came into the office. McLeon sat the fake minister down in a chair and said to the detectives, "Sometimes the citizens can be a help, he must have been surprised as hell when Richards let him have it. Tom Richards, he's a real estate salesman, but he used to be in the ring. Couple up on Olmstead, the woman had just come home from the market when the doorbell rang. And the husband was watching TV in the den, and came to see who she was talking to. He'd seen the story in the paper, and he clobbered the guy. He was just coming to when I got there."

"Very gratifying," said Varallo. He and Delia looked at him. The fake minister was just as he had been described and you could see why the women had trusted him. He was a tall, well-built man in his mid-thirties, with thick smooth brown hair, the neat little Van-dyke beard, and he was wearing a black suit with a stiff clerical collar.

He said glumly, "I'd be obliged if you'd take the cuffs off, I'm not going anywhere." Varallo nodded at McLeon, who unlocked the cuffs. "Surprise you can say," said the minister. "How the hell could I know there was a husband at home? There wasn't a second car in the garage." He felt his jaw. "That bastard really landed one on me, damn it." McLeon handed over the knife, a horn-handled knife about nine inches long.

"Suppose we hear your name," said Varallo. McLeon went out to get back on tour.

"Decker. Adam Decker," said the minister. He had a pleasant baritone voice. "It just shows you what can happen when you're fool enough to go outside your own line. I never stooped to that kind of thing before, my God, the heists with a knife, I need my head read. But I've been in a kind of cycle of bad luck the whole damned last year. The stars gone wrong or something." He took a pack of cigarettes out of his breast pocket and lit one.

"So you feel like talking," said Varallo.

Decker looked at his cigarette moodily. "Look," he said, "I'm a con man, that's my line. Oh, I know your routine, for God's sake, you'll print me, so you'll find out I've got a little pedigree back East, I've only done one stretch, when the Bunco cops caught up to me about five years back. That time I was running a bucket shop peddling fake stocks and bonds to the marks, and I didn't get out of town quick enough. Up to about four months ago, I was teamed up with a pal— I thought he was a pal—at the same racket, back in Newark, when the damned bad luck hit me again. That lousy bastard ran out on me and took most of the profits. The damned fool, he'd been playing around with a woman and he got scared of her husband, and they skipped town. I was stranded without much in the way of assets, and I just felt as if I wanted to get a long ways off."

"So you came to California?" said Varallo.

"Well, I always heard there were a lot of suckers out here," said Decker frankly. "And it's another piece of bad luck why I picked this damned burg. While I was in Dannemora, I shared a cell awhile with a fellow named Hewlett, a damned nice fellow, who hailed from here originally. He was in for bigamy, he'd acquired about four wives and they ganged up on him. A very nice guy. And I thought it might change my luck to start over here." Decker sounded pleased to have somebody to talk to openly. "Well, it didn't. Aside from the old heap I drove West, I didn't have much else, just about enough to pay a couple of months' rent on some cheap office and put the ad in the local paper under Business Opportunities. And rents don't come cheap in this damn town. I got a hole-in-the-wall place in a building down on South Glendale, and by God, I've been living hand to mouth, waiting for the marks to show."

"And not many turned up, I take it," said Varallo.

"Hell and damnation," said Decker, "there don't seem to be as many easy marks out here as I always heard. I roped in a few, but I sure as hell wasn't making the profits very fast. Bill had left me about half the stock we had, the pretty printed certificates on the nonexistent companies, you see, and that was about all I had. In fact, the only excuse I've got for stooping so low as to pull the robberies was that the rent was due again and I only had about enough to buy a few meals."

"And what gave you the idea about the missionary societies?" asked Delia.

Decker laughed ruefully. "The old ladies," he said. "I just

needed an excuse to get them to open the door. You can see that. I had the clothes—these clothes— I was working a pitch with Bill last year where I showed up as a satisfied client to get the new marks roped and tied, and nearly everybody trusts a clergyman. Do you mind if I go to the washroom?" he asked suddenly. "I'd like to get rid of this damned beard."

Varallo said, surprised, "Well, I'm afraid we haven't got any shaving facilities on the premises."

"Oh, it's just glued on," said Decker, "and it's damned itchy."

"Let's hear the rest of the story first," said Varallo, and he shrugged.

"I think you noticed the women at the market, didn't you?" said Delia.

"That's where I got the idea," he said simply. "I'd gone to a market for some supplies—I'd been warming up canned stuff on a hot plate at the office—and there was this woman ahead of me at the checkout counter, she had the cart piled full with expensive stuff and when she opened her purse I could see she had a hell of a lot of cash. The idea came to me all at once, she was a nice-looking old lady, and I thought it'd do no harm to try a dry run on it. I spotted her in the lot, she was getting into a Caddy, and I followed her up to a big house north in town. It looked like money all right. No second car in the garage. I was ashamed of myself," said Decker, "pulling such a crude stunt, but there was all that cash for the taking if I could get it." He looked at the knife on the desk. "You don't suppose I'd ever have used that, I'm not a violent man, I've never laid a hand on anybody in my life and I wouldn't have hurt the old ladies."

Delia said, "You knocked one of them down and broke her arm."

"I didn't know she broke her arm, I'm sorry about that. I know most churches have these tracts put out in their lobbies, there for the taking, and I hit a few churches and got a little collection, just as window dressing, you know. And I bought that knife," and he looked at it disgustedly. "I got out these clothes and the fake beard, and I went back up to that house and tried the pitch. And she fell for it like a lamb, as soon as I showed her the knife she handed me the cash. There was five C's there, and I tell you I was damned glad to see it. Well, next day I landed a good mark at the office, a retired navy man, a CPO, and he was going to be good for a couple of thousand but he couldn't lay his hands on it for a month or so. So I had to hang on until then. I'd had my fill of this damn place, I was thinking I must have been nuts to come all the way out

here, away from my usual stamping grounds. And if I could just
hang on until I got the mark's two G's, I'd head back East, I've got
contacts back there and the luck might change. But by the time I'd
paid the damned rent there wasn't much left of the five hundred,
and I had to eat till the mark came through. I thought the markets
were a good place to spot the old ladies. I figured most of them
shopping in the middle of the afternoon were likely to be the ones
who didn't work, and they'd be too old to have kids at home, and if
there was a husband he'd be out at a job. The next one I tried
didn't fall, wasn't interested in the missionaries, but after that I got
another one to let me in, and she had about ninety bucks in her
bag, and I noticed she was wearing a nice diamond ring, so I took
that. Me!" said Decker in self-disgust. "Acting like a common
hood, robbing the old ladies with a knife and dropping the loot off
at a pawnshop! I was ashamed of myself."

Varallo said, "So now let's talk about Edith Ferguson, Decker."

"Who?"

"The one you ended up killing."

Decker jerked bolt upright in the chair and stared at them.
"Killing?" he said. "I never killed anybody, what the hell do you
mean?"

Delia said, "You probably didn't intend to kill her, but you did,
you know. Maybe she tried to hang onto her handbag, and you
gave her a shove in struggling with her, and she fell down against
the coffee table. Is that how it happened? And she fractured her
skull and died."

He said wildly, "I don't know what the hell you're talking about,
I never did anything like that! The only one I hurt any was the one
that lost her balance and fell down, for God's sake, and I never
meant that to happen—"

Varallo said coldly, "We didn't have to look at the scene twice to
know that was you, Decker, you left a couple of the missionary
tracts right beside the body." And they could guess that he had
panicked when he realized she was dead, the gentlemanly con
man unused to violence; he'd grabbed the cash from the handbag
—and the jewelry they'd heard about later—and run.

"For Jesus' sake, you trying to frame me for a homicide? I never
did anything like that— Nothing like that ever happened!"

"Up on Tamarlane Drive," said Delia. "It was Friday afternoon." The autopsy report on Edith Ferguson had put the death
between four and midnight that day; if the body had been found
sooner, the doctors could have been more specific.

His eyes were wild. "That's a Goddamned lie— Tamarlane Drive, I don't even know where the hell that is. For Jesus' sake, I don't know anything about this! Sure, I told you about the old ladies, you got me on the robberies and there's no way I can get out of that, but you're damned well not going to frame me for a killing!"

"Come on," said Varallo, "there was her handbag with the cash missing, and a wad of jewelry, and the pretty missionary tracts beside the body. It's two plus two, Decker. We don't think you intended it, it was an accident, but you were responsible for her death."

"The hell I was," said Decker. "I don't know anything about an old lady with a fractured skull, I pulled off four robberies like that, and all those women were perfectly O.K. when I left with the loot —only that one slipped and fell down—and I never meant to knock her down, she just lost her balance. My God, what kind of frame are you trying to set up on me?"

"No frame, we're telling you straight, the evidence is that you were there."

"I deny it," said Decker instantly. "I'll deny everything I've said, and that's all you get out of me." All the easy geniality had disappeared; his mouth was tight and his eyes were wary. He wouldn't utter another word.

Varallo took him over to the jail to book him in, and Delia applied for the warrant. When Varallo came back, she was sitting smoking quietly and hadn't started to type the final report.

Varallo sat down and ran a hand through his tawny crest of hair. "Of course it's circumstantial evidence," he said absently. "It remains to be seen what the D.A. wants to call it. God knows it's true enough that the ones like Decker, the con men, aren't given to the violence. That was probably just a simple accident, he shoved her a little too hard and she banged her head on the table."

"Probably," said Delia. "Did you read the autopsy report, Vic?"

"Well, I looked at the cause and time of death, why?"

"There was just one funny little thing," said Delia. "There were some bruises on the top of both her shoulders, as if somebody had taken hold of her there."

Varallo said incredulously, "To bang her head on the table deliberately? Decker? But that's funny." He thought, and said, "You know what probably happened, she fell against the table, and when she didn't get up he realized she was hurt and took hold of her to try to rouse her. Death isn't always instantaneous with a fractured skull, and he saw she was badly hurt and he lost his head and ran."

"And," said Delia, "forgot he'd left his missionary tracts behind. That could be. He didn't realize we'd connected him to it by those, and admitted all the rest of them all open and frank."

Arthur Ferguson had called in the week before to say that there was some of his stepmother's jewelry missing; he had given some vague descriptions, of a big emerald ring, several diamond rings, a diamond-set dress watch, some earrings. They would be getting a search warrant for Decker's office, but very probably Decker would have already pawned that stuff.

It was nearly the end of shift. O'Connor came in grinning his shark's grin and said, "That search warrant just came through. I want Lew and Leo—" The rest of the men were drifting in at the end of the day, and he pounced on Wallace and Boswell, gave them a hasty rundown on the Reyes girl. "I went down and spotted the house on Chestnut Street, and the warrant's just in. We'll be doing some overtime. I'll call Katharine. These Goddamned punks have been manufacturing the angel dust in that rear house, I'll swear, and I wish they'd blown themselves to kingdom come. Most of that damn gang is over eighteen and we've got some of their prints on file— The lab'll be doing some overtime too. By God, we'll nail some of those damned punks for a little heavier charge for a change!" He plunged for his office to call Katharine. "And," he shot back over his shoulder, "this isn't the whole answer to all the angel dust floating around the county, but it's something, one factory we can shut down."

Wallace said, "Damn it, I had a date tonight. Yes, yes, all very gratifying, but it's a damn nuisance." He sat down at his desk and started to dial the phone. "We were going out to a dinner theater in Hollywood, damn it. She's a nice girl, I've only dated her twice, and when I stand her up like this she'll probably never go out with me again."

Boswell yawned, "I just hope we get to have dinner before we pull off the raid."

As might be expected on a Saturday night, two new heists went down, at a liquor store and an all-night pharmacy. There were five witnesses, all told, and they all thought they'd recognize pictures. Some of the day crew would be shepherding them downtown if they didn't make any mug shots in the local records. There was another pileup on the Ventura Freeway. Just before the end of shift a Traffic man came across a body. It was lying in the street along Pacific Avenue, and Harvey went to look at it. When he came back, he said, "Doesn't look like anything complicated, probably another drunk, or he passed out of natural causes, or maybe broke his skull when he fell down. There was some I.D. on him, he was a Pedro Cardenas, Stanley Avenue." They left the report on the night's activities on Forbes's desk and went home.

O'Connor usually took Maisie up into the hills for her weekly run on Sunday morning, but today he was hot to round up all the punks. The Guerreros gang they all knew; if a few of them had been running the factory for manufacturing angel dust, they'd all know about it. Last night the raid had uncovered a very complete little factory, and they'd confiscated a respectable amount of the finished product and more of the raw ingredients.

The house on Chestnut Street, with its tiny rear guesthouse, was owned by Juan Delgado, according to the neighbors, but he'd been in a nursing home awhile and the house was empty. The neighbors didn't know about any relatives. However, one of the gang members known to the Narco men was Tony Delgado. There hadn't been anyone in the house when they descended on it last night, and there was still legwork to be done. The place was filthy and in the wildest disorder, but Taggart had picked up quite a few prints. The Reyes girl was still in the hospital, and Gene Thomsen went down to get her prints; Delgado was over eighteen, as was most of the gang, and they'd get a couple of them for the rape, too; the girl would identify them.

They knew several of the gang hangouts, and roped in Varallo and Forbes for more manpower. By noon they'd brought in nine of the punks and were talking to them separately in the big office. None of them would admit anything. The only thing O'Connor got out of Delgado was the sullen information that that house was his grandpa's, and the old man, he'd be damned mad at the cops for messing it up, only he was in a kind of hospital and didn't know nothing; he was dying of old age. "Which you aren't very likely to do," said O'Connor genially, "if you go on fooling around with the angel dust."

Three of the gang had illegal amounts of pot on them, and another one was carrying heroin. When the lab finally sorted out the prints, with any luck they'd have a charge on a good many of the punks. They all got lodged in jail, however temporarily, and hopefully by this afternoon some of the prints would be identified.

Delia had gotten hold of Gonzales before O'Connor could tag him to help out with the gang members. "Sister Star's supposed to be home today," she said, "and I'd like to take her by surprise." She hadn't any intention, of course, of leaving the arrest until the appointment made for Monday afternoon; any lawyer worth the printing on his degree could label that entrapment.

"That one," said Gonzales. "You don't want to tip the other one off that we're interested, if she isn't home yet."

"We can go and ask," said Delia. They took Gonzales' car down to the shabby old house on Kenilworth Avenue, and Delia left him sitting in the car at the curb and pushed the doorbell on the front porch. The little dried-up woman opened the door.

"Is Sister Star here yet?" asked Delia politely.

"Why, yes, but—" She peered at Delia. "You're one of the new clients, I remember your face, but I think I gave you an appointment tomorrow—" Delia turned and beckoned Gonzales, who got out of the car and started up the walk. Delia produced the badge.

"We've got a warrant for your sister's arrest, and a search warrant for this house," she said. The little woman opened her mouth wide and began to scream loudly. Delia and Gonzales went past her into the shabby, crowded living room. Another woman appeared in the doorway of the room beyond that, a woman of majestic proportions with black hair in a thick coronet braid around her head, a heavily jowled fat face. She was draped in a tentlike caftan robe of violent purple.

"Agnes, oh, Agnes, it's the police, they're going to arrest you—"

Delia showed her the badge. "Miss Agnes Dooley? You're under arrest."

The big woman plumped herself down in a dilapidated old armchair. She said in a deeply disgusted tone, "Oh, for God's sake." She looked consideringly at them. "The other one, yes, but I'd never have taken you for a cop," she said to Delia. "Are you sure you're not making a little mistake, dear? I don't claim to be a fortune-teller, I know that's against the law, I'm an accredited minister of the Spiritualist church. I'm a practicing psychic, and however ignorant the cops may be on the subject, the parapsychology's a perfectly respectable study, the universities teach courses in it, you know."

"That may be," said Delia gravely, "but I don't suppose the courses include practicing the old gypsy switch, Miss Dooley. I'm afraid you didn't quite succeed in removing all of Mr. Carpenter's material instincts. He took a look inside that manila envelope on the way over to Catalina."

She came out with one startling flat obscenity. "Oh, Agnes!" wailed the other woman.

Miss Agnes Dooley said, "Well, so that's that. That little damned fool, he's the last one I'd have expected to get suspicious, but people are funny— You think you've got them all labeled nice and neat and they go and do the unexpected thing. Lucy, you stop your sniffling and go call Brady." She looked at the detectives coolly. "That's my lawyer, I'm allowed to call my lawyer, aren't I?"

"Certainly," said Delia.

"And you'd better pack a bag for me. Put in a few packs of cigarettes, and enough clothes to last a couple of days. Brady'll bail me out, and you'll have to tell tomorrow's clients I've been taken ill or something."

"Oh, Agnes, they just don't understand your great gift— It says right in the Bible, 'the laborer is worthy of his hire'—"

"Don't dither, Lucy, we've got over this sort of thing before."

And the clients who found Sister Star so spiritual-minded would be all too ready to believe that the ignorant, soulless law was persecuting what it couldn't understand, reflected Delia. Miss Dooley accompanied them to jail quite readily, having exchanged the caftan for a more conventional tailored suit. They booked her in, and the matron searched her overnight bag and led her off. Delia and Gonzales went back to the house. It wouldn't, of course, be any help even if they came across Mr. Carpenter's two thousand dollars; cash wasn't identifiable. But they might turn up some other evidence.

What turned up might be interesting, but it wasn't legal evidence. The room off the dining room was fitted up as a kind of occult studio, with a gilt-framed drawing of the zodiac over the fake hearth, a bookcase holding the expectable works on astrology, occultism, white witchcraft. A folding table held a rather handsome deck of tarot cards. On the mantelpiece was a row of fat wax candles in various colors, in ceramic holders. "The ceremonial candles," said Delia. Gonzales was looking around, stroking his mustache. "I should think she's a pretty crude operator, it's wonderful what people will swallow."

"The other side of the coin," said Gonzales seriously. "It's all of a piece with the trappings of church, the confessional box and the robes and all the rest of it. People have got to believe something, you know. If it isn't one thing it's another."

In the closet of the front bedroom they found what probably consisted of her costumes for impressing the clients, several flowing robes in various colors. One of the kitchen cupboards held a rather astonishing variety of liquor. "So spiritual-minded," said Delia. In a drawer of the desk in the living room they came across four thousand dollars in cash. "And I'll bet part of it is Mr. Carpenter's. I wonder who meekly handed over the rest of it."

"God knows."

The other woman was watching them with all the fascination of a rabbit watching a snake. In the plastic notebook in the dining room was a list of scheduled appointments for the coming week, thirty or thirty-five of them. "At ten bucks a time," said Gonzales respectfully, "we're in the wrong business." And in a drawer in a bedroom chest was another notebook listing names, with little cryptic notations attached, obvious reminders of the client's particular interests. Looking for husband, ran one: play up tarot, try intellectual pitch, suspicious: swallow anything about past lives.

"Really, it makes you tired," said Delia. "And she'll be convicted of the fraud and spend about six months in on a year's sentence, and come right back to business at the old stand. Even if any of the clients know she's been in jail, and I wouldn't doubt that the sister might hand them some line that she's taking a brush-up course in psychic knowledge at a Tibetan monastery, they'll just put it down to persecution against a great psychic."

"We're only here to ferret them out," said Gonzales. "The one thing we can't do is put sense in people's heads."

As they went up to the front door, the other woman said timidly, eagerly, "That's a very good idea. I'd never have thought of it by myself."

"What?" asked Delia.

"Oh, the Tibetan monastery. That's what I can tell people, it's a very good idea."

They went back to the office and Delia typed the final report on it.

The search warrant came through for Decker's office about noon on Sunday. Varallo and Forbes were both damned bored with those vicious punks by then, and went out to execute it. If they should come across any of Edith Ferguson's jewelry, that would be some useful evidence, but they didn't really expect to by what Decker said, and by all logic, he'd pawned all the jewelry as soon as he acquired it, and they hadn't any really specific description. Arthur Ferguson had said vaguely, some diamond rings, the watch, the emerald ring, diamond earrings, and between one pair of diamond earrings and another there wasn't much to choose.

The con man down on his luck had had to settle for a shabby and ancient two-room office in an old, tired building on South Glendale Avenue. He had probably used the better part of the stake he had in furnishing the place from secondhand furniture stores. The front room held an old desk, a desk chair, a couple of plastic upholstered chairs, a plastic upholstered loveseat. There were sleazy beige drapes across the one window. He'd had, of course, to install a telephone, hoping to take calls from the gullible marks who had read the classified ads listed under Business Opportunities.

They rummaged in the desk, but all it held, in a bottom drawer, was a little stack of the pretty printed paper, the spurious stocks and bonds he'd been peddling to the marks. The company names were pompous and pretentious: South African mining stock, Alaskan oil stock, Middle East imports.

"When you come to think," said Varallo, "it must be a hell of a way to live, swindling silly citizens. Only one con man out of a thousand ever makes it big."

"And most of them do it legally," said Forbes. "Mostly in politics." Varallo laughed. "And it's a funny mentality— A lot of them are damned smart boys, they could go right to the top on the right side of the ledger, but they'd rather be con men, they get a kick out of taking the marks."

In the tiny room behind the front office was the makeshift living quarters, an old folding cot with a single blanket, an electric hot plate, plastic dishes stacked on an open shelf, a row of canned goods, instant coffee, a box holding some plastic tableware. "The con man down on his luck," said Varallo. "They're all frustrated actors, the extroverts, but damn it, Jeff, I know the man's a crook, but there's something likable about him."

"That's what they trade on. Well, there's nothing here. All that jewelry is long gone, we'll never get a smell of it."

"Seeing what the evidence is on the Ferguson homicide, I wonder what the D.A.'s office might call it. Probably involuntary manslaughter, which it was for ninety-nine percent sure."

Forbes grunted. "Well, this has been a waste of time."

Delia had just gotten back from a belated solitary lunch—it was Mary Champion's day off and Varallo and Forbes had gone out with that search warrant—when the hospital called. Everybody else was busy with the gang members and the new heists, and Katz was on his way out with John Poor, swearing about a new burglary. The hospital said that Orley was much improved and could be talked to.

Frank Orley still looked pale and ill. He was sitting up in the hospital bed nearest the door in a two-bed room, and the other bed was occupied by an elderly man looking comatose. Thinking of what Frances Hendrix had said, Delia wondered how Orley was feeling about Frances now. He looked younger than twenty-one; he'd been recently shaved and he was in a clean hospital gown. He had a long, narrow face with a sloping chin, his dark hair was thin and stringy, and he was picking aimlessly at the blanket with one stubby-fingered hand. He didn't seem much interested in the badge, or the fact that the police wanted to ask questions.

Delia sat in the straight chair beside the bed. "You know, Frank," she said, "Mrs. Hendrix says she doesn't want to bring any charges against you. For threatening to kill her. But there'll be some military police coming for you, you'll be punished for desertion."

"I suppose," he said in a thin voice. "I suppose I will. I don't mind the Army. They tell you what to do and when to do it and you don't have to figure things out for yourself." He moved restlessly in the bed. "I wouldn't mind staying in the Army, I guess. Whatever they do to me for running away."

"How did you get the idea that Frances had been your girlfriend? She says she never was, you know."

He was silent, looking down at the blanket, and then he said miserably, "I had a hell of a time. Just a hell of a time, trying to get back to California. I picked up some rides, but not many. And I hadn't hardly got out of Kansas before I was running out of money. I walked a lot. And I had to buy stuff to eat and, once, I stayed overnight at a motel, and then I didn't have hardly any money left at all. But I had that gun. I stole it from Al Feldman back there, when I ran away. Yeah, I wanted to kill Francie— I've been in love with Francie ever since we was in school together, see. And that guy she married, too. It seemed like it was the only thing I could think of. I wanted to kill them both. And I had just a hell of a time. I thought everything was gonna be all right when that guy picked me up, he said he was going to Phoenix. But that's still a ways from California, and I only had about ten dollars. So when we come back to his car that time, I took out the gun and held him up. I never did anything like that before, honest. And I'm sorry now, because he was a nice guy, he bought my lunch. He had about a hundred bucks on him, I took that—and I took his car—and I lit out. But I got lost, see. I never did no cross-country driving, and I couldn't read the signs so good. And I got lost. And then the car started actin' up on me, it was kind of an old car, and the battery was awful low, and finally it conked out on me. I didn't even know where I was, and I walked a long ways till I come to a little town and there was a gas station, and the guy said it was some place in Utah. And he took me back to the car and towed it in and fixed it up, it had to have a new battery and some other things—and then I didn't have hardly no money again, it took nearly all the money I'd got from that other guy. But the guy at the gas station, he told me what road to take, get to Phoenix and over here, the numbers to watch for. Only then I had the accident with the car, and it did something to it so it wouldn't run no more."

"How did you come to do that?"

"I was awful tired, all that walking, and it was night, I guess I must have fell asleep while I was driving. Anyways, the car was in a ditch and it wouldn't run. And if I'd had enough money I could have got a bus in Phoenix, it was somewhere right near Phoenix that happened, but I didn't have enough money. I only had about five dollars and after I bought something to eat I didn't have even that much. So I started walkin' again. But only two guys picked me up and they wasn't goin' very far down the road. So I was walkin'. Seems like I walked miles and miles and that day it was awful hot out on the desert, but when it got to be night it was awful cold and I only had the jacket. I forgot to say, when I had the accident with the car I took that guy's two suitcases, and my uniform was kinda dirty so I put on one of the suits, it didn't fit me too good and all the shoes were too small. I thought I could hock the rest of what was in there, but the man at the pawnshop said he didn't take clothes. And I couldn't carry the suitcases any farther when I started walkin', so I just left 'em along the road. And finally, after it felt like I'd been walkin' for days and days, a man picked me up and said he was goin' to San Bernardino. I hadn't had anything to eat in a long time, and I thought some of trying to hold him up, but he was a big, tough-looking guy and I didn't. He left me off in the middle of town, and after a while I stole a car. A guy at school once showed me how to hot-wire a car."

"We know about that, Frank. You still wanted to kill Francie?

But you know she was never your girl, she was just friends with you, and—" Delia hesitated.

He said wretchedly, "You don't have to say it. She just felt sorry for me, I know. She just felt sorry, and wanted to be nice. All the way, I kept thinkin' about doin' it—shootin' them both . . . but I really knew all the time—" His voice trailed off miserably.

"Knew what?"

"That it was all just in my head," he said desperately. "Somethin' I was just pretendin' was so. See, most of the other guys in barracks, they had relatives and girlfriends to write letters to them, and I just had Francie's letters and she didn't write very often—and I'd told them she was my girl, so they'd know I had a girl like all the rest of them. And some of the guys, when they got an overnight pass, they'd pick up with the hookers, but I didn't want to do that. I was just pretending Francie was my girl, that she loved me like I love her— And then I got the letter, and she said she was going to get married—and she wouldn't write me no more . . . and I . . . and I . . ." He was silent a long time, and then he said, "But right there at the last, I was just so tired, so awful tired. I kept on goin', I'd come all that way to do it—it was still in my head I had to do it—and I got to that place she said they were goin' to live, but everything was all kind of foggy because I was so tired. I remember lookin' at the mailboxes to get the apartment number and that's about all."

"And you know now it was all for nothing, don't you, Frank? It would have been a terrible thing if you had killed them. There wasn't any real reason, do you understand that now?"

Orley burst into weak tears. "Yeah, I know, I know that. I really knew it all along, but it was all kind of like a dream—just pretending that Francie was really my girl, and then she'd gone and married another fella and I had to get back at her— Nobody but Francie ever went out of their way to be nice to me— I never had no relatives of my own, there was just the foster homes and some of the people were O.K., but I never stayed anywhere very long— And I wasn't ever any good at school— I never had any real good friends. And I knew, I knew all along, that Francie was just sorry for me— But I had to pretend." He mopped his eyes with the sleeve of the hospital gown. "I want to ask you something," he said hoarsely. "I want to ask you to do something for me."

"What's that, Frank?"

"Will you please tell Francie I'm sorry. I'm awful sorry if I scared her. I'd never want to hurt Francie anyway. She was always so nice to me."

Delia said gently, "We'll tell her that, Frank."

Varallo had arranged the lineup at the jail for Monday morning. All four of those women unhesitatingly identified Decker as the fake minister, even minus his clerical collar. He hadn't been allowed to take off the little Vandyke beard, and the jailer said he'd been cussing about that. He didn't have any money to hire a lawyer and make bail; when he was indicted, the court would appoint a public defender for him.

They had finished rounding up the amateur actors on Saturday, and pinpointing as best they could the probable customers who had bought or rented Thorpe's porn movies.

The witnesses to the two heists on Saturday night had made two mug shots at the R. and I. office, downtown, and the detectives were now looking for those men. Unfortunately they were both off parole and had changed addresses, so it might be a long hunt. Varallo had just dropped back to the station early on Monday afternoon to report the results of the lineup to Delia, when Gene Thomsen came in with a couple of official lab reports.

"We can't do anything for you on that homicide last Friday night, I'm sorry to say. We didn't pick up any prints there except Tansy's. We got the gun and the slug out of him from the morgue, and I dug those slugs out of the wall in his office, and they all match, an old S. and W. .32 revolver. But no prints, not even on that smashed glass from the display case. There were just a few smudges on the other cases, and some of his in the store and the office, that's all. I expect he kept everything all polished up to impress the customers. But we've got the answer for you on that other heist, the one at the coin dealer's on Saturday. It does beat all hell," said Thomsen, shaking his sandy head, "just how damned stupid these punks can be." He offered Varallo the couple of Xerox sheets in his other hand. "You'd think a kid of two would know better. Here are these two low-life types—Roy Dodson and Arnold Engel—they've both got pedigrees, Engel with us and Dodson with L.A. Two counts of armed robbery, one of assault for Dodson. And so they've got to know their prints are on file, and their ugly mug shots. So they walk into that place in broad daylight and go pawing through that safe, while the proprietor has the chance to get a good look at them. We got a mess of Dodson's prints off the safe and a couple of Engel's off the glass top of the counter in front. My God, talk about stupid—"

Gonzales laughed. He'd come in just after Varallo and was postponing getting back to the legwork, with Rosie curled up in his lap. "So where do we find them?"

"That's the kicker," said Thomsen, sounding perversely disgusted. "They're both still on parole. All you'll have to do is make a couple of phone calls to Welfare and Rehab to find out where they are."

"Oh, for God's sake," said Gonzales. "And where did anybody get the notion it takes brains to be a cop? Stupid, you can say."

Varallo picked up the phone.

Anita Reyes identified Tony Delgado and one of the other gang members as the rapists, and O'Connor applied for that warrant happily.

Everybody else was out hunting the heisters. Varallo and Gonzales picked up the two identified ones, having been told by their respective parole officers exactly where to find them, and Dodson and Engel were astonished and aggrieved to be dropped on. Dodson still had some of the gold in his possession. Tomorrow was going to be a busy day, and it was Delia's day off, so they'd be shorthanded. They hadn't gotten an autopsy report on that body found on Saturday night, Pedro Cardenas, but Gonzales had found the address to break the news and it seemed that he'd been a solid citizen, holding a steady job. He'd been a widower living alone in a cheap apartment. Sometime they'd get the autopsy report and find out if they had a homicide to work.

The D.A.'s office was still apparently thinking about what charge to bring on Chesney, but Murphy would be indicted tomorrow along with a couple of heisters from last week. Varallo and Forbes would be in court on that for part of the day at least.

On Sunday night another heist had gone down, at an all-night pharmacy, and the heister had taken a shot at the pharmacist when he was a little slow opening the register. He wasn't badly hurt, but he didn't think he'd recognize a picture, so on that they were reduced to the tedious routine of looking for possible suspects out of Records.

When Varallo and Gonzales had booked Dodson and Engel into jail, late Monday afternoon, they came back to the station and tossed a coin for which of them would do the final report on it.

Gonzales lost, and uncovered his typewriter resignedly. "Just about have time to do it before the end of shift," he said.

A messenger came in from Communications and put a manila envelope on Varallo's desk. He glanced at the inscription. It was the autopsy report on Martin Tansy. He didn't look at it right away, he could guess what it would say; but Delia slid it out of the envelope and started to read it. A minute later she said sharply, "Vic, look at this!"

Varallo took the single sheet from her and scanned it briefly. At the bottom of the brief page the last line stood out clearly. *Conclusion as to cause of death: suicide.*

"What the hell do they mean?" said Varallo, startled. "It was Murder One, the heister . . . all the evidence— Suicide, for God's sake!"

CHAPTER TEN

"Goulding signed it," Delia pointed out.

Varallo snatched up the phone and called the morgue. After a delay he got hold of Dr. Goulding and said, "What the hell are you giving us on this autopsy report on Tansy? The man was shot by a heister, for God's sake, and you're labeling it suicide?"

"Well, that's what it was," said Goulding mildly. "I take it you didn't see the body."

"No, it was reported to the night watch—"

"And they'll be experienced detectives too," said Goulding, "but naturally they wouldn't examine the body in detail, preserving the scene for the lab men. I didn't need more than a glance at it, Varallo. You've heard of cadaveric spasm?"

"Oh, my God," said Varallo quietly. "You don't mean to say—"

"That's right," said Goulding. "When he was brought in, he still had that gun in his hand, and we had a hell of a time prying it loose. It happens at the instant of death, you know, the muscle spasm, it's a reflex action, quite unpredictable, sometimes it happens and sometimes it doesn't. But if you get a corpse with a bullet wound and a gun fixed to it by the cadaveric spasm, that says suicide with no ifs, ands, or buts."

"Oh, my God," said Varallo. "Yes, I see— But the scene—" He stared into space and after thirty seconds Goulding asked if he was still there.

"Can I answer any other questions for you?"

Varallo said absently, "I don't think so, Doctor," and hung up the phone. And then he said, "But, my God—" He got up. "Come on," he said to Gonzales, "we're going to look at something, Gil." But he took up the autopsy report to read it in more detail first. Martin Tansy had been a very robust and healthy man, no sign of any disease.

"What's bitten you?" asked Gonzales. Varallo passed on what Goulding had said.

"Oh," said Delia. "Oh, I see."

"Yes," said Varallo. "Have you got that address in La Crescenta? You might call Laura and tell her I'll be late." The keys to Tansy's gift shop had been handed over to the wife when the lab had finished its examination. Varallo and Gonzales drove up to La Crescenta and got them back from Mrs. Tansy, who looked surprised at the request.

"Had your husband seemed worried or depressed lately?" Varallo asked her.

"Well, he'd been very worried about the business, sales were way down, and the rent there was so high— He'd said he was sorry he'd risked taking that lease, but it was such a good location he thought it was worth taking the chance. But even over Christmas the sales were poor, and he'd had to go into our savings account to pay the rent last month."

Varallo asked, "Did he have any insurance, Mrs. Tansy?"

"Oh, yes, Martin was a great believer in insurance, and he had a big life policy. That was another thing that had been worrying him lately, the premium was due— He wanted to be sure, if he died first, I'd be provided for— He had a policy that would pay two hundred thousand dollars. But why are you asking about that? Have you found the man who killed him?"

Varallo just said, "We'll let you know, Mrs. Tansy."

On the way downtown, Gonzales said, "That'll be the answer, part of the answer. The insurance policy wouldn't pay off in case of suicide. But he wouldn't have left all that on the premises, Vic, he wouldn't dare— What in hell would he have done with it?"

"I thought about that," said Varallo. "He could have just shoved it in a paper bag and put it in the trash dumpster behind the store— And if he did that it's long gone. But there'd have been some risk that it would have been spotted, at that. Jewelry, it doesn't take up much space— I think it's worth a look. The autopsy report spells it out for the insurance company, but we may as well get what evidence we can."

Most of the shops in that big shopping mall were closed when they got there, only the couple of restaurants open. Varallo unlocked the door of Tansy's Fine Gifts and groped for a light switch; the overhead lights came on and showed them the little shop, with its display of costume jewelry in the glass cases, the gift items on open shelves, at the rear the smaller display case with its glass smashed. Under the bright fluorescent lights it all looked queerly forlorn and neglected.

Gonzales said, "A look at his books should tell the story, how the business was on the rocks, and he wasn't a young man, he must have felt he was too old and tired to start over."

"That's the picture," said Varallo. "Do you hear something?" He headed for the little rear office. There, the mute testimony of death still remained, a bloodstain on the worn carpet, the lab technicians' dusting powder here and there. Varallo went past the desk and looked into the tiny lavatory. "I wonder," he said. The water in the toilet tank was making a continuous rushing sound, monotonously overflowing with the water carried off by the overflow valve. Varallo went back to the desk and called the lab. Ray Taggart had just come in. Varallo told him where they were. "When you were here on Friday night, was the john running?"

"I seem to remember it was," said Taggart. "I didn't do anything about it, not my business, and I was busy."

"Well, come and look at it now," said Varallo.

By the time he got there, they had the top of the tank off, and they'd taken a look but hadn't touched anything. "I'm not a plumber," said Taggart plaintively. "What do you want me to do?"

"If you've got some kind of tool to get into the bowl— I think something's clogging up the works right there." But Taggart hadn't any appropriate tool. They cast around for something to use and finally Varallo used the handle of the lavatory brush to poke around, and presently it connected with something and he drew it out with a long glittering gold necklace caught around it.

He sighed. "So there we are," he said. "All right, Ray, we can leave the rest of the job to a plumber. That poor desperate devil, he'd thought it all out carefully, and he'd planned it just fine, only he didn't allow for the cadaveric spasm, probably didn't know anything about it."

Gonzales said, "And it took some guts, Vic. He couldn't see his way to going on, maybe facing bankruptcy, and he wanted to be sure his wife got the insurance. So he set up the fake heist. The insurance wouldn't pay up if it was an obvious suicide. He banged his hand on the wall to show he'd been in a fight, gashed his finger to show the ring had been torn off, smashed in that case— He probably figured he'd drop the gun after shooting himself, and that was risky, but he couldn't do anything about it, he'd hope we'd think the heister just got in a panic and forgot the gun, dropped it."

"And the supposed loot will all be down there," said Varallo, "caught in the toilet tank. He thought he'd flushed it away and nobody would ever find it. Poor devil. He couldn't know he'd get trapped himself by the accident of the cadaveric spasm."

They left the toilet still running. Tomorrow they'd get a plumber up here and fish up all the supposed loot.

Varallo got home late, and he didn't often bring the job home with him, but he was feeling a little sad and sorry about Martin Tansy, who'd made such a gallant effort to provide for his wife. He told Laura about it over a drink, and she said she was sorry they'd ever found out about it. "You approve of defrauding the insurance companies?" asked Varallo.

"Oh, insurance companies, they've got all the money in the world, and he'd paid in all the premiums. It's just a shame she won't get the money, that's all."

"Yes, his bad luck about the cadaveric spasm, but you couldn't expect the doctors not to notice it."

It was Hunter's night off. Rhys and Harvey sat around until nine o'clock, when they were called out to a heist. It was the parking lot at one side of a rather classy restaurant out on Glenoaks, and the victims were a well-dressed middle-aged couple. "My God," said the man, "I know the crime rate's up, but this is a decent part of town, damn it, and there were people all around. We'd just got back to the car when this bastard came up and shoved a gun at us—" They'd had dinner at the restaurant and were just starting home.

"Could you describe him?" asked Rhys.

"Well, I don't know that I could, he was a big fellow, I got the impression he was fairly young—"

The woman said helpfully, "He had pretty long hair and he was wearing jeans and a T-shirt."

Whoever he was, he'd gotten about seventy bucks and the man's wristwatch, an expensive one. There wasn't much to do about it, of course. They could put the description of the watch on the pawnbrokers' hot list, and it was barely possible that it might be spotted. That was the only call they had all night.

On Tuesday morning Varallo got a plumber to the gift shop, and he recovered all the gold jewelry and Tansy's diamond ring from the trap of the toilet. Varallo wondered absently where Tansy had gotten the gun; the wife had said he didn't have one, but they'd never know that and it didn't really matter. He went up to the house in La Crescenta and broke the news to her. The son and his wife were there; they'd just been arranging the funeral at a local mortuary.

Mrs. Tansy said blankly, "Suicide? But it was some robber who broke in—" He had to spell it out for them, and she broke down. "I don't understand, Martin hadn't any reason to kill himself, why should he commit suicide?" The last thing in her mind was the insurance money, but the son took that point instantly. He took Varallo aside while his wife ministered to his mother, and he said heavily, "He set all that up himself, didn't he? He wanted to be sure that Mother got the insurance. And all for nothing. Damn it, it's not fair— He worked so hard all his life to make a success in business— And to have it all end like that— Well, there it is, nothing to be done about it." Varallo handed the keys back to him and left thankfully.

There were still the heisters to hunt for, and O'Connor and Wallace were still busy with all the paperwork on the gang members and the manufactory. The autopsy came in on Pedro Cardenas, and it didn't pose them any more work; he'd died of a coronary. The manager of the apartment house where he'd lived had told them he'd worked the swing shift at a small-parts factory on San Fernando Road, and it was likely he'd been on his way home, just gotten off the bus, when he'd died in the street. Nobody at the apartment building knew anything about any relatives, and when Varallo had taken a look at the apartment he hadn't found an address book there, so there wasn't anything they could do about that. He'd had a bank book showing some modest savings, which would pay for a funeral.

At two o'clock that afternoon one of the squads reported a new body, and Varallo and Gonzales went out to look at it. It was in a car parked on a side street off South Central; it was the body of a pretty young dark-haired woman in a green pantsuit. It looked as if she'd been beaten in the face, but there was no obvious cause of death, and it was an awkward place for a lab man to work. Thomsen came out and first dusted the handbag beside her on the front seat, and didn't find any liftable prints. Varallo opened it and looked at the plastic slots in the billfold; there was about twenty dollars in a change purse. There was a driver's license for Valerie Heilbron, an address on Concord Street. By the registration in the glove compartment, the car was hers, an old Chevy. They went up to that address and found it was an old apartment house. There was no answer to the bell, so they tried the door across the hall and

talked to a young blonde woman who told them her name was
Beatrice Getzoff, and of course she knew Valerie. "We went out to
dinner together last night, it's awful expensive to eat out but
you've got to get some pleasure out of life once in a while." They'd
gone to Pike's, and then they'd gone to the Ace High Bar, on
Central, because there was an awfully good piano player there.
"And I left about nine-thirty, we'd gone in separate cars, because I
always have to be home by ten, when Harry comes home, my
husband, he drives a bus for the city and his last run ends at nine-
thirty, he don't like me going out at night but life's a drag, you've
got to have some pleasure."

"She was still in the bar then?" asked Gonzales.

"Yeah, she said she'd stay on some, why?" They told her about
Valerie and she began to cry. Between sobs she managed to answer a few questions. Valerie worked at a dress shop in the Galleria, she wasn't married, she'd gotten divorced last year, and of
course she was a good, respectable girl; she wouldn't go picking up
strange men; well, if some guy got talking to her there and he
seemed all right she'd have talked to him, but they hadn't any call
to insinuate she'd have picked up a strange man— Well, she had a
sister in Eagle Rock, her name was Angela Bauer, her mother lived
back East.

They had the keys from her handbag and looked at the apartment, found an address book, and called the sister to break the
news. That bar would just about be open now, and they went
down there, but they might have known it would be useless. The
bartender who was on nights wouldn't be on duty until six o'clock.
It was a fairly good-sized bar, and if it had been at all crowded
nobody might have noticed the girl at all, to say whether she'd
been talking to anyone. The bartender might not know any of the
customers by name, and they'd be at a dead end. The night watch
could do some poking around and ask. They went back to looking
for the heisters.

"For once, the day watch leaves us something to do," said Rhys,
glancing over Varallo's note. The middle of the week was usually
slow and it was better to have some action to go out on than to sit
around the office. He and Harvey went down to that bar and
talked to the bartender and the cocktail waitresses. The bartender
didn't know anything to tell them, but one of the waitresses remembered Valerie Heilbron, not that she knew her name. "Kind
of a little dark girl about thirty, yeah, she used to come in with

another girl, a washed-out blonde, and I remember times I was waiting on them they called each other Valerie and Bea. Yeah, she was in last night— Yeah, she had a green pantsuit on— They were at one of my tables. The other one left and later on this girl, the dark one, she was talking to a guy at the next table. Gee, no, I don't know who he was, how would I? We get some regulars in, she was one of them, but a lot of people just drop in, I don't think I'd ever seen the guy before. Well, I guess he was sort of young, but it's dark in here, you know, I couldn't say at all what he looked like."

"Handful of nothing," said Harvey. "But the damnfool girl was asking for whatever she got, taking up with a stranger at a bar." They went back to the office and Rhys typed a note for Varallo. They were just thinking they wouldn't get another call, with the clock just on midnight, when the dispatcher called up an assault. Rhys went out on it alone. It was clear up on Honolulu Avenue in Montrose. The squad-car man was Bryson, and he was talking to a big fat man in the parking lot alongside a single building. Ten feet away, a man was lying on his back on the blacktop, with some kind of suitcases scattered around him.

"Better not try to move him, Mr. Clymer," Bryson was saying. "The ambulance ought to be here any time." He greeted Rhys with relief. "This is Mr. Clymer, he owns this place." There was a neon sign still flickering over the front door: HONOLULU SUPPER CLUB. "He says the fellow's name is Gearhart, it looks as if he's been assaulted and robbed, his pockets are turned out, and all his stuff thrown around—"

"Archie Gearhart," said the fat man, looking concerned. "A very nice young guy, he's the drummer in the combo. See, I got a combo to play here three nights a week, the people like to dance— I didn't plan it that way when I opened this place, but a lot of my regular customers are older folk. Well, middle-aged, there's a lot live right around here, and I built up kind of a regular clientele, you could say. They like to come in a few evenings a week, have a snack and a few drinks, play a little gin in the card room, and nights the combo's on they dance. The combo plays all the old stuff for them, see, the stuff from the forties and fifties. But the older ones don't stay late, the combo packs up at eleven-thirty and I close at midnight. The others in the combo are Bert and Tom Fuller, they're brothers, Tom's the piano player and Bert's on sax. Archie's the drummer. They just left, I was going around closing down the place, I was at the back door ready to turn off the lights when I heard a sort of commotion out here in the lot and looked out, I saw two guys running off and Archie lying there with all his traps thrown around—"

Gearhart was a young fellow, and he was out cold. There were a snare drum and a big bass drum beside him, and a black metal case open with the contents scattered around, brass cymbals, a lot of different drumsticks. The ambulance was just coming up. "I'd better call Tom," said Clymer, "to come and get all Archie's traps."

"Did you get any kind of look at the men?" asked Rhys.

He shook his head. "Archie was probably just starting to load the traps into his car—that's his car there—and Bert and Tom had already left. The drummer's always got a lot more to carry than the other guys in a band."

One of the ambulance attendants said, "He doesn't look too bad, his pulse is O.K." They loaded Gearhart into the ambulance, and Rhys did a little swearing. It was past the end of shift, but he'd have to go back to the station to leave a note for the day crew on this. Gearhart would probably be sitting up and taking notice tomorrow, and might have gotten a better look at the pair who jumped him, might even know who they were.

On Wednesday morning, O'Connor and Forbes had to be in court to cover a couple of indictments. Varallo had gone to talk to last night's assault victim, and everybody else was out looking for heisters. Delia was holding down the office alone about eleven o'clock when a woman came in and looked around. Her gaze rested on Rosie, who was curled up on Varallo's desk chair, with mild surprise. "I'd like to talk to somebody, a detective, who knows something about Edith Ferguson. Are you a detective?"

"Yes, that's right." Delia told her her name and gave her a chair, and the woman sat down. She was in her late sixties, a medium-sized woman with a neat figure despite her age, and gray hair professionally cut and waved. She was very well dressed in a tailored navy suit and white blouse. She had probably once been very pretty, with a heart-shaped face and large blue eyes. "My name's Garvin," she said. "Rose Garvin."

"Yes, Mrs. Garvin, what's it about?"

She drew a long breath. "Well, I just hope the police have the imagination to understand it," she said. She was looking distressed about something, but there was a grim look in her eyes too. "I'm going to have to take up some of your time to explain."

"That's all right, just take your time and tell me about it."

Mrs. Garvin settled back in the chair. "Well, first I'll tell you that

Edith Ferguson was my oldest and closest friend, we'd known each other for fifty years. Oh, she had other good friends too, who knew her well, but she wasn't much of a one for socializing or gadding around—neither am I—and she detested bridge or card games of any kind. I expect I saw more of Edith than anybody, we thought the same way about things, we could always talk to each other, if you see what I mean. I'm going to miss her just dreadfully," said Mrs. Garvin suddenly. "But I know she's all right and I'll see her again. We used to go out to lunch together several times a week, or she'd come to my place—I live in La Cañada, by the way—or I'd go to hers. You see, I only heard she was dead on Monday."

"I see," said Delia. "Of course it must have been a shock to hear she'd been killed. We found the man who did it, you know, and it probably wasn't intentional, just an accident."

Mrs. Garvin eyed her thoughtfully. "Now, you just hear me out, Miss Riordan. I only got home on Monday, I've been on a cruise in the Mediterranean with my daughter and her husband, I've been gone six weeks, and of course I'd been sending Edith postcards and a few letters, but naturally she didn't write to me. And as soon as I got unpacked and straightened around I called her, that was Monday night, and I was surprised she didn't answer, because she never goes out in the evening, she can't drive after dark. I was afraid she might be ill—though she never is. Anyway, I called Beatrice Radford, she's another old friend, and she told me about Edith, how she'd been murdered, the robber breaking in and killing her for the money and jewelry. Well, of course it was a shock, a terrible shock, and I sat there crying like a silly old fool— because death doesn't really matter at all, we just go off to some other place. I'd missed the funeral, of course, not that that mattered either, that was last week, but it wasn't until I talked to Ruth Trissell last night— Beatrice had called her to tell her I was home —that I heard what was supposed to have happened." The grim look in her eyes hardened. "Beatrice had just said the robber broke in, but Ruth told me about this fellow, she said there'd been a story in the *News-Press* about him, it was at the funeral that Arthur's wife had told her about it, that he was the one who killed Edith. This man getting women to open their doors to him, pretending to be a clergyman and talking about missionary societies, and he'd robbed other women."

"Yes, that's right," said Delia.

Mrs. Garvin said thoughtfully, "I wasn't the only one who knew some of Edith's opinions, though I knew her better than anyone

else. Ruth Trissell probably didn't see anything wrong about it—
she's a very conventional woman and Edith was a kind woman, she
wouldn't trample on anybody's beliefs, Ruth wouldn't have known
how ridiculous that was. I'd imagine that Arthur just told everyone
the same tale, the robber breaking in. But Jean Ferguson told Ruth
the real story of what was supposed to have happened. She never
did know enough about when to keep her mouth shut, she's an
obnoxious woman."

Delia regarded her with interest. "Just what are you implying,
Mrs. Garvin?"

"Now, you listen to me, Miss Riordan," she said in a hard voice.
"I knew Edith Ferguson better than anybody in this world. It was
lucky for Arthur that I was away, and I've no doubt he recognized
the fact. By the time I got home it would all be over, poor Edith
killed by a robber who broke in, and if I ever heard the rights of it,
well, it'd be over and done with, and I'm just a foolish old lady with
a bee in my bonnet. But I'll tell you this, Miss Riordan, Edith was
like me, she didn't have any use for churches or clergymen or
religious dogma. She believed in reincarnation, as I do myself, and
as far as missionaries are concerned, she thought—the way she
used to put it—that it was pretty damned arrogant of these pious
Christians to go to somebody else's country and tell them they
were worshiping all the wrong gods. I can tell you, if that man had
come to her door talking about missionary societies, she'd have
shut it in his face. Oh, she'd have been polite about it, just said she
wasn't interested, but that's what it would have amounted to.
She'd never have opened the screen door to take his brochure just
to get rid of him. Nobody got into the house that way. Do you
understand me?"

Delia said slowly, "Yes, I see. But those tracts were right beside
the body, Mrs. Garvin."

"I daresay," said Mrs. Garvin in a peculiar tone. She sat forward
in the chair. "I'll ask you to put up with my being long-winded. As I
say, Edith and I knew each other in and out. I knew all about her
affairs and she knew all about mine. When she married Albert
Ferguson—that was thirty-seven years ago—he was a widower
with a boy. He was a good fifteen years older than Edith, and I
didn't like him much, but she wanted to get married. I'd been
married about four years then, and Ellis and I were very happy.
He died just last year. Well, Albert was the kind of man who made
money, he was in real estate, he had his fingers in a lot of financial
pies, as it were—oh, all strictly legal, of course—which is probably

more than can be said of his son. Maybe it would have been different if Edith had had any children of her own, but she didn't. She tried her best to act like a mother to Arthur, but he was just as cold-blooded and coldhearted then as he is now, and she never got near him. And of course he took after Albert, and he was the apple of Albert's eye, Arthur could never do anything wrong as far as Albert was concerned. But I will say, he made a perfectly fair will—Albert, I mean—seeing that Edith hadn't any children or any relatives left. There was something like eight or nine million in stocks and bonds and income property. He left the realty company to Arthur, and half of everything else to Arthur and half to Edith, but her half was tied up in a trust and it reverts to Arthur on her death."

Delia sat up straighter. "Oh, I see."

"All she owned that she could will away was the house and her personal possessions, and she's left those to my daughter. After Arthur was grown up, she never saw anything of him, he and his father would discuss business at the office, and after Albert died, Edith wouldn't lay eyes on Arthur once a year, neither of us liked that mercenary little bitch he married, and she was too proud of her fine figure to have any children. But, about four months ago, Arthur started to come around trying to get Edith to lend him money. Oh, he tied it all up in fancy language, just a temporary setback and he'd soon be flush again. He's a gambler, you know, he'd take any risk for a good profit. Of course, Edith had a very good income, but she didn't like Arthur and she wasn't about to hand over any of it. We talked it over and came to the conclusion that he'd gotten through most of the money Albert left him—bad investments and gambles, and they've always lived up to the hilt of what they had, cars and that big house and parties and all Jean's fancy clothes. He knew he'd get all the rest when Edith died, and she was sixty-five but strong as a horse, not even any of the chronic aches and pains of old age," and Mrs. Garvin smiled wintrily. "She could have lived to be ninety. And now I'll tell you something else. Just before I left on this cruise, I think that Arthur was planning out some way to get Edith killed."

"What?" said Delia. "How do you mean?"

"Well, it looked fishy to both of us. He'd never had any time for her before, and there he was trying to persuade her to come down to their beach house at Coronado, talking about the nice sea air. He keeps a motorboat down there, and maybe he thought he could get Edith to go for a ride in it. Easy enough to push her

overboard, and she couldn't swim. Only, Edith wouldn't have
been such a fool. That was just a little idea we both had, and—" She
looked uneasy. "It was mostly a joke between us, but when I think
it over— About the last thing I said to her before I left for New
York, I said, watch out for Arthur, don't let him coax you into that
boat—and it was only half a joke. Well, I won't apologize for committing slander, but I think what could have happened is that
Arthur saw the story about this fake clergyman and saw how he
could use it to murder Edith. She'd have let Arthur in, you know—
she didn't like him, but she wouldn't have been afraid he'd do
anything, well, crude, in her own house in broad daylight."

And Delia thought, those bruises on Edith Ferguson's shoulders.
The once she'd seen him, Arthur Ferguson looked like a big and
powerful man, and she had been small and thin. Before she'd have
had time to scream or struggle he could have gripped her by the
shoulders and cracked her head against that table with all his
force. If the first blow hadn't cracked the skull, there'd have been
more, and even though the larcenous clergyman hadn't exhibited
violence before, still there'd be evidence left. If Decker could pick
up those free tracts in the churches, so could Arthur Ferguson.
But, by the autopsy, the skull had been fractured by the one blow
to the temple where the bone was thinner. Leave the tracts beside
her, the circumstantial evidence was plain on the fake clergyman.

"Well, do you believe me?" asked Mrs. Garvin challengingly.

"I rather think I do, Mrs. Garvin. But nobody would ever be able
to prove it, you know."

"And that other man—you said you'd caught him—he'll be held
responsible. But I swear to you, Arthur did it. And I could suggest a
way to prove it, Miss Riordan. He told the police the man had
stolen Edith's jewelry, it's missing. Well, I know that greedy little
bitch Jean Ferguson, and she'd never let Arthur just throw that
away, and he wouldn't take the risk of pawning it. Edith had some
very distinctive pieces. I could identify everything, there was that
emerald ring she always wore, a big rectangular stone with dia-
monds all around it, and other things— If you got a search warrant
for that house and looked, I'll bet you'd find it all."

"But we haven't any probable cause to ask for a search warrant,"
said Delia.

"I see," said Mrs. Garvin. "I suppose you'd know." They looked
at each other and she got up heavily. "Well, I've said my piece, it's
all I can do. Thanks for listening." Delia watched her out. She
thought that Mrs. Garvin was probably quite right, and that was

exactly what had happened. But there wasn't anything to do about it.

Archie Gearhart hadn't been much hurt, a mild concussion, and the hospital would release him this morning. He was a sharp-looking young fellow with a little mustache. He told Varallo, sounding amused, "I never saw either of them before, they were just two long-haired louts about eighteen. They were in the club last night, and I guess they had the idea that all musicians are stoned on dope half the time. One of them came up to me on the break and asked if I could tell him where to buy some pot. I just told him to get lost. But I'm pretty sure it was that pair that jumped me, went over me and all the traps looking for the dope."

"Just the simple, crude thing," said Varallo. "We'll never pick them up, of course."

"Well, at least they didn't kill me," said Gearhart, "and all the traps are O.K."

It was the same sort of thing as the Valerie Heilbron homicide, except that she'd been killed: anonymous and unworkable.

And when they all heard what Delia had to say about Mrs. Garvin's tale, they were inclined to agree that Ferguson had probably set up that murder, but they couldn't touch him for it.

Decker was up for indictment the next day, and along with him Howard Chesney, who was being charged with Murder One: the D.A. was setting an example to avenge a fellow lawyer. Delgado and the other punk would be indicted for the rape on Friday. And they hadn't caught up to these heisters yet.

On Wednesday night another heist got pulled at an all-night pharmacy on Los Feliz, another stupidity with two clearheaded witnesses anxious to look at mug shots. On Thursday about noon, Delia was down in the Records office waiting for those two to look through the books, when she was summoned upstairs to take a phone call.

"Miss Riordan?" Rose Garvin's voice was high and excited. *"I told you so— I told you so!* And what a stupid thing, to start wearing it right away— But she didn't know I'd be there of course."

"Who?" asked Delia.

"That mercenary little bitch— Arthur's wife— Jean Ferguson. The lawyer asked me to come into his office this morning, something about Edith's will—she left me her grandfather clock—and the Fergusons were there, and Jean was wearing Edith's emerald ring! Of course I could swear to it— I told you they'd have kept all that jewelry! And I can identify all of it. And when Arthur told you it was all stolen— Now have you got a legal reason to get a search warrant?"

The search warrant came through about three o'clock, and Delia and Varallo took Mrs. Garvin with them to the Fergusons' big, pretentious house in Flintridge. The wife was there alone, a rather gaudy blonde with shallow china-blue eyes, and she was badly frightened at the sight of the warrant. "That's the ring," said Rose Garvin triumphantly. "I pretended not to notice it this morning. Where's the rest of Edith's jewelry that you pretended was stolen?"

Ferguson came in while she was eagerly and positively identifying the diamond-studded watch, the earrings, a gold necklace, and several gold bracelets, and he began to bluster.

"What the hell's going on? What business have the police got here anyway?"

But his wife was in a panic now, and she screamed at him, "They know— They know all about it! You had to be so smart, you said nobody'd ever suspect it wasn't that other fellow killed her— After you saw that story in the paper— But they know, and now we're in real trouble, not just all those debts—"

"Shut up!" he said. But he hadn't said it soon enough. She was the kind who would come apart and tell all she knew. They took them both back to the station to hear all the details.

Before he started home, Varallo went over to see Decker at the jail and told him he was off the hook on that homicide, and why. Decker let out a long breath. "Well, that's one hell of a load off my mind," he said. He looked younger and less distinguished without the neat little Vandyke beard. "I'd have hated like hell to have a thing like that tied to my pedigree the rest of my life. I'm not a violent man, and I'm ashamed of myself for pulling those damned crude robberies. I'm much obliged to you for telling me, I'll sleep better tonight." He accepted a cigarette and a light. "I don't expect I'll do more than six months or so, and brother, am I going to make tracks East. I've had enough of California, believe me. And I've got contacts back there."

Delia was tired when she got home, but it had been an interesting day. Henry was chattering away as usual, and greeted her brightly. "Hello, Delia dear! You're a very pretty girl, dear! Did you have a nice day?" She replenished his dishes before she got dinner.

When she had cleaned up the kitchen, she was rummaging in her handbag looking for a ballpoint pen to make out a shopping list for tomorrow, when the door chimes sounded loudly. Startled, she jumped and dropped the bag, and its contents scattered all over the floor. She went to the door. Henry was silent, voraciously sucking an orange.

In the hall outside were her two neighbors, the middle-aged man with glasses and the tall dark one. "My name is Peabody," said the older man fussily. "I'm afraid I don't know yours." She told him. "I do not like to intrude on anyone's privacy, but my mother is becoming quite alarmed and I must say so am I, and I decided it is necessary to ask some questions. We are your neighbors, my mother and I, and this is your neighbor on the other side, I asked him to accompany me, as he might be concerned too. Ever since you have moved in, Miss Riordan, we have been worried about the very strange sounds from this apartment, a very peculiar voice, sounding like some deranged person, quite irrational. One can't make out the words, but the tone is quite irrational and, ah, alarming. My mother is a semi-invalid and alone all day, and we have become quite disturbed—"

"Can't say I've heard anything myself," said the other man easily, "but I've been doing some overtime and I don't leave the balcony door open."

"A person could cross from your balcony to ours easily, and if this person is deranged in some way—there it is again!" said Peabody agitatedly. Henry had finished his orange.

"Oh, for heaven's sake," said Delia. "You'd better meet Henry." She opened the door wider.

Henry was pleased at visitors. He screeched and stretched his bright blue wings. "Awk! Did you have a nice day? I like a little sugar in my tea. Yo-ho and a bottle of rum!"

"I'm very sorry if he's disturbed you," said Delia. The other man laughed.

Peabody said, "Oh. A parrot. I see. Well, of course that explains the matter. I will reassure my mother." He turned to the door, and then his eyes riveted to the scattering of objects on the carpet. Among them, of course, was the snub-nosed Colt .32.

"Miss Riordan," said Mr. Peabody sternly, "may I ask why you possess a pistol? I disapprove of guns in private hands, they are extremely dangerous."

"I'm required to carry it," said Delia crossly. "I'm a police detective." She picked up the badge from the floor and showed it to him.

"Oh, really," said Peabody stiffly, and marched out.

"Give us a kiss, dear!" said Henry.

The other man suddenly collapsed in laughter. He leaned on Henry's cage and whooped with mirth. "Peabody," he gasped, "his name would be Peabody—" He got out a handkerchief to wipe his eyes. "A deranged person. And Henry. What a name for a parrot!" He had a rather craggy face with a square jaw and shaggy eyebrows over shrewd blue eyes. He took something out of his breast pocket and held it out. "Sergeant Dan Fitzgerald, L.A.P.D., Valley Division," he said solemnly.

"Oh!" said Delia, looking at the badge. And of course that was why he had seemed familiar. He was the counterpart of every officer she'd ever worked with. Whatever they looked like, they all carried around the invisible aura that said, This is a cop.

"I say, let's all have a little drink!" said Henry loudly.

"Now, I'd call that a damn good idea." Dan Fitzgerald smiled down at her. "What about it?"

The Heilbron thing got shoved in Pending; she'd been strangled, and they'd never know who had done it. It was a busy weekend, with three more heists and the inevitable burglaries for Katz to swear about. They hadn't heard anything else about the apologetic rapist or the nut with the scissors cutting off the women's hair, but they would both probably surface again. And Ferguson would be indicted for Murder One next week.

Delia was typing a follow-up report on the latest heist, on Monday afternoon, when Varallo came back to the office after lunch and stopped by her desk. "Say, there's a movie Laura wants to see, opening at the Alex on Wednesday. You can come baby-sit."

Delia stopped typing, but didn't look up immediately. She'd never turned down the Varallos before. It was the accepted thing; if they wanted to go out, Aunt Delia stayed with the children. "Oh, I'm sorry, Vic," she said, "I can't. I've got a date."

P012 "Oh," said Varallo. She heard the surprise in his voice, and glanced up to see the curiosity in his eyes. "Er—who with, if you don't mind my asking?"

To her horror, Delia felt herself beginning to blush, and was immensely relieved when the phone started ringing. She said, "I'll tell you sometime," and reached for the phone hastily.

ABOUT THE AUTHOR

LESLEY EGAN is a pseudonym for a woman who has written over fifty mystery novels under her own name and two pen names. Her most recent novels as Lesley Egan are *Crime for Christmas*, *Little Boy Lost*, and *Random Death*. Ms. Egan lives in California.